Ava's Place

Novels by Emily Beck Cogburn

Louisiana Saves the Library

Ava's Place

Published by Kensington Publishing Corporation

AVA'S PLACE

EMILY BECK COGBURN

KENSINGTON BOOKS
www.kensingtonbooks.com

KENSINGTON BOOKS are published by

Kensington Publishing Corp.
119 West 40th Street
New York, NY 10018

All Kensington titles, imprints, and distributed lines are available at special quantity discounts for bulk purchases for sales promotion, premiums, fund-raising, educational, or institutional use.

Special book excerpts or customized printings can also be created to fit specific needs. For details, write or phone the office of the Kensington Sales Manager: Kensington Publishing Corp., 119 West 40th Street, New York, NY 10018. Attn. Sales Department. Phone: 1-800-221-2647.

Kensington and the K logo Reg. U.S. Pat. & TM Off.

eISBN-13: 978-1-4967-0012-4
eISBN-10: 1-4967-0012-0
First Kensington Electronic Edition: February 2017

ISBN-13: 978-1-4967-0011-7
ISBN-10: 1-4967-0011-2
First Kensington Trade Paperback Printing: February 2017

10 9 8 7 6 5 4 3 2 1

Printed in the United States of America

For my family. All y'all.

CHAPTER 1

For the fourth day in a row, the rumbling, exhaust-spewing pickup blocked the playground entrance.

Ava stopped her rattletrap van a few feet away, in an actual designated parking spot. She took a deep, calming breath and tried to channel some of the Zen mind-set that seemed to come so naturally to her yoga instructor, Summer. She closed her eyes and pictured the young woman's cheerleader ponytail and soft black yoga pants. *Breathe in, breathe out. Relax your toes, ankles, knees, face.*

When Ava opened her eyes again, the truck was still there, expelling foul diesel fumes. Summer's smooth voice was gone, replaced by the booming bass of a rock song as the door to the pickup opened. A man in a baseball hat lifted a little girl from the extended cab and carried her to the playground.

Ava flipped down the van's visor and opened the mirror. She'd long ago given up trying to cover her freckles with makeup. Pancake foundation made her look like a creepy horror movie doll, so she just used mascara and eyeliner around her green eyes to draw attention away from her Little Orphan Annie cheeks and nose. She touched up her red-orange lipstick and snapped the mirror closed.

It wasn't only Truck Guy giving her stress. Getting three children ready for school was never easy, but that morning everything had gone wrong at once. Her oldest, James, spilled Lucky Charms on his only clean pair of uniform pants while he was desperately trying to finish his spelling homework. Middle child, Luke, had to have a peanut butter sandwich with the crusts cut off because he absolutely could not eat school lunch again. Meanwhile, Sadie, the youngest, had flung every item of clothing she owned onto the floor. Ava couldn't wait until Sadie was old enough to go to public school and wear the burgundy and navy uniform. Life would be simpler when the poor child didn't have to decide between pink shorts or pink striped shorts.

Ava had dropped the boys off at school seconds before they'd be marked tardy. Now only Sadie was left. Ava was already tired. She loved the parenting roller coaster and didn't want the ride to be over, but sometimes the ups and downs were too much. On the flip side, so much time was spent waiting for something to happen, just listening to the clicking of the chain as it carried the car slowly to the top of the hill.

"Don't want to go to Sadie's class!"

Ava turned and looked at her three-year-old daughter. Sadie hugged Fluffy the cat and Sparkle the teddy bear, her constant companions. "Come on, you're going to have fun."

"No!"

Ava cursed, but only inside her overworked mind. Sadie's favorite teacher had a second job as a public school bus driver and, as a result, arrived at the day care at nine thirty. "Ms. Bee will come in later. I told you that. You only have to go to the other class for an hour." She slung her purse over her shoulder, got out of the van, and slid the back door open.

Sadie wore a pink dress decorated with hearts, pink striped bike shorts, and pink sneakers. She moved in little kid slow motion, carefully placing Sparkle and Fluffy in the empty seat across from hers, picking up a stray M&M from the floor and examining it before popping it into her mouth, and then hanging one foot out of the van as if testing water in a pool. Ava reached past her and grabbed the bag with the nap sheet and blanket.

The moment Sadie's sneaker hit the asphalt, Ava closed the van door and took her hand. Sadie wasn't capable of walking quickly to the playground. She pulled Ava in different directions as she bounced, skipped, and then stopped to examine the flowers when they got to the patch of grass along the fence. Thanks to Truck Guy, they had to stay close to the chain link to get to the gate. AC/DC's "Thunderstruck" blared from the stereo, and the truck released an especially noxious cloud of exhaust as they passed by.

Ava's stilettos sank into the grass as she unlatched the gate. She yanked the shoes free and led Sadie onto the playground. They walked under a live oak with thick, moss-covered branches like something out of a creepy fairy tale. Directly ahead, a hole in the ground served as a sandbox. Twin boys shoved toy trucks through the sand while a stout-legged girl tried to drape herself upside down on a plastic climbing dinosaur. The rest of the kids chased each other or ran with no discernible destination. It was still early August, so the children would have most of their outdoor time in the morning, when it was relatively cool.

Truck Guy stood near the sign-in sheets with his daughter by his side. Ava deliberately looked away, focusing instead on a crying boy sitting in time-out against the storage shed. Sure, the man looked like he belonged on the cover of a romance novel, but that wasn't why she'd checked her makeup before getting out of the van.

Sadie gripped Ava's hand tighter, and her pigtails bobbed as she searched the playground. "Where Ms. Bee?"

"She'll be here later, just like I told you," Ava said.

"No!" Sadie let go of Ava's hand and flung herself down full-length onto the kid-trampled grass. Her whole body writhed as she sobbed with a level of anguish appropriate to the imminent destruction of the world.

Ava squatted beside her daughter, teetering a little in her high heels. Sadie's distress made her feel like her own world was ending. She was also desperate to calm her before the entire playground became convinced that she was torturing her daughter. "Sadie, it's going to be okay. Ms. Bee will be here in one hour. I promise. You will survive until then. The other teachers are nice. No one's going to make you eat liver and onions or dig ditches."

Sadie ramped up her fire engine noise. Ava put her hand gently on her daughter's head, only to have Sadie slap it off. "Go away, Mommy!"

"Sweetheart, go have fun with your friends."

"No!"

Feeling the eyes of all the parents and teachers on her, Ava went to the table with the sign-in sheets. She did the best she could as a parent, but there always seemed to be someone giving her nasty looks when her children cried in public, talked too loud, knocked over a glass in a restaurant, or transgressed in some other inexcusable manner. Sometimes she just wanted to disappear.

Truck Guy had finished signing in. He and his daughter stood on the edge of the pebble-filled area with the swings, slide, and teeter-totter. He released her hand and she trotted toward the slide. As he turned to leave, he glanced in Sadie's direction. Ava imagined that his gaze was disapproving. She glared back at him. He didn't know that when Sadie was in one of her fits, nothing worked. Santa Claus could show up and she'd keep screaming. Besides, he had no right to judge. His own daughter's crooked pigtails were already coming undone, and she wore sandals that would be full of playground pebbles within ten minutes. Not to mention that his truck was still running and she could smell the exhaust all the way on the other side of the playground.

Ava scrawled her signature next to Sadie's name. She squatted down beside the sobbing girl again. "Ms. Bee will be here soon, I promise. I love you, but I have to go to work now."

Sadie wailed louder, and Ava nominated herself for the worst mother in the world. After three children, tantrums still left her helpless and flustered. Perhaps it was her fault that Sadie threw fits in the first place. Certainly her mother thought so. On one of her infrequent visits, she'd hinted that Sadie's moodiness was a direct result of Ava's permissiveness. If she was stricter with the children, all her problems would be solved, according to her mother. But Ava had long ago resolved not to emulate her parents, who were cold and distant, taking the attitude that children were to obey, not question. Besides, as a single parent, Ava hardly had the energy or time to fight every battle.

A tall, African American woman left her post by the swings and walked over. Ms. Shondra never acted frustrated, no matter what the children did. Ava wished she knew what her secret was. Meditation? Low blood pressure? Prescription medication? Bungee jumping on weekends?

Ms. Shondra bent down and took Sadie's hand. "Come see, baby." The teacher tilted her head toward the gate, indicating that Ava should get away while she could.

Ava walked quickly back across the playground. Truck Guy with his muscular back and pumped-up biceps was right ahead of her.

Jared had seemed like the perfect boyfriend when they'd met in graduate school at Columbia. He'd asked her out by passing her a note during their Mass Communication 750 class. It read: *How about some individual communication after this mass communication? At the coffee shop?*

In retrospect, the note wasn't actually very clever, but it had made her smile. She had nodded yes and spent the rest of the class period sneaking glances at his profile—straight nose, half-smiling lips, stubble where he'd missed a spot shaving his chin. Instead of the coffee shop, they ended up at the campus pizza parlor, drinking beer, and eating thick slices of pizza. She listened to his stories about growing up in a small town in Ohio, reading the *New York Times* in the library, and dreaming of the big city. He'd known since elementary school that he wanted to be a journalist, the kind who ferrets out corruption and wins Pulitzer prizes. Ava had been less sure. She liked writing, and her professors told her she was good at it, but she'd never been a newshound. Jared's enthusiasm was infectious, though.

They'd spent graduate school passing notes during their classes and celebrating turning in their term papers with drinks at their favorite bars. They had an easy, jokey rapport that made their friends envious. In private, they had surprisingly little to say to each other. It didn't matter, though, because Jared was always working. He wrote for the campus newspaper and interned at one of the local weeklies. Ava studied a lot, but she found herself with more time than Jared. As soon as they graduated and got married, she became pregnant. He took a job at the *Saint Jude Gazette*, and they made the trip south in a rented truck, stopping often for snacks of boudin and cracklins, neither of which Ava had ever had before. The midsize Louisiana paper hired her as a stringer, paying her by the story, until she had James.

After the baby was born, the household took a *Leave It to Beaver* turn. Since she wasn't working, Jared expected Ava to cook, clean, iron his shirts, and take care of the baby by herself. The arrangement seemed fair, and Ava was happy to have time to spend with James. He was an easygoing baby. By the time Luke was born, she began to feel restless and wonder why Jared spent so much time at the office. Did he really need to go out for drinks after work so many nights? Couldn't he do a load of laundry once in a while or cook dinner one night, just to give her a break? She was at least able to talk him into watching the kids occasionally so that she could write stories for the *Gazette*, and she relished the time to be an adult.

Then, he got a job at the *Chicago Tribune*. He hadn't even told Ava he was looking. That bothered her more than anything. He'd been telling her less and less about work. They exchanged necessary information about the children and not much else. Worse was the way he broke the news. Ava was already pregnant with Sadie and lying on the couch feeling tired and just nauseated enough to make moving seem like a bad idea. The boys were in bed. Jared came in and looked down at her. She could read his expression. He thought she was lazy, pathetic, and fat. For once, she didn't care.

"I'm moving to Chicago," he said.

Ava's mouth went dry. He was moving? By himself? It didn't make sense. "What are you talking about?"

"I got a job at the *Chicago Tribune*. I start in two weeks."

"You're going by yourself?"

"I want to get an apartment downtown, by the office. I don't want to commute. I think you'd be happier staying here." He crossed his arms across his chest.

Ava sat up, fighting the nausea and fatigue. "If you leave without us, we're done. You can get a lawyer or I will."

"I'll do it." With that, Jared went into the bedroom and shut the door.

* * *

Truck Guy got into his vehicle. At first, Ava thought he was leaving, but no, he was actually driving the pickup to the entrance of the combined church and day care. Apparently, he couldn't walk like everyone else. He'd probably leave the stupid truck running while he went inside, too.

As she trotted toward the day-care part of the building to drop off Sadie's nap sheet and blanket, Ava watched him get out of the truck—sure enough, leaving the engine on—and go inside. She silently cursed her stiletto heels as they sank into the grass again. Cute, impractical shoes were one of the few indulgences she still allowed herself. She spent the rest of her money on fruit snacks, school uniforms, plastic toys, and school lunches.

When she stepped onto the blessedly hard pavement, she sped up as much as she could. She was sure she looked ridiculous trying to run in the three-inch heels without falling flat on her face.

She was concentrating so hard on not tripping over her own feet that she didn't notice Truck Guy standing in front of the door, holding it open for her. She stopped on the sidewalk and tried to catch her breath. He didn't need to see her gasping like a fish.

He smiled and in that brief moment, some of her anger faded. His blue eyes were soft and his expression sympathetic, as though he understood exactly how difficult her morning had been. Ava ducked her head, ashamed. Maybe she had misjudged him. She mumbled a thank-you, raced up the stairs, and shoved Sadie's blanket and sheet into her cubby. By the time she made it back to the parking lot, the wheezing truck was gone. She laughed at her own disappointment. After all, cute guys were trouble and she didn't need any more of that.

CHAPTER 2

Ford eased up on the clutch as he pulled his temperamental truck out of the day-care parking lot. He didn't understand why the tall redhead had been giving him nasty looks. He thought her daughter was in Nelly's class, but he had trouble keeping track of the little girls sometimes. There were at least four blondes with pigtails, including his own daughter.

He turned off the loud rock music that Nelly liked and drove toward the Louisiana A&M campus. He had no time to worry about Redhead Mom, even if she was stunning with her long legs and smooth-looking skin. Breakfast was the busiest time at the café and he hated that he couldn't get there any earlier. Ever since Marion divorced him and moved to New Orleans, he hadn't been able to work as much as he should. He practically lived at the café on weekends, while Nelly stayed with Marion, but during the week, the best he could do was nine a.m. to three p.m. Bobby Joe didn't seem to get it. Childless, his brother had the attitude that anything domestic was woman's work. Ford snorted to himself and rested his arm on the open window. Marion was an emergency room doctor and she worked long hours.

It didn't make sense for her to have primary custody. Ford loved his job, but he made less than one-third the money she did. Sacrifices had to be made and, truth be told, he'd much rather spend time with his daughter.

Ford parked his truck behind the café and killed the engine. He patted the dashboard. He hoped it would start again when he finished his shift. Two hundred thousand miles was a lot. He'd ask Bobby Joe to look at it over the weekend, but he knew what his brother would say: "You can't polish a turd." The truck was dying, which made him think, as he often did, that time was going by too fast.

Bobby Joe's pickup was parked next to the Dumpster. It wasn't in much better shape than Ford's, but Bobby Joe was a decent mechanic and he kept the twenty-year-old engine running with spare parts and elbow grease. His brother also didn't have to drive to New Orleans every weekend so his kid could have some kind of relationship with her mother.

Ford got out of the truck and pushed a pile of empty bun pallets away from the back door of the café. The orange plastic trays went farther than he intended, and the top one slid off onto the asphalt. He straightened the stack and shoved it against the café wall. He'd come out and move them later, if the bread man didn't pick them up. The back driveway was so small that delivery trucks had to unload in front. Real estate was precious in the campus area. The location was great for business, though.

He opened the back door and went inside. The kitchen smelled of freshly baked biscuits and industrial soap. As usual, Bobby Joe had cleaned the stainless-steel countertops and put everything away after finishing his prep. Ford took a black apron from the hook on the wall and hurried to the front.

Bobby Joe was breaking eggs into a bowl. He turned toward the grill to stir a fry pan–sized mound of hash browns and bacon bits with a metal spatula. "Nice of you to show up."

Ford tied on the apron and joined him, reading the order tickets hanging from a string over the sandwich board. "You got this veggie omelet?"

"Not yet," Bobby Joe said.

Ford glanced out into the dining room as he sprinkled vegetables onto his end of the grill. All of the seats at the counter directly in front of him were occupied. He recognized most of the customers sitting on the 1950s-era stools as well as the ones in the vinyl-covered booths. The café décor, from the blue flowered curtains to the black-and-white tiled floor, was original, as far as Ford knew. When they bought Rosie's, the brothers had agreed that they didn't want to change anything, even the name. Bobby Joe liked to joke with people about where Rosie was. Some of his favorite lies were: "Oh, she's in back, making her special biscuits"; "She died some years back in a tragic fryer accident"; and "She's serving time out at the Louisiana Correctional Institute."

Since the café was within walking distance of Louisiana A&M, many of the regulars were professors and staff. In the brief moment Ford took to survey the dining room, he spotted the grungy French professor who always requested off-menu pecan pancakes, two chemists in their stained jeans and T-shirts, and the married couple from the history department. The usual groups of undergraduates wearing baseball caps and flip-flops were scattered throughout, but Ford didn't know most of them. Students came and went too quickly.

He whisked some eggs, added salt and pepper, and poured

them onto the grill. He let the omelet cook for a minute before turning it and folding the vegetables inside. "Biscuits or toast with the omelet?"

"White toast," Bobby Joe answered. "Next order I need is Frenchy's pecan pancakes and bacon."

Ford tossed two slices of bread on the grill and reached for a clean plate. He watched the dining room over the counter. Todd was waiting tables today. The dreadlocked African American man reminded Ford of himself at that age—recently graduated from college and not sure what to do next. Ford had suggested making him a manager and maybe later a partner, but Bobby Joe thought he was still too immature. Watching Todd talking to a table of undergraduate girls while more customers arrived, Ford thought that his brother might be right.

"Order up, Todd!" Ford held out the omelet and toast that he knew had to belong to the English department secretary at table three.

Todd disengaged from the girls and grabbed the plate. "Got it, boss."

Ford shook his head at the young man's back and started on the pecan pancakes. At least Todd listened to him. He might like to chat with the customers a little too much, especially the female ones, but he worked hard and never complained. Ford made a mental note to talk to him about his future.

The rhythm of the café was familiar and comforting. Ford liked to joke around with his brother and occasionally entertain a lonely customer. Cooking was calming, even during the breakfast and lunch rushes. He felt at home cracking eggs, tossing salads, frying catfish for po'boys. All his frustrations and problems seemed to dissolve in the controlled chaos of service.

However, as Ford tried to settle into his routine while

pouring pancake batter and scrambling eggs, he felt off-kilter and didn't know why. *The woman on the playground.* There was something about her. He slid his spatula under a pancake and flipped it. Burnt. He tossed it in the trash, made another circle of batter on the grill, and dropped a few chopped pecans on top. He had to concentrate. It was no use thinking about the angry redhead. She clearly didn't like him.

He plated the pancakes and yelled, "Pecans up!"

"Frenchy French French always gets his little side of bacon. Always," Bobby Joe said. "Did you take an extra stupid pill this morning?"

Ford tossed two strips of bacon on the grill. He didn't bother to answer his brother. "What else do you need?"

"Those eggs, plus bacon and toast. After that, biscuits and gravy. Side of scrambled eggs."

Ford turned the bacon and put bread onto the grill. Which kid was the redhead's? He couldn't remember a single carrot-topped child on the playground. He seasoned the eggs and flipped them with his spatula. Maybe the girl who was screaming and lying on the ground was hers. That might explain why she had looked so angry.

"Come on, come on. Where's the bacon?" Todd held up the plate of pancakes.

Ford got the bacon off the grill and plated the scrambled eggs and toast. He slid both under the warmer before going to the back for the biscuits. He put two in the microwave and stirred the cream gravy. It smelled incredible. Ford was starving; he'd forgotten to eat breakfast again. There would be time for a breather after the rush was over. He hurried back to the front with the biscuits.

He'd been gone for a minute at the most, but in that time, three more orders had come in. Bobby Joe had started another batch of their popular hash browns and he was scrambling an egg at the same time. Ford read the next ticket and gathered the ingredients for a Western omelet. Now there was no space in his brain for anything except the food. But he knew that the redhead would be invading his thoughts again, whether he liked it or not.

CHAPTER 3

Ava put her oversized leather handbag down in her cubicle. The previous year's round of layoffs, right before Ava had joined the paper as a part-time worker, had halved the staff of the Entertainment department, leaving a bare minimum of two editors and four writers, not counting her. The empty cubicles were depressing, especially since many of the axed employees had left small tokens behind: a cutout of a newspaper headline that read "Good-bye and Good Riddance," a broken *Saint Jude Gazette* mug, old phone directories, half-used notebooks. Every time Ava walked by the empty desks that no one had bothered to clean out, she thought about the long careers of the absent writers and editors, some of whom had been her mentors when she first started in the business.

When she first worked as a stringer for the *Gazette*, Ava usually wrote stories on nights or weekends. After Jared left for Chicago, she had to quit because he wasn't there to watch the children. But two years later, she decided she needed to write again—for the money and also for her own sanity. She knew the paper had just laid off many of the older editors and reporters, but maybe they needed someone part-time who would work cheap.

One morning, after dropping the boys off at school and Sadie at day care, she drove over to the *Gazette* offices. Dressed in her most conservative navy blue suit and her favorite slingback heels, she stood in the parking lot and shaded her eyes to look at the mirrored *Gazette* building. The paper had moved from the downtown office where she and Jared had worked pre-kids. Ava was glad not to have the ghost of her ex-husband hanging around the place where she was hoping to find employment, but the downtown building had history and atmosphere that the new one lacked. The old newsroom had been located on the third floor, with windows overlooking the Mississippi River. Wooden cubicles divided the space, many of them cluttered with yellowing newspapers, reporter's notebooks, and journalism awards, evidence of the many years of occupation by old-school reporters. The bland rented building in front of her could have been a bank. In fact, two floors of it were sublet to Louisiana A&M Credit Union.

Ava went inside and walked up to the guard, who was shielded behind glass. "I'm here to see Rocky Dufresne," she said.

The young African American woman gazed at her and apparently decided she wasn't a threat. "Go on up," she said. "Fourth floor."

The walls near the elevator were decorated with a mock-up of the paper dating from the day the *Gazette* had moved in, two years previously. Two years since Jared left, years of joy and bitterness, changing diapers, brushing little teeth, cooking hot dogs, supervising school projects.

Ava shook her head, punched the elevator button, and waited. Across from the elevators a rusty printing press from the early days of the paper was displayed under glass next to a TV tuned to an insipid morning show. On the screen, a woman with a straw-colored helmet of hair showed viewers how to make a fall wreath using fake leaves and wire. The future of news.

When the elevator came, Ava got in and pushed the button for the fourth floor. As soon as she stepped out again, she smelled mildew. The office was exactly like she'd expected—gray carpet, gray cubicles, white window blinds. She had no idea where Rocky's desk was, and there were no signs or arrows. If she turned one way, she'd come to a bank of cubicles below a TV playing ESPN. That had to be the sports department. The other two choices were hallways leading to mazes of cubicles. She turned right and pretended that she knew where she was going.

After a few steps, she realized she was in the Entertainment department, which contained *Bon Temps*, which ran on Fridays, *Sunday Features*, and the daily *Life and Leisure* section. Most of the cubicles were empty because of the layoffs, but she recognized the faces in the few that were occupied. The survivors were Geoff Rodgers, a constantly dour man who gravitated toward stories about war heroes; hat aficionado and society writer Norma Winter; and food writer Marilyn Hendricks, who liked finger sandwiches and vintage clothing. Ava approached Marilyn, remembering her as the friendliest of the bunch.

"Ava Olson! I haven't seen you in a coon's age!" Marilyn swiveled in her chair and examined Ava. She wore a Kelly green dress with a wide belt, and her hair was dyed copper red. "How are the children?"

"In school, thank goodness."

"I know it! What brings you to our neck of the woods?"

"I'm looking for Rocky. I'm hoping he has some work for me."

Marilyn's red-painted lips turned down slightly. "He just might. No one left but us chickens."

"Who'd you lose?"

"Kevin retired before the shake-up started. Sharon was moved out to the Acadiana Bureau, Jessica and Lynn took the buyout."

"The buyout?"

"A retirement package they gave to some of the oldsters. It was an offer-you-can't-refuse kind of thing." Marilyn shook her head. "It's so empty in here now."

"It is."

Marilyn's phone rang, and she reached past her flower-painted coffee mug to grab it. "Rocky's in the far corner. Good luck."

Ava avoided the other reporters on her way to the editor's desk. Rocky's cubicle was next to a window, but with the mini-blinds and the tinting, it might as well have been a wall. His metal desk in the downtown building had suited him better. Flanked by open bookshelves and lit by sunlight from the nearby window, the old space had a literary feel.

Ava guessed that the closed black cabinets around Rocky's new desk contained books, but there was no way to tell. A few novels were lined up against the gray fuzzy cubicle wall, along with a picture of a boy grinning next to a birthday cake. Rocky had lost his wife to cancer and was raising his grandson for reasons he never revealed. His shoulders hunched slightly as he edited a story on his computer screen.

"Hey, Rocky," Ava said.

He turned around slowly. The editor hadn't changed in the two years she'd been away. He was short and muscular, with close-cropped gray hair, and he wore a plain white shirt and gray pants.

"Ava. Good to see you again. What have you been up to?" he said.

"Raising three kids on my own and attempting to hold on to my sanity."

"Sounds familiar. Grab a seat. There are plenty now."

Ava brought over a black office chair and sat down. "I'm sorry about your department. Losing everyone, I mean."

"The Great Purge, yes. The big Cheez Whizzes have cut the pages of all the sections, too. There's hardly room for book reviews anymore, though they can always find enough space for the pictures of the debutantes and society ladies at their benefit parties. Also, since Lynn took the buyout, I am now editing both the *Bon Temps* section and *Sunday Features*."

Ava didn't have as much time to read the *Gazette* as she used to, but she knew that *Bon Temps* was the Friday section that highlighted movies and events for the coming weekend, and *Sunday Features* contained book, art, and theater reviews. "Well, maybe this is the wrong time, then. I came to ask if you have any steady work for me. It doesn't have to be full-time."

Rocky's gaze was searching and, Ava thought, sympathetic. "Well, you're in luck, depending on how you look at it. The guy who used to type up our calendar of events for *Bon Temps* got a job on the copy desk. The position is half-time, and you can write at least one story a week. Advance stories. You can do the interviews over the phone for the most part. No weekend stuff."

Ava wanted to jump up and pump her fist in the air like her son Luke did when he found out they were having pizza for dinner. "I'll take it," she said.

Ava sat down and turned on her computer. It had been almost exactly a year since she'd accepted the job. Even though the work was often tedious, she didn't regret her decision.

Rocky crossed the coffee-stained, industrial low-pile carpet and leaned against the wall of her cubicle. The editor was two inches shorter than her. Ava had thought about wearing flat shoes to work so she wouldn't tower over him, but her boss didn't seem to care. Rocky, in his own words, "rolled with the punches."

"Here's your calendar stuff." He held out a battered manila folder containing the week's press releases and notices from various organizations.

Ava stood up to take it and set the folder down next to her computer. "Do you want to buy a raffle ticket for Luke and James's school?"

"What do I win?"

"Two bucks for a chance on a tablet computer."

"Sure, I'll bite. Put a note on the envelope and set it over there. Maybe you'll get some takers. Did you get attacked by a gang of vicious toddlers this morning?" Rocky pulled a black wallet from his pocket and extracted two dollars.

"Not that I know of. Why?"

"You have a smiley sticker on your butt and a twig in your hair." He reached up and plucked a stick from her messy curls.

"I'm just full of surprises." Ava twisted around and peeled the yellow smiley from the back of her skirt. Had Truck Guy seen that? Completely embarrassing. "Any other decorum violations I should know about? Lipstick on my teeth? Toilet paper sticking to my shoe?"

"Not that I can see. Check with me later." Rocky filled out the raffle ticket and handed it to her.

"Thanks, boss man, I owe you."

"Not if I win. How are the rugrats doing?"

"Sadie threw a fit this morning because her favorite teacher wasn't there when I dropped her off. Luke insists that his shoes are too small even though they're falling off his feet. James desperately needs some handheld video game thing. The drama is worse than a daytime soap," Ava said.

"Yup. It never ends, until all of a sudden it does. The

days are long, and the years are short, you know," Rocky said. "When my kids were young, I thought some of their soccer practices and band concerts would last forever. Now they don't need me anymore. Except Mike. It's not easy, but raising my grandson has been an unexpected blessing. He's already six, though. Life moves quick, especially when you get old like me."

"I know. I try to remember that, but it's hard when you're walking around with smiley stickers on your butt all morning. I think I'm losing my mind."

"Lost mine a long time ago. Good riddance." Rocky went over to the low bookshelf in front of the windowsill and started opening his mail, mostly packages containing brand-new books and galleys of soon-to-be-released books. He'd told her once that getting all those books was like Christmas every day. The ones he didn't keep and review, he gave away like a literary Santa Claus.

Ava sat down in her office chair and pulled off a sticky note for the raffle ticket envelope. Dealing with the kids' schools sometimes seemed like more work than her job. She was supposed to make an "All About Me" book for Luke with no fewer than thirty pages, including pictures of his family, pets, and favorite things. She also had to bring an individually wrapped, healthy snack for seventeen kids twice a month, and the list of supplies for Luke's class contained twenty-eight items. James's list was shorter, but she'd had to purchase new uniform shirts and pants since he'd outgrown the ones from the previous year. Then there were parties, fund-raisers, field trips, and always, always homework.

Ava finished her note and set the raffle ticket envelope on the windowsill. Looking out the tinted window that made even the sunniest day seem like twilight did nothing for her outlook on life. A black extended-cab pickup in the parking lot reminded her of Truck Guy. Yet, there was no reason to think about him. She had enough to worry about without obsessing over where he parked his stupid, huge vehicle. And she certainly shouldn't be imagining how he might look without his hat—or his shirt. Someone like him had to have a wife or girlfriend, and even if he didn't, he wouldn't be interested in a frizzy-haired divorcée with three kids.

"Whatcha looking at?" Rocky asked, opening a brown envelope containing a romance novel with a shirtless man on the cover.

Ava glanced at the book and felt her face go hot. "Nothing. Just daydreaming."

"Here, maybe you need this. Spice up those daydreams a little." Rocky put the novel in her hand. "It's not like I'm going to review it anyway."

"Anything else look good?" Ava said, trying to change the subject.

"Sure, there's the new Robert Olen Butler. He's always interesting. Do you want it? You know the deal—review the book, get it for free."

"Why don't you pay people to write reviews?" Ava asked.

"The editor before me used to farm them out to her friends and relatives, who of course were hacks. After that, the managing editor decided that it would be a volunteer thing. Works out okay, because I do most of them myself and I have a few professors at A&M who are used to writing for free." Rocky tore open another envelope.

"I don't have time for pro bono work."

"I understand. You have the kids to support. Doesn't that big-shot husband of yours send you anything from Chicago?"

"Ex-husband. Not as much as he should. He claims reporters don't make very much money. What I think is that certain reporters spend too much of their cash in bars." Ava tucked the romance novel under her arm.

"He's still living the swinging single life? No second family yet?"

"No. He didn't seem to want his first family. Not that I'm bitter about that or anything."

"Well, it took me two go-arounds to figure marriage out."

"You were married before Inga?" Ava asked. Rocky seldom talked about his wife, who had passed away from cancer before Ava and Jared came to work for the paper. Ava wasn't sure how long she'd been deceased, but she'd always assumed it was after their two children were grown up.

"Right out of college. Lasted a whole year. Some of us just have to get it wrong before we get it right." Rocky opened another book and added it to the growing pile on the windowsill.

"I'm not holding out hope that I'll ever get it right."

"Why? You're young."

Ava glanced out the window again. The truck was gone. "I'm thirty-five."

"So?" Rocky said.

"And I have three kids."

"Some men actually like kids. We're not all beer-swigging, skirt-chasing barbarians."

"What about you? You didn't remarry."

"No one could replace Inga. Never. Never. Never." Rocky threw the envelopes in the recycle bin and took the books back to his desk.

Ava went to her cubicle. She wanted to read the romance novel, but instead, she opened the newspaper's word processing program and brought up the calendar file for the week. She typed in the Catacular Ball benefit for the local pet adoption agency, a teen vampire party at the library, two plays at local theaters, and the Shrimp and Petroleum Festival. She yawned and looked longingly at her empty travel mug. She appreciated the flexible hours of her job and Rocky, who was understanding about doctor's appointments, field trips, and school project emergencies. Still, the drudgery of data entry put her brain into hibernation mode. She went to the office kitchen for a fresh cup of coffee, came back, and began typing again.

Two hours later, Rocky's voice startled her out of a near-stupor. "Damn it!"

She stood up quickly, stumbled, and almost fell, catching herself on the desk just in time to avoid sprawling out on the carpet. Her left foot had fallen asleep in her stiletto heel, again. She hauled herself to her feet and looked around.

Ava and Rocky always got to work early because of their children's school schedules, but many reporters came in later since news didn't really start happening until lunchtime. During the three hours they'd been in the office, writers and editors had drifted in and the room was as full as it ever got. But no one was working.

By the window, Geoff Rodgers was talking to Rocky and looking more dour than usual. He stroked his push-broom mustache and frowned. Norma Winter pulled the brim of her pink bucket-style hat down over her face as she whispered something to Marilyn Hendricks. After a moment, Norma sat back down at her desk and blew her nose on a wad of pink tissues.

Marilyn spotted Ava and wove around the cubicles until she reached her desk. "You haven't heard the news?" she said.

Ava leaned against the cubicle wall. Her foot still hurt. "No, what?"

Rocky walked over, on his way back to his desk. "The *Times-Picayune* is going to three days a week. People are being laid off as we speak."

"Right now?" Ava's lethargy was gone. Like the *Gazette*,

the *Picayune* had been reduced in size in recent years. The book section had been eliminated, and some of the local news had been replaced by wire stories. But it was unthinkable that the largest newspaper in the state could become a three-day-a-week tabloid, like a country rag from some small town. The self-destruction of the *Pic* was not even good news from a competitor standpoint. Though New Orleans was only eighty miles away, the *Gazette* had never been a rival to the *Picayune*. Tacit agreement kept each paper out of the other's territory.

"When people started showing up for work this morning, the managing editor brought them into his office one at a time to tell them whether or not they get to keep their jobs." Rocky scratched his stubble-topped head. "They're saying it's going to be more Web-based, but that's crap. They're just gutting it to save money and squeeze as much profit out as they can. All those people laid off. Probably at least eighty. I can't believe it. I wonder if Herbert Boudreaux is going to be fired. And Grace Smith. She's been there forever."

"I hope we're not next," Ava said. "How will the *Gazette* survive if the *Pic* can't?"

"I don't know. The largest city in the state will have no daily newspaper. It's a new world, Ava. We're in the wrong industry at the wrong time. I'm going to make some calls." Rocky went to his cubicle and picked up the phone.

Marilyn sat on the windowsill bookcase and crossed her stocking-covered ankles. "We're barely surviving. Our section has been reduced to nothing, staff has been cut so much that if an editor gets sick, it's panic time. You should think about another career while there's still time, Ava. You're young enough to start over, unlike the rest of us. We have to hang around until they send us to the glue factory. We don't have anywhere else to go."

"I don't want another career. They'll have to drag my dead body out of here," Ava said. Sure, typing the calendar stuff could be boring, but writing stories was endlessly interesting. That part of her return to the *Gazette* made all the data entry worthwhile. Now that it might be taken away from her again, she was ready to fight for it. She and Jared used to joke about being dinosaurs waiting for the meteor to hit. It didn't seem so funny anymore.

"I guess we all go down with the ship, then," Marilyn said, jumping off the bookshelf and returning to her desk.

CHAPTER 4

Ava balanced her tablet computer on her lap and bent over awkwardly to type on the tiny keyboard. The other parents waiting for the start of the day care's Summer's End program gossiped, read the program flyer, and took out cameras or cell phones. Ava couldn't afford to be that relaxed. Even though it was Friday and the story wasn't due until Tuesday, she had to finish it. Working over the weekend with the kids at home was impossible, and she had to compile the weekly calendar on Monday. She adjusted her bottom on the hard pew and caught the tablet just before it slid onto the tiled floor.

The Summer's End flyer was on the pew next to her, but she hadn't had time to read it. She thought Sadie was going to sing and talk about what she wanted to be when she grew up or something. Luke had spilled his Froot Loops on the sheet of lines that Sadie was supposed to memorize, and Ava had never gotten around to asking the teacher for another copy. In fact, she'd completely forgotten about the program until she'd seen all the kids dressed up when she dropped off Sadie. Luckily, Sadie didn't seem to notice that all her classmates wore frilly frocks or bow ties while she had on her usual shorts and knit dress.

At least Ava had managed to interview the circus ringmaster early so that she could attend the program. Not surprisingly, Carl Rogers loved to talk, which made Ava's job easy. He claimed that when he was a baby, he'd been bounced on the knee of one of the great Barnum & Bailey ringmasters. Clearly, he'd told the story a hundred times, but it was still entertaining. Ava learned that while most circus performers were third- or fourth-generation carnies, the Rogers family had been circus super fans instead. Apparently, there were actually people who followed circuses around the country like Grateful Dead groupies.

As she wrote the story, Ava's mind kept straying back to Rocky's comment that they were in the wrong industry. Four days had passed since the announcement about the demise of the *Picayune* and she still couldn't believe it had actually happened. Even though she hadn't shared Jared's lifelong dream to be a reporter, she'd quickly fallen in love with the job. She liked writing, but more than that, she was excited to find out how things worked. She loved interviewing and learning about the lives of a variety of people from rock collectors to circus performers. The only downside was that she felt like second fiddle to Jared. He'd won Louisiana Journalism Association awards every year he worked at the *Gazette*, something she never could have accomplished as a mere stringer. And then there was the little matter of him landing a job at the *Chicago Tribune*.

Ava folded the computer into its case with the keyboard. She couldn't send Rocky the story yet because the church didn't have publicly accessible Wi-Fi. She would have to wait until the program was over and go to a coffee shop. Just thinking about it made her fidget with impatience. She turned around, searching for any indication that the program was going to start, just in time to see Truck Guy entering the back of the sanctuary.

He wore the same outfit as the last time she'd seen him—black T-shirt, jeans, and work boots. He'd taken off his baseball hat and his curly blond hair was matted against his head. Without the cap, his pale blue eyes stood out against his tanned face. She nearly dropped the computer again as she reached down to put it in her bag. She hadn't been able to stop thinking about him, no matter how hard she tried. Silly as it was, she was disappointed every morning when she dropped off Sadie and his daughter, Nelly, was already on the playground. Would he sit next to her in one of the few seats left near the front, or would he stay in the back and risk not being able to see his daughter? Heavy steps sounded on the tiled floor and stopped right behind her. She pretended to read the program.

"Is this seat taken?" he asked.

Ava shook her head and he slid into the pew. He smelled like bacon. She was starving, as there hadn't been time to get lunch after the interview. Her stomach grumbled, and she hoped he didn't hear. She snuck a sideways glance at him. Short blond stubble stuck out from his chin. He rested his scarred, rough-looking hands on his lap. No ring, she noticed.

The school director came up to the microphone. Ms. Tanasha was a no-nonsense woman who wore stylish pantsuits. She always made Ava feel disorganized and inadequate, especially when she gently reminded her that she'd forgotten to pay Sadie's tuition for the month or sign up to bring treats for the children's beginning-of-the-year party.

"Parents, grandparents, friends, relatives, I want to thank you all for coming out to this program and for all you do. . . ." Ms. Tanasha began.

Ava tuned out her speech about the greatness of all the teachers and students at the day-care school. Waiting to send Rocky the story made her nervous. She wanted him to at least get a chance to glance at it before he went home for the weekend. The kids got out of school in just over an hour—leaving not enough time for her to go back to the office. Maybe she could sneak out and find some Wi-Fi so she could send the story after Sadie finished singing or whatever.

Truck Guy was doing his own part to raise her blood pressure. She couldn't remember the last time she'd been close to such an attractive man. If she moved her hand just a little, she would be able to touch his. She imagined she could feel the heat from his body and it weirdly made her shiver. God, when had she turned back into a teenager? Just because he didn't have a ring didn't mean he'd be interested in her. Besides, she was here to watch Sadie's program, not daydream about a man she didn't even know. He wasn't paying attention to her anyway. He was apparently actually listening to Tanasha's boring speech.

When the school director finished talking, Truck Guy reached into his shirt pocket and took out a stick of gum. Ava's fantasy of him asking her on a date at the end of the program suddenly disappeared. Jared had chewed gum all the time, even though he knew she hated it. He claimed that if she was exposed to it more, she'd get over her revulsion. The only result was that she began to realize that he was an insensitive jerk. To be fair, Truck Guy wasn't trying to torture her. He had no idea that the sound of gum chewing was like fingernails on a chalkboard to her. It was too late to switch seats. She edged away from him.

Truck Guy popped the stick of gum into his mouth and started chewing, cow-like, his whole jaw moving back and forth, back and forth. In her ears, the smacking of gum and saliva drowned out every other sound in the room. Jared's unsolicited advice had been to just not let it bother her. Ignore it, he said. But the wet sounds invaded her brain like tiny alien soldiers, increasing her agitation.

One of the teachers, a huge woman stuffed sausage-style into a black dress, herded her two-year-olds onto the stage. She patiently guided the squirming children to their places while the kids waved to their parents, examined the flower arrangements by the pulpit, and grabbed each other's clothing. Ava tapped her foot impatiently.

Pop, pop. Truck Guy was amusing himself with his gum. If Ava turned her head away, she would appear to be gazing out the window rather than watching the program. She clenched her teeth and tried to take a yoga breath. It didn't work. She could barely pull any air into her lungs.

The two-year-olds sang their songs and exited the stage as slowly as they'd come. If she didn't tell Truck Guy to knock it off during the break, she'd go crazy. She tapped him on the arm.

He stopped chewing and turned to look at her. When he wasn't smacking his gum, he was gorgeous. Ava almost changed her mind about confronting him, but she wouldn't be able to sit through the program listening to his disgusting mouth noises. "Can you please spit out the gum?" she said, trying to sound nonchalant.

He stared at her as though he couldn't process what she'd said. After a few painful seconds, he silently stood up, left the pew, and walked up the side aisle to the back of the church. Ava slumped down in her seat. Now she felt like the jerk. He might miss his daughter's program because of her. She hated herself for getting irritated. Why couldn't she just tune it out, like a normal person? Clearly there was something wrong with her. For that matter, she could have just found another seat, sparing the poor guy the humiliation of being reprimanded. Anxiety had muddled her thinking and it hadn't occurred to her to move. Dumb.

As the three-year-olds took their places, she watched the back doors. When the children began their first song,

Truck Guy returned and leaned against the back wall, no longer chewing gum, she noticed. Sadie and another little girl held hands, singing loudly and out of tune. The boys on either side of them stood silently, staring out into the crowd with blank expressions of either indifference or terror. One of the other girls lifted up her skirt and chewed on the hem. Another started picking her nose.

After finishing their songs, the children took turns saying their names and what they wanted to be when they grew up. When it was Sadie's turn, she stepped up to the microphone and said, "My name is Sadie. I want to be a toy maker and make toys for children."

This was news to Ava. Usually Sadie said she wanted to run a cupcake shop with her mother. Too bad Ava couldn't bake anything except brownies from a box mix. Her daughter's plans for the future always kept them together forever, which was fine by Ava. Sometimes they were going to have a store, or be princesses or fairies. Ava dreaded Sadie actually growing up and having her own life. Ava would be alone, without her precious little shadow. Ever since Jared left, the future had been a yawning tunnel of emptiness. She pictured herself in a tiny apartment, begging her children to visit. She had no husband, no siblings, and few friends. What was she going to do after the children were grown? Learn to knit? Watch soap operas?

She slipped out of the pew as the four-year-olds assembled. Truck Guy was still leaning against the wall. As she started up the aisle, he left. She tried to catch up, but her high-heeled sandals limited her speed to that of an overcaffeinated octogenarian. She followed him through the front door and out into the parking lot. "Hey," she called out, breathing hard from her attempted sprint.

He stopped and waited a second before turning around. He put on his hat and pulled it low over his eyes.

"Hey, I'm sorry. I just can't handle gum-chewing," Ava said.

From under the bill of the cap, he gave her a pathetic, puppy-dog look. "You have something against *me* and I don't know why."

"I do not!" Ava was shocked. She'd never even talked to him before. Why did he think that?

"Come on, the other day on the playground. You were giving me the stink eye."

"No, I wasn't."

He folded his arms across his chest. "Tell me. I can handle it."

"I was mad that you parked your truck right in front of the playground and left it running. That's all. It was stupid of me. I was in a bad mood because I was going to be late to work and Sadie was crying and I can't afford the school supplies for my older kids plus the tuition for her . . . just a million things," Ava said.

"I park right in front because I'm always terrified that Nelly is going to get hit by a car. I know it's crazy, but I have nightmares about it. And I leave the truck running because a lot of times in the morning, if I shut it off, it won't start again."

Ava held out her hand. "Ava. I'm sorry."

"That's your name? Ava?" He took her hand and squeezed it gently, his rough skin contrasting with the careful touch.

"Yeah."

"I'm Ford. Anyway, you should apply for a scholarship for Sadie. That might help."

"I guess I could."

"Yankees never want to ask for help."

"You figured out my dark secret." It usually took people about two seconds to realize that Ava wasn't from Louisiana. Some even managed to guess the state.

"Wisconsin, right?"

"Dairy land, yes. And before you ask, we do have more cows than people."

"That's okay. Louisiana has more alligators than people." Ford reached into his pocket, took out a set of keys, and bounced them on his palm. "I have to get back to work. No more evil looks, okay? I'd rather you just tell me. Like with the gum."

"Okay." Ava wanted to explain that she wasn't really as obnoxious and obsessive-compulsive as she seemed, but he was already walking toward his truck. She found herself hoping that it wouldn't start so she could give him a ride to wherever he was going. But the engine turned over and a few seconds later he was gone.

Ava got into the van and sat for a minute, thinking. She had to go somewhere with Wi-Fi, but the coffee shop only sold soggy croissants and too-sweet muffins. There were a few restaurants nearby in the strip by the A&M campus. Maybe it was the smell of bacon on Ford, but she was hungry for breakfast food.

Ava hadn't eaten at Rosie's Café since Jared moved to Chicago. She hated taking the children to restaurants, except for fast food. If Rosie's hadn't changed in the years since she'd been there, the food would be good and bacon-y. Better yet, the café was nearby and the counter meant she wouldn't have to eat at a table by herself. As she walked in, her stomach grumbled again. The place smelled like hamburgers, bacon, eggs, and French fries. Choosing what to eat was going to be difficult. She wanted everything, in large quantities. She took a seat at the counter and immediately almost fell off the stool.

"Are you stalking me?" Ford said, from behind the grill.

Ava gave herself a mental slap to the forehead. She hadn't

noticed earlier that his cap had the name of the café on it. Or maybe she had noticed and that had given her subconscious the idea to come to Rosie's. She tried to act businesslike as she opened her tablet. "I'm innocent, I swear. I just need Wi-Fi so I can turn in my story. And something to eat."

Ford flipped the hamburgers he was grilling onto buns and started dressing them with lettuce and slices of tomato. "I guess I could serve you if you aren't too irritated by any of my other personal habits."

"You're not still mad at me about the gum, are you?" Ava asked. "I'm sorry it bothered me so much."

"Nah. You're a customer now. I try never to be mad at anyone who eats my food. What can I do you for?"

"The Wi-Fi password. Please."

"Password is bacon199. You want a sandwich?" Ford said.

"Yes, please. I think I forgot to have breakfast and I missed lunch somehow." Ava typed in the password and then finally e-mailed Rocky her story. Concentrating was difficult, not just because of her hunger. Knowing that Ford was a few feet away was pleasantly distracting. A little voice inside her head kept telling her that he was sexy even with the apron tied around his waist. She told the voice to shut up and stared at the computer screen. That stupid voice had said similar things about Jared and, aside from the children, all her ex had brought her was trouble. Or at least, it seemed that way now.

When she looked up, Ford was placing raw shrimp on the grill. He turned and took a po'boy bun from a bag. "I'm going to make you the best sandwich you've ever had. Any objections?"

"I guess I can handle that." Ava admired his backside as he brushed melted butter on the bun and opened it onto the grill. So what if she enjoyed the view? She could appreciate the way his jeans hugged his waist and followed the shape of his legs down to his tan work boots without worrying so much. Her tablet pinged. There was a typically concise message from Rocky: *Got story. Reading.*

Ford took the bun off the grill, then went further back into the kitchen and returned with an unlabeled glass jar. "This is just something I've been experimenting with." He sliced open an avocado, mashed it with a fork, and mixed in yogurt, lime juice, salt, and pepper.

"It really doesn't look like you're making a po'boy," Ava said.

"Just wait." Ford spread the avocado mixture on the bun and added pickled vegetables from the jar. He topped the sandwich with the shrimp and handed her the plate over the counter. "Iced tea?"

"Sure. Unsweetened."

The sandwich was beautiful—pink, plump shrimp, vibrant pickled cucumbers and carrots, and that tangy avocado sauce. Ava took a bigger bite than she meant to, but she didn't regret it. The sauce was perfect with the spicy shrimp and salty vegetables. Ford was right; she'd never eaten anything like it. The po'boy bore no resemblance to the average restaurant sandwich with dry, deep-fried shrimp and limp lettuce and tomato. This was the food of the gods.

He grinned as he set the tea in front of her. "Hungry, huh?"

Feeling silly, Ava nodded again. She had too much food in her mouth to even consider speaking. She probably would have been speechless with amazement anyway. The man was cute and he could cook. Something was wrong with the universe if he didn't have a girlfriend.

Ava took a long drink of cold tea. Before she could say anything about the sandwich, Ford turned away again to fill fry baskets with frozen potato sticks. She checked her e-mail again. Rocky had written, *Story fine.*

Ava relaxed and finished the sandwich. Normally, she couldn't eat more than half of a po'boy, but this time she devoured every bite.

Ford plated a cheeseburger with French fries and came back to the sandwich station. "I take it you liked the food," he said.

"Yes, thanks a lot. I hardly ever manage to eat breakfast anymore. Getting three kids ready for school is like trying to walk through a hurricane. I'm lucky if I get coffee."

"I can't imagine having three. Just dressing my little princess is a trial. If I try to put the wrong clothes on her, she goes into full-blown meltdown. And God forbid I try to get her to use the toilet."

"I don't have the energy for that fight with Sadie right now." Ada drank the last of her iced tea. "I'm on kid number three and I'm still scared of potty training."

The kitchen door swung open. The man who entered bore a passing resemblance to Ford, though his hair was dark and thinning on top. He put on a Rosie's cap and tied an apron around his waist. "I see you scared away all the customers while I was gone. I knew you were ugly, but not enough to empty out the place," he said to Ford.

"Well, you should know. At least Mom didn't make me sleep outside." Ford took a rag from beneath the prep station and wiped down the counter. "Ava, this is my somewhat obnoxious brother, Bobby Joe."

"Pleased to meet you. Glad we have one customer left," Bobby Joe said.

"You'd better stop talking and start working because I have to leave in ten minutes to go get Nelly," Ford told him.

"Yeah, yeah, Mister Mom." Bobby Joe took a stack of nearly empty prep containers and went back through the kitchen door.

"Lunch is on the house," Ford said to Ava.

"No, I can't let you do that." She reached into her bag for her wallet.

"Sorry, we don't have a shrimp po'boy on the menu. I can't write you a ticket."

"Now you're making me feel really guilty for asking you to spit out the gum. You have to understand that my ex was the most obnoxious gum chewer on the planet."

"I understand. I have some bad associations with my ex too. Though they mostly involve her terrible cooking. Come back sometime. I'm always here, unless I'm driving my little princess around."

"I will if you promise to make me that po'boy again. Why isn't it on the menu?" Ava asked.

"My brother. He really runs the show around here." Ford shrugged.

"Tell him I liked it and I'll come here as often as I can if he adds it to the menu." Ava shouldered her bag. "I have to leave now, though. It's time to get the kids from school."

"Thanks for coming in. I'll see you around."

Ava thought he seemed a little sad as he began wiping down the counter, like maybe he didn't want her to leave. She told herself that it was her imagination. But when she reached the door, she looked back and he was watching her go. He smiled and waved.

CHAPTER 5

After Ava left, Ford finished cleaning up and headed for the back door. Bobby Joe was dicing onions at the prep table. He scraped them into a plastic tub. "Cute chick."

"She's the mother of one of the kids in Nelly's class," Ford said.

"Too bad."

Ford untied his apron. He didn't want to talk to his brother about Ava. "You'd better get your lazy butt on the grill because I'm leaving."

"Someday Jeanie and I are gonna have a kid and then you'll be screwed."

"Does she want to?"

Bobby Joe shrugged and stacked the onions on top of a container of sliced tomato. "I don't know. She wants to go back to school and get her master's right now."

"Good for her," Ford said.

"Good for nothing." Bobby Joe picked up his *mise en place* and went to the front.

Ford tossed his apron in the laundry hamper and left. He had to crank the engine three times before the truck turned over. He kept putting off asking Bobby Joe to look at it, because he hated that his brother was a better mechanic than him. He should have taken auto shop instead of chemistry in high school. It wasn't like he had any use for the periodic table anyway. Bobby Joe was always the practical brother. If it wasn't for him, Ford would still be sitting around in a studio apartment trying to figure out what to do with a degree in American history. Marion always said he was un-ambitious, that his brother was the one with all the ideas. In fact, Bobby Joe had encouraged him to marry Marion, when he wasn't sure he wanted to accept her proposal. That hadn't worked out so well, but the café had. So what if it was the brainchild of his little brother?

Ford gave the truck a little gas and pulled out of the café lot. He knew that he probably wouldn't see Ava when he picked up Nelly, but he found himself hoping anyway. He got the impression that she wasn't a woman who smiled a lot. He would like to make her laugh every time he saw her. Now, there was a practical goal.

When he got to the school, she was walking to her van. Besides Sadie, she had two elementary-school-age boys with her. Both had carrot-red hair and their mother's long legs. The older one walked slightly hunched over, as though try-ing to seem smaller. In contrast, the younger one bounced along with childish enthusiasm. Ava looked tired. She held herself much like her older son—head down, auburn hair cascading around her face. She didn't appear to notice his truck. Ford wanted to get out and say something to her, but he was afraid she wouldn't want to talk to him. Okay, maybe he was just afraid, scared of being shot down, discarded again like a used-up paper towel. He'd been there too re-cently with Marion. Ava was gorgeous and she had a think-ing-person's job. He was just a guy who flipped burgers for a living. He sometimes wondered if that was why Marion left. Was he boring? She seemed to think so. Last he'd heard, she was dating another doctor. Maybe they talked about bedside manner together. The thought made him smile. Probably not. Marion had always had a policy against discussing work at home. He thought it was stupid. There, he admitted it. He'd hated all her stupid rules. Everyone had to stay at the table until the whole family was done eating, Nelly had to take a bath every night, even if she didn't need one. Her toys had to stay in her room and he had to line up his shoes neatly on the mat and hang up his keys as soon as he got home. Living with her was like being in a military compound.

Ava and her kids got in the van and left. Ford felt painfully alone as he headed for the door. Fridays were the worst, because he had to take Nelly to New Orleans to be with her mother for the weekend. The drive down was always fun, with the two of them singing along to Nelly's favorite AC/DC album. But the return trip without her was miserable. He usually found himself worrying about whether Marion was too hard on her, wondering whether he let her watch too much TV, and dreading the long, empty hours until he could bring her back home.

He trudged up the steps to Nelly's classroom and got her sheet and blanket from her cubby. As soon as he appeared at the door, Nelly ran toward him. "Daddy!"

Ms. Bee smiled. She had short, curly hair and red reading glasses on a beaded chain around her neck. Ford felt like a giant next to her. He took up too much space in her little classroom with its wee chairs and kid-sized bookshelves.

"She had a good day today," the teacher said. "We ate turkey sandwiches for lunch and painted pictures."

Ford tried to sound cheerful. "Great!"

"I peed the potty," Nelly said.

"She did a good job," Ms. Bee said. "Kept her pull-up dry all day."

"Fantastic! What a good girl, Nelly!" Ford said.

"See y'all Monday," Ms. Bee said.

"Bye!" Nelly skipped to the door and Ford followed, pink sheet and blanket tucked under his arm.

Nelly insisted on opening the gate when they got outside. In response to Ava's complaint, Ford had put the truck in one of the parking spots rather than leaving it in front of the door. The strip of asphalt between the sidewalk and the pickup seemed miles long even though it wasn't more than a few feet. Nelly was so small and the cars and trucks—his especially—were huge. She could be crushed like a bug so easily. Anxiety rose in his throat and threatened to choke him. "Let me carry you," he said.

"No!" Nelly twisted away from him and started to run into the parking lot.

Panicked, Ford grabbed her arm. Even though none of the cars were moving, in his mind she was inches from being killed.

"You hurt me." Nelly looked up at her father with big, watery eyes.

"I'm sorry. But you can't run in the parking lot. You have to hold Daddy's hand."

"Okay."

Once she was buckled into her car seat, Ford relaxed a little. She was safe. Would he have an anxiety attack every time Nelly walked across a parking lot? "We have to go see Mommy now."

"No."

Lately, Nelly automatically said no to everything, so Ford didn't take her comment very seriously. He turned the key and nothing happened. The battery had to be dead. At least he hoped that was all it was. He rested his head against the steering wheel.

"What wrong, Daddy?" Nelly said.

"The truck is broken."

"Oh."

Ford knew that his brother wouldn't be happy about having to leave the café to come help him. Darlene, the night cook, probably hadn't arrived yet and Todd made omelets as tough as rubber. Ford lifted his head, took out his cell, and dialed Marion instead. "We're going to be a little late," he told her voice mail. "I'll call you when we're close."

"Come on, honey. Let's walk." Ford got out of the truck and put Nelly on his shoulders. She grabbed his hat and held on.

The neighborhood around the school was mostly student housing for A&M. The houses and dilapidated apartment buildings had dying plants and thrift store couches on their porches. The students they passed smiled at Nelly sitting on Ford's shoulders. Ford eyed the scraggly-haired, bearded college boys. In a decade, guys like them would be trying to court Nelly. He could see the wisdom of locked towers like the one in her *Rapunzel* book.

By the time they arrived at the café, Ford's shirt was soaked with sweat. He put Nelly down and led her inside.

Bobby Joe looked up from the sandwich he was assembling. "What are you doing here, Ford? Gonna teach Nelly to make scrambled eggs?"

"Truck won't start. I need your jumper cables."

"Shoot. You think it's the battery?"

"I hope so. Otherwise, it's the alternator." Ford changed into the extra Rosie's T-shirt he kept behind the mustard jars.

"Okay, you take over. I'll get you a new battery and put it in. Your truck's at Nelly's school, right?"

"Yeah." Ford washed his hands and tied on an apron. Bobby Joe would handle things, as usual. Even though he was younger, he'd always been the take-charge kid—at least when it came to putting the wheel back on the wagon or changing the oil on Dad's old Chevy. That hadn't changed too much. Sometimes letting his brother take over—make most of the decisions regarding the café and even help him choose his apartment after Marion left—made Ford feel like a child. But it was easier to just go along.

Ford set Nelly down at a table and gave her a kid's menu and crayons. Too bad he hadn't thought to bring some toys.

"You still taking Nelly to New Orleans?" Bobby Joe asked.

"After I get the new battery. I have to. Marion will kill me if I don't."

"You're coming back after, right?"

"I'll be here to close, don't worry." Ford examined the tickets and started making hamburgers. He put some fries on for Nelly. He was glad for the excuse to have her around a little longer. She had flipped the menu to the blank side and was drawing a rainbow.

Two hours later, they were on the road with a new battery. Ford tapped on the steering wheel impatiently. The delay meant that he now had to face rush hour traffic out of Saint Jude. He sipped his Coke and turned on the radio.

"AC/DC!" Nelly cried.

"Okay." Ford put in her favorite CD instead. Marion thought he shouldn't give in to Nelly's demands, but he couldn't see the harm in playing the music she liked or letting her eat fries. Marion could say what she wanted; she didn't spend every day bathing her, feeding her, helping her do puzzles, fixing her impossible hair. She had the idea that she was shaping Nelly into a certain kind of person by taking her to dance lessons, making her listen to Mozart, and feeding her wheat germ. Most of the time, Ford just tried to get through the day. Keeping her fed, clean, and relatively happy was enough to wear him out. Not that he minded. Before he knew it, she'd be a teenager and want nothing to do with him. He had to enjoy her childhood while he could, especially since his dream of having a large family had been squashed by Marion. One child was plenty, in her view.

Ten miles out of Saint Jude, the traffic opened up and Ford nudged the truck to seventy miles per hour. He'd been right about the battery. That was all it needed, for the moment anyway. Nelly was looking out the window. The passage of vehicles on the road seemed to mesmerize her.

Ford punched Marion's number on his cell. "We'll be there in fifteen minutes."

Marion blew air into the phone. "You're two hours late."

"The battery on the truck died."

"She missed her dance lesson."

Ford wanted to make a sarcastic remark about Nelly's future career as a prima ballerina being ruined, but he settled for rolling his eyes and a simple "Sorry."

Marion answered the door of her condo wearing a white outfit that was either a sweat suit or a pantsuit. After the divorce, she'd cut her brown hair short and dyed it an unconvincing blond. She was pixie-like, with delicate features and tiny feet. The new hairdo made her look like Peter Pan. She bent down to greet Nelly. "Hello, darling."

Ford felt like a stranger in his ex's condo. She'd bought it after moving to New Orleans and decorated it with new furniture and knickknacks. It was the sort of place most people would live in after their kids grew up—the couches and chairs were white and the stone table was for setting drinks on, not for kids' art projects. Nelly's things were confined to her room behind the kitchen.

"What's new with you?" Marion asked Ford.

Ford watched Nelly open her small suitcase and take out

her favorite stuffed animal, a purple pony. "Same as always. Business is good at the café. How about you?"

"I'm still dating Nate, in case you're wondering. Other than that, nothing. Would you like to sit down?"

Ford didn't want to hang around and chat, but he understood the importance of maintaining their relationship. He sat on one of the armchairs and Marion took the other.

"I can't stay long because I promised Bobby Joe I'd get back to close for him. He's been there all day and he needs a break," he said. "I'm sorry we were late and Nelly missed her lesson."

Nelly wandered off to her room, dragging the pony by its tail, but leaving the bag on the living room floor.

"Have you ever thought about getting a bigger building for the café? You could hire more people to help you, make more money, and have some time off once in a while," Marion said. "Maybe you could afford a new truck too."

Ford gritted his teeth. Marion was trying in her own way to be helpful, but she didn't understand that he wasn't like her. He didn't feel like he always had to improve things. Marion wouldn't be content to own one small café—she'd want a chain of restaurants. One of the last fights they'd had was over when Ford was ever going to grow up and stop being just a fry cook. That was when Ford realized she was never going to accept him for who he was. "Bobby Joe and I like to keep it simple. We're happy with our little café and just a few cooks. If we expanded, we might make more money, but it would end up being a lot more work," he said.

"That's not necessarily a bad thing. Working harder, I mean," she said.

Spoken like someone who spent seventy hours a week at the hospital, which Ford was pretty sure Marion did. "I guess I'm just lazier than you, Marion."

"I didn't mean that."

"I know you didn't. But it's true. I don't work as hard as you and I accept that. I'm never going to be one of those guys who owns ten restaurants. That's just not me. I know that was a big part of the problem between us and I'm sorry about that."

Marion leaned her head back against the chair, like she often did when she was thinking. "Yeah, I guess it was. We didn't understand each other very well."

Ford wasn't sure that was exactly right. It was more that they couldn't live with the differences. He wanted a family that ate dinner together every night and played board games on rainy days. She wanted to become a highly successful emergency room doctor. Neither of them realized at first how incompatible those two visions were. But, he wasn't going to argue that point with her. It was over now and all they had to do was get along for Nelly's sake.

"Let me say good-bye to Nelly and then I'd better get going," Ford said.

"Okay." Marion stood up. "I guess you'll pick her up on Sunday as usual?"

"Yeah. Early in the afternoon so we can visit my mom, if that works okay for you."

"That's fine. She just has piano lessons at one o'clock, so any time after two is fine."

Ford went to Nelly's room. She was building a house for Pony using fabric-covered foam bricks. The rest of her toys were lined up on a bookshelf—wooden blocks, board books, puzzles, fabric donuts that had to be stacked by size. Everything was designed to teach her something, like shapes, sizes, or simple math. Ford preferred to buy her plastic ponies and play food.

"Hi, Daddy. You go now?" Nelly said.

"Yes, I have to go to work, sweetie. I'll see you Sunday. Have fun with your mom."

"Okay." She came over and hugged him, Pony still dangling from one hand. "'Bye."

Back in the truck, Ford started the engine and thought about changing the CD, but left it in instead. Even though he'd heard "Back in Black" hundreds of times, the AC/DC song always made him feel a little better. The music wasn't enough to melt away those eighty miles, though, or to erase the fact that Marion had a new boyfriend and he was still alone.

CHAPTER 6

The inch of coffee at the bottom of Ava's *Gazette* mug was cold. To acquire more caffeine, she would have to shove her aching feet back into her black-and-gold three-inch stilettos and hobble to the office kitchen. That wasn't going to happen.

Instead, she decided to appeal to her boss's better nature, or at least to his own need for caffeine. "Rocky, doesn't a hot cup of chicory-enhanced dark roast sound good right about now?"

He glanced over at her. "Yeah, it does. Are you asking or offering?"

"Asking. Pretty please."

"It's the shoes again, isn't it?" Rocky got his mug and walked to her desk.

"They look so good, but hurt so bad," she said.

"Have you ever thought about bringing a pair of sneakers or something, just for emergencies?" Rocky asked, taking her coffee mug.

"Do you really think tennis shoes would match this dress?"

"No, but we're reporters here, not fashionistas. Look

at Norma Winter. She doesn't exactly worry about what matches. Today, she's got on a pink hat with peacock feathers and a green-and-white-striped dress," Rocky said.

"So, that's what I should aspire to?" Ava raised her eyebrows.

"No, I'm just saying the bar is pretty low."

"I'm going to die of caffeine withdrawal before we finish this conversation."

"Fine, fine. I'll hurry. I don't want to fill out a bunch of paperwork about some reporter dying from lack of coffee," he said.

"You'd do it anyway. Because I'm so charming and lovable."

"Something like that." Rocky rolled his eyes and headed toward the office kitchen.

Ava leaned back in her chair and stared at the water-stained ceiling. She hated Fridays. Not so much the promise of the weekend ahead—Saturdays and Sundays with the kids were usually fun—but because of the drudgery. The previous Friday, she'd had her circus story to write and Sadie's school program to get her out of the office. This week, she'd written her story for the next edition already, putting her almost a week ahead of the deadline. The calendar was due on Wednesday, so that was already done. Which left only one thing: the dreaded dining guide.

Even in the age of the Internet, the *Gazette* continued to run a list of local restaurants. Whenever she had nothing else to do, Ava was supposed to call and verify the hours of operation and whether each restaurant was still in business. Since there were hundreds of listings, by the time she got to the end, it was always time to start over again. That morning, she'd flipped back to the beginning—American Cuisine, whatever that meant. She'd called Applebee's first and worked her way through Quizno's, talking to bored waitresses, clueless busboys, and distracted "sandwich artists."

Ava had had worse jobs in her life, but that fact didn't make her feel much better. She tried not to think about Jared writing investigative stories about the state of prisons in Illinois or changes to the welfare system. The *Chicago Tribune* editors would never ask their prizewinning journalist to call the Number One Chinese Restaurant to find out whether they were open on Sundays. Ava still held out hope that someday, somehow, she could lose the calendar and dining guide duty, but keep her job.

"I never found the ceiling tiles to be all that interesting." Rocky set Ava's mug on her desk.

"I was having a moment," Ava said.

"Excuse me. Didn't mean to interrupt."

"Thanks for the coffee." Ava took a sip.

"You're welcome. I'm sorry you have to do the dining guide today. I wish I could give you a better assignment," Rocky said.

"It's not your fault the industry is imploding."

Rocky took a drink from his own mug. "It's more like a slow-moving forest fire."

"Thanks. That makes me feel so much better."

"Your circus story looks good. Grab a copy. Oh wait, I forgot that you can't walk."

"Please bring me one, my thoughtful, noble, and wise boss."

Rocky took a copy of the *Bon Temps* section from under his arm and tossed it onto her lap. "You're a good writer. That's why I put up with you and your shoes. Listen, I heard a rumor that there might be some full-time jobs opening up in New Orleans."

"At the *Pic*? It's dead, remember?" Ava said.

"Not dead, just dismembered. No, at the *Gazette*. We might be finally invading the Big Easy. There's talk of setting up a bureau or maybe even starting a separate paper just for our Mardi Gras–obsessed friends down there."

"Interesting."

Rocky leaned against the cubicle wall. "Just rumors. And if it happens, I imagine they will hire some of the laid-off *Pic* writers. But there's no reason you couldn't apply. It's worth a shot."

"I don't know. I really don't want to move to New Orleans," Ava said. "The kids like their schools, I have a house. . . ."

"Don't you want a full-time job? Don't you want to stop typing in the stupid events calendar every week? Come on, Ava."

"Besides, like you said, they'll probably just hire some of the *Pic* writers."

"You'll never know if you don't try," Rocky said before he went back to his desk.

Ava opened the paper he'd given her and found her story. The circus had provided photos of trained tigers and acrobats. The ringmaster grinned at her from one of the pictures. He had sounded like someone who would be svelte with sleek black hair, but he was actually bald and thick around the middle.

The article reminded her why she was in the business. It wasn't a great work of literature, but she'd loved writing it. People would pick up the newspaper and read the story, or at least skim it. Maybe they'd get excited about the circus and buy tickets. It would be nice to be a full-time reporter, but the idea of relocating to New Orleans was scary. She'd heard that the public schools down there weren't very good and she couldn't afford private school tuition. Getting a new house, a pediatrician, a dentist, car repair shop, and just finding her way around seemed impossible. It would be ten times harder than moving to Louisiana with Jared. Back then, they'd had each other for support and no children to worry about yet. No, she didn't want to move. She would make more money, but it wouldn't be worth it.

She took a long drink of coffee and flipped to the next page of the dining guide. Rosie's Café was at the top.

She sat up straight and put down her mug. What would she say if Ford answered the phone? She couldn't pretend she didn't know him. Should she mention the sandwich he'd made for her or promise to come in for lunch again and pay for her own food? Maybe she ought to ask about his daughter and invite them to go to the circus or something. But then, he would think she was only interested in him as the father of Sadie's friend. And she wanted more, or she thought she did. The idea was crazy. So, he made an incredible sandwich and looked good in jeans. That didn't mean they were soul mates.

She picked up the phone, reminded herself that she had a job to do, and dialed the number.

"Rosie's Café. Ford here."

Ava could hear sizzling, talking, and the clanging of dishes in the background. Her pulse sped up as she imagined Ford holding the phone to his ear while turning hamburgers on the grill. "Um, this is Ava. You know, Sadie's mom? Um, I'm calling to verify your hours of operation for the *Gazette*'s dining guide."

"We're open every day, six a.m. to midnight," Ford said. "Anything else?"

"No, that's it, thanks." Ava slammed the phone down and slumped in her chair. He didn't sound interested in her at all. In fact, he sounded irritated. That settled it. He didn't like her and she was too old for crushes. She'd have to just forget about romance. Anyway, she was fine on her own.

The three years since Jared had left hadn't been perfect, but being alone was better than being with the wrong person. When she thought about all the hours she'd wasted worrying about Jared, asking herself when he was coming home, where he'd really been, whether she had done something to drive him away, she was furious, mostly at herself. She wasn't going to be a sucker again.

Ford didn't have to like her. She was just the mother of his daughter's friend. Even still, he could have been a little more polite. Fine, well, she wasn't in a very good mood either. Did he think she wanted to call all these restaurants? That she made the whole thing up just to bother him? She was leaning back to look up at the ceiling tiles again when she saw Marilyn standing outside her cubicle.

"Darling, you hung up that phone so hard, I was afraid you were going to break it," Marilyn said. She wore a vintage navy blue polyester dress belted just above her waist and matching ankle-strap heels. She was balancing a plate of cookies on one hand and extended it into Ava's cubicle. "Try these. I want to feature them in my *Bake This!* column."

Ava took a cookie, even though she really didn't feel like eating.

Marilyn set the plate down on the windowsill. "Now, tell me all about it."

"Oh, it's nothing," Ava said, trying the cookie. "This is incredible, though."

"Thank you. The secret is to combine butter and shortening. Butter for flavor and shortening for texture. There's a life lesson in that somewhere, but I don't know what it is."

"If a food writer position opened up in New Orleans, would you apply for it?" Ava asked.

"Gee, I don't know. My kids are grown and moved away, and my husband is deceased, so there's nothing really holding me here. But starting over is scary, isn't it?"

Ava resisted the urge to ask for another cookie. "Rocky wants me to apply if there's a full-time job in entertainment. But I'd hate to make my kids move schools, especially James. He's old enough now that it would be hard for him to lose his friends."

"I had to move my kids here from Lafayette when they were in elementary school. They weren't happy at first, but they adapt. It might even be good for them. Sometimes challenges make us grow. Another life lesson," Marilyn said.

"It's starting to sound like a good idea. I could apply, anyway."

"Do it." Marilyn picked up her cookie plate. "You deserve a full-time job."

Marilyn brought her treats over to Rocky. Ava sighed and studied the list of restaurants again. Nothing was keeping her in Saint Jude, that was for sure.

CHAPTER 7

Ford tossed the cordless phone on the counter. He was officially an idiot. A beautiful woman had called him and all he could do was recite the café's hours of operation. Granted, she'd phoned during the lunch rush, but he could have at least asked her to call back at a less busy time. He'd been in a bad mood because of Marion, as usual. Nelly didn't know enough to keep her mouth shut around her mother. For some reason, Marion had waited until that morning to call and lecture him about what he fed their daughter. "Nelly told me that you let her have fries and ice cream every day. That's hardly a balanced diet. Honestly, who's the adult in your house?"

Nelly was exaggerating. She didn't have fries every day. They did eat ice cream after dinner because it was a nice little before-bed ritual and Nelly liked to pick the flavor. Ford didn't care what his ex thought. A nightly scoop of fudge ripple was not going to make his daughter obese.

"Ford, your bacon's burning," Bobby Joe said. "Who was that on the phone?"

"No one. The newspaper. They wanted to check our hours or something."

"Nice of them to call during lunch." Bobby Joe was

working salads and sandwiches. He layered a po'boy bun with mayonnaise, lettuce, and tomato and then added ham and cheese.

"Yeah, well, whatever." Ford lifted the bacon off the grill and threw it in the trash. He had to get over his funk about Marion and find a way to make it up to Ava. She'd probably already written him off.

Ford backed the truck into a space in the day-care parking lot. He really wanted to see Ava, but he'd look like a stalker if he sat and waited for her. Anyway, it was 2:55 and her van wasn't in the lot. He'd almost certainly missed her, but he didn't want to call the newspaper. He hated talking on the phone, especially to apologize.

When he got to the classroom, only Nelly and a boy named Steve were left. Ava must have come and gone.

"She had a little accident," Ms. Bee said.

Ford glanced down at Nelly in alarm. He'd been so busy thinking about Ava that he hadn't even looked at his own daughter. She didn't appear to be hurt. He bent down and hugged her. Instead of the pink dress she'd insisted on wearing that morning, she had on shorts and a T-shirt.

"She had a messy diaper and pulled it down before I could get to her," the teacher said. "Her clothes are in this bag."

"I'm sorry," Ford said. He exhaled. That kind of accident he could handle.

"It's okay. I'm sorry her dress got messed up. Don't forget to bring another backup outfit for her Monday," Ms. Bee said.

"I will. Thanks." Ford looked down at Nelly. Her hair was falling out of its pigtails again.

He took her hand and she pulled away. "No, Daddy." She bounded into the hallway, leaving Ford to say a hurried good-bye to Ms. Bee before running to catch up with her.

When they arrived back at the apartment, Ford stumbled as he took off his boots. He was exhausted. The night before, Nelly had woken up screaming. He'd stayed in bed with her and coaxed her back to sleep. After returning to his own bed, his worries had kept him awake. Should he have tried harder to make it work with Marion? Should he sell his share of the café and get a job where he didn't have to sling burgers nights and weekends? Was Marion right that Nelly's diet of milk, cereal, chicken nuggets, and fries was dooming her to a life of bad health?

"Daddy, I want to watch TV." Nelly jumped onto the couch that Marion had bought when they were first married. The fabric was ripped on one arm and dotted with stains that Ford lacked the skill and initiative to remove.

"Okay, just for a little while." Ford turned on the television and went into the bathroom. Bobby Joe had helped him install a miniature washer and dryer above the toilet so that he wouldn't have to use the filthy Laundromat near campus. He stuffed in the soiled dress and a few of his dirty work shirts from the hamper.

After starting the cycle, he went to Nelly's room to pack some extra clothes before he forgot. He'd allowed her to pick the paint color for her room and naturally she'd chosen pink. Her twin bed was covered with a princess comforter pulled back to reveal a group of stuffed animals. Toys spilled out of the various plastic tubs lined up against the wall, a stark contrast to the neatness of her things at Marion's condo. Ford knew he should clean and organize the room, but he was too tired.

He got out a T-shirt and tiny shorts from the pink plastic two-drawer dresser he'd bought at a discount store and brought them back to the living room. Nelly was absorbed in a cartoon with talking trains that rolled their creepy eyes and moved through a weirdly static countryside. He stretched out on the couch, stared at the ceiling, and thought about Ava. He'd been planning to ask her out on a date and now he had to apologize instead. Trying to catch her at the day care probably wasn't going to work. He'd have to call her. He was as nervous about it as a teenager who dialed a girl's number over and over again, trying to work up the nerve to let the call go through. After a few minutes, he fell asleep. In his dream, trains invaded the café and ordered coal instead of bacon and eggs.

CHAPTER 8

Ava parked the van and searched for a little blond girl on the day-care playground. For a moment, she was hopeful, but then she spotted Nelly on the seesaw. She opened the door of the van and got out quickly, angry at herself. It didn't matter that Ford had already come and gone. He'd made it clear when she called Rosie's last Friday that he didn't want to talk to her. She could take a hint. Jared had more than hinted that she was boring. He hadn't directly accused her of turning into a soccer mom, but he'd implied it. He'd started not-so-subtly asking what books she'd read lately or whether she'd even opened the newspaper. He wanted her to read every article he wrote. Before the children, they had read all of each other's work and even proofread it when there was time. That was fun, but after Luke was born, she couldn't do it anymore. She'd get halfway through one of his articles before a kid interruption. Plus, if she sat down on the couch or a comfortable chair, the children climbed on her. She got in the habit of never sitting down except to eat. There was too much to do anyway: endless laundry, dishes, cleaning, cooking, mediating fights between the boys. She'd finally told Jared that he'd have to get over his aversion to housework if he wanted her to have an intellectual life. He'd decided to leave her instead.

Ava opened the van door and Sadie jumped out. She took off at a run toward the playground with Ava following as fast as she could. Good thing she'd worn the two-inch heels instead of the higher white pair she liked best with her yellow-and-white dress. "Sadie, wait for me," she called out.

Sadie stopped at the gate and peered through the chain link. "Charlie!"

A boy with bowl-cut brown hair ran across the playground and threw himself against the gate. Sadie grabbed the chain link with both hands and rattled it like a desperate prisoner.

"Hold on," Ava said, shooing both kids away and opening the gate.

The children crashed together in a painful-looking hug. Then they joined hands and ran toward the swings.

Ava walked to the table with the sign-in sheets. Ms. Shondra and some of the other teachers sat on wooden bleachers watching the children play. "Your daughter has a boyfriend," Ms. Shondra said.

"I see that," Ava said.

"No matter where we put them for nap, they manage to scoot their cots together."

Ava scrawled her name on the sign-in sheet and watched Charlie and Sadie swing for a moment before she went back to the car. She was glad her daughter was happy, but she wondered how long it would last. Would Charlie break her heart for another little girl tomorrow?

Ava didn't like the look on Rocky's face as he approached her cubicle. Normally, nothing much bothered him. He'd weathered the firing of many of his colleagues and the death of one editor he'd worked with for years. The destruction of the *Picayune* had affected him deeply, though, and seeing him rattled that day had been disconcerting. Now something else had happened, but as he got closer, she could see that he was angry, not sad. That was even more unusual. Anger was definitely not Rocky's style.

"You're not going to like this," he said, holding out a page proof. The flimsy newsprint flopped around as he laid it on her desk. "I don't know why Judith McCoy took it upon herself to rewrite this article, but I can't do anything about it. I hear tell her uncle is not happy with her current position, and they're going to make her an editor soon. I guess she decided to test out her skills on your article, unfortunately."

The piece of paper Rocky had given her was a mock-up of how the newspaper page would look when it was printed, complete with pictures. Editors were given copies to make final changes before the paper was "put to bed," as the old school newspapermen used to say. This page contained an article Ava had written at Rocky's suggestion. It was supposed to be about ten things to do with young children after school or on weekends. Scanning the text, she didn't recognize a single sentence.

"'Slither over to the reptile exhibit at the zoo'? *'Monkey Fun* swings into the Imax Theater this weekend'? 'Kids will go ape over the new primate-themed mini-golf at Fifth Street Park'?" Ava read out loud. "I didn't write any of this. It's embarrassing! And it still has my byline!"

"I know. It makes me sick. I don't know if cutesy is supposed to be our new style. If they force me to write like this, I might have to take early retirement," Rocky said.

"Why did she leave my name on it? Judith's byline should be on this crap. I would never write like this," Ava said.

"We're better off not fighting her. Judith is young and she has an information technology degree. She's into social media and whatever is out there now. She's up-and-coming. I'm old and obsolete."

"So, what does that make me?"

"I'm not sure, Ava. We just have to keep doing our jobs the best we can. Have you talked to Mann about positions in New Orleans yet?"

"No. What's the point? They don't want me. They want young and happening. I don't stand a chance."

Across the room, Judith talked on the phone in her cubicle, a sardonic grin on her face. Her gold-highlighted hair was cut in layers and she wore wide-legged pants with a tight, white shirt. At nearly six feet tall and about 180 pounds, she dwarfed almost everyone in the office. She'd curled her lip dismissively when Rocky introduced her to Ava, apparently not impressed by the part-timer. Judith had been forced on the section a few months previously by her uncle, who happened to be the publisher of the newspaper. Rocky had taken an instant dislike to her and had parked her in the far corner. She handled some social media promoting as well as writing semi-competently about art and plays. Rocky gave her just enough assignments to keep her from complaining.

"Damn it. I work hard. You work hard, and we do a good job. We shouldn't be treated like this." Ava handed the page proof back to Rocky. "I don't even want to read this."

"Neither do I. I'm sorry, Ava. I wish I could tell you this won't happen again, but I have no idea what will happen around here anymore. Things are changing," he said. "We have to play by their rules or get out of the industry."

Ava dropped the boys off at school the next morning with their bake sale brownies, homework, and raffle ticket money. Watching them walk into the building made a lump form in her throat—her babies were growing up too fast.

They were still so vulnerable. Luke's socks didn't match and James's shoes were beginning to look like they'd been tossed around the locker room too many times. Luke trailed behind his big brother, stopping to examine a leaf on the ground or an interesting rock on the sidewalk leading to the front entrance of the school. At ten, James was tall-kid awkward. He looked painfully skinny, even though he could eat three peanut butter sandwiches in one sitting. His navy uniform pants had to be cinched tight with a belt so they didn't fall down his narrow hips.

Five-year-old Luke was sturdier than his older brother. He still had some of the fearless, oblivious toddler in him. More curious than wary about the world, he rushed right in to play with any boys he could find.

The children went inside the building and the heavy doors closed behind them with a *bang* that Ava imagined she could hear through the closed van windows. In the backseat, Sadie sang the alphabet song in her sweet, small voice. She was so different from the boys. More sensitive and empathetic. Ava worried about her more than Luke and James combined. Like her, Sadie bruised easily.

Ava drove to the day care and parked as close as she could get to the playground just in case Sadie decided to make a run for it again. Even though it wasn't eight thirty yet, the air was sticky with humidity that foreshadowed the day's heat. Ava was more than ready for winter to begin. One of the few things she missed about Wisconsin was fall, which didn't really exist in Louisiana. Summer lasted until October, when it was replaced by an uneasy winter without leaf changes or snow.

The teachers clustered together in the shade of the big oak while the children ran between swings and slides. Sadie and Ava both scanned the playground as they walked up to the gate, but neither of them found what they were looking for. Sadie's friend Charlie wasn't there, and neither was Ford.

As soon as they walked through the gate, Nelly came up and took Sadie's hand. "Let's go play."

"Wait." Ava took a comb from her purse. "Can I fix your hair?"

Nelly's pigtails were so loose that strands of hair flew around her face, getting in her eyes and mouth. She brushed them away with her hand. "Okay."

Nelly stood still while Ava quickly took out the elastics and redid the pigtails. Her blond hair was finer than Sadie's thick mop and Ava had to wind the bands around five times. Barrettes would have helped with flyaway strands, but she didn't have any. "Is that okay?"

Nelly nodded, glancing over Ava's shoulder. Ava turned. Ford was behind her, his big arms folded over his chest. He must have been talking to one of the teachers on the other side of the tree. She couldn't tell whether he was glad that she'd helped Nelly or not because his face was partially hidden by his Rosie's cap. Even though she knew he didn't like her, Ava was absurdly glad to see him. Against her will, a little thrill of electricity shot through her body. Sadie and Nelly ran toward the swings together, and Ava wished her life was as simple as theirs.

"Hey, thanks. Hair is not my thing," Ford said. "And sometimes she just won't stay still for me. Cries and cries."

"I let Sadie watch TV while I do it," Ava said. "Or sometimes she plays with the barrettes in the basket."

"I'll have to try that." He took off his hat and folded it. "I've been wanting to talk to you. Can you have coffee with me?"

"When?"

"How about now?"

"Sure. Okay." Ava strove for a casual tone of voice. There

was no reason to get her hopes up. He might want to talk about parenting or little girls' hairstyles. The idea that he could want parenting advice from her was so funny that she had to stifle a laugh. Most of the time she felt like a complete parenting disaster. She was pretty good with little girls' hair, but the harder stuff made her crazy.

"Meet you at Campus Coffee in five minutes?" he said, straightening the hat and putting it back on.

"Sounds good." Ava smiled as she saw Charlie and his mother approaching the gate. It was nice to think that she and Sadie might both get their wishes.

Ava paid for her coffee with change she dug out from the crumb-encrusted seats in the van. Being constantly broke was getting old. The child support Jared sent never seemed to be enough. Maybe it really was time to apply for one of the jobs that Marilyn kept telling her about. Ava usually deleted the e-mails even though she knew the food writer was just trying to be helpful.

Ford wasn't among the tables of students with laptops. He might be really mad at her and having a practical joke at her expense. No, he clearly wasn't that type of guy. Sure, he'd been short with her when she called the café, but he wasn't mean. At least, she didn't think so. On the other hand, she'd never thought Jared would move across the country without her. She was a lousy judge of character. The best thing was to work and forget about men. She sipped the too-hot coffee and opened her iPad. Still no e-mail from the professor in charge of the animation festival. Rocky wanted the story before five o'clock, so she'd have to call Dr. Mills or even walk over to his campus office if necessary.

Another ten minutes passed. Ava started to feel stupid. Ford was going to stand her up. So what? He was just a dis-gustingly good-looking guy she sometimes saw on the playground when she dropped off Sadie, that was all. She got out her phone and started dialing the professor's number.

She glanced up before pushing the "call" button. Ford had arrived. His anxious expression made it seem at least possible that he hadn't been late on purpose. She put away her phone and waved.

He walked toward her, not bothering to order anything first. "I'm sorry. Bobby Joe called and insisted that I bring him a bunch of eggs first because the supplier was late. I wanted to call you, but I don't have your number."

"I can fix that." Ava gave him one of the business cards she'd made up for herself. Since she was a contract worker, the *Gazette* didn't provide them. Yet more evidence of her second-class status at the paper.

"Nice. I don't have any of these." Ford tucked the card into his wallet.

As he put it away, Ava had a moment of regret. As a reporter, she was used to giving out the cards with her cell phone number on them. But this was different, personal. For the first time, handing over the card made her feel vulnerable.

"I'm sorry I didn't talk to you more when you called the café. I was sort of surprised. And we were in the middle of lunch rush," Ford said.

"I didn't even think about that. Sorry. I had this huge list of restaurants and my brain was liquefying. I hate cold-calling. I went to school to be a reporter, not a telemarketer."

"I thought you *were* a reporter."

"I'm a freelancer. So sometimes I end up doing the stuff no one else wants to do. It's okay. As long as they pay me," Ava said.

"Yeah, well, I'm part owner of Rosie's and I still have to clean the grease traps."

"That must be fun."

Ford shrugged. "I like working at the café. I'd go crazy in an office all day. It was my brother's idea. He figured that I'd cook and he'd do the books and whatever. But it doesn't work that way. We both do everything. We have to. Never thought I'd see Bobby Joe frying eggs, but he does an okay job."

"What about Nelly? Does she go to the café with you?"

"Not usually. She gets bored pretty quickly, and Bobby Joe is always afraid she'll stick her hand in the fryer. So basically whenever she's in school or with her mother, I'm at the café. That's okay, though. I don't have anything else to do really."

"Work. Kids. That's it, right?" Ava said. "I mean, that's the way it is for me."

"Pretty much." Ford looked at his hands. They were crisscrossed with burns and scars, no doubt caused by kitchen knives and deep fryers.

"I'm okay with that most of the time, but sometimes I miss having my own life. I used to write fiction."

Ford raised his eyes. "I used to write songs. I was no Tom Petty, but I was okay. Still get out the guitar sometimes when Nelly's in bed, but most of the time I'm too tired."

"I don't even try," Ava said.

"You should. Write, I mean."

Ava shook her head. "I don't know. I never got anything published anyway."

"So what? I'll never get a record contract, but that doesn't mean I shouldn't write music."

"My ex used to say that every reporter has an unfinished novel in a drawer somewhere. Except him. He put all his energy into his career. Which is why he's at the *Chicago Tribune* and I'm here."

"Being a workaholic is overrated," Ford said. "I should know—I was married to one. Speaking of work, I have to get back to the café. Bobby Joe will kill me if he has to handle the whole breakfast shift by himself."

Ava drank the last of her coffee. "Well, you have my number."

"Yeah, but I'm not gonna call. I'm going to ask you on a real date right now."

"Tell me your proposal and I'll consider it," Ava said, feeling the rush of electricity again.

CHAPTER 9

"Aren't you going to hose the grease off yourself before you go on your date?" Bobby Joe asked.

Ford lowered a fresh basket of potatoes into the deep fryer. "I figured you wouldn't let me off that early."

"I ain't your boss, but if I was, I'd tell you to get your butt out of here and clean up." Bobby Joe filled a coffee cup and slid it across the counter to a bearded philosophy grad student who was pretending to read Descartes.

The student raised a bushy eyebrow. "Dude, you should totally go change and stuff. You can't meet a girl smelling like fries."

Ford glanced at the clock. If he left immediately, he'd have time to shower and put on fresh jeans. "Yeah, okay. Since y'all are such dating experts."

"Get going," Bobby Joe said. "And don't let the door hit your fat butt on the way out."

Ford parked his truck in Ava's driveway. The grass around her house was more of a weed patch than a lawn, with creepers climbing up the siding almost to the windows. He made a mental note to offer to mow it. Since moving into the apartment, he missed yard work, grilling, and gardening. But he couldn't afford to keep the house when Marion moved to New Orleans. Besides, he and Nelly didn't need a lot of space. When he married Marion, he'd hoped to have three kids. Marion had kept putting off getting pregnant, though. She was ambitious, determined to show everyone who doubted her that she could be a successful doctor. Ford admired her drive and passion, until he realized that it meant family would always come second. First, she had to finish medical school and then her residency. And by the time Nelly came along, their marriage was already falling apart.

Ford really didn't want to think about Marion or the kids he'd never have. He got out of the truck and walked up the sidewalk to Ava's front door. The house needed a pressure wash and a coat of paint. It was pink, not an unusual color in Louisiana. Nelly would love it, if he ever brought her here. He pressed the doorbell and waited.

Ford didn't know what he expected Ava to be wearing, but certainly not four-inch red heels, black skinny jeans, and a sequined tank top. He was glad he'd listened to his brother and at least changed into a fresh black T-shirt. Dressing up wasn't his style. He had one suit that he wore to funerals and weddings.

Before he could tell Ava she looked good, however, Sadie grabbed her leg and started wailing. A teenage girl with a face full of acne tried unsuccessfully to pry the toddler from her mother.

Ava dropped into a crouch. "It's going to be okay. I'll be back in a couple of hours. Your brothers and Ms. Sandy will take good care of you. She might even give you a lollipop."

"Stop crying, Sadie." One of the boys appeared from behind the babysitter and took his sister's hand. "Mommy's coming back later. Let's go watch TV," he said soothingly.

"Okay." Sadie sniffed and followed her brother.

Ford wondered whether he was making a mistake. Anything that happened between Ava and him would affect their children, no matter what they did. But he couldn't help it. In the four days since their coffee date, he'd thought about her constantly. He'd wanted to call, but he was afraid of being too pushy.

"You might want to bring socks," he said to Ava.

"Why? What are we doing?"

"All I'm going to tell you is you won't be in those heels very long."

"I can live with that." Ava walked down the hallway toward the back of the house.

The living room/kitchen was comfortably cluttered. A papier-mâché chicken perched on top of a pile of books on the mantle next to a painting of men and women with oversized heads bent over cotton plants under an enormous orange sun. The kids' homework was spread out on the kitchen table along with a random scattering of pencils and crayons. After her outburst, Sadie had lined up an assortment of toys on the scratched coffee table and the stuffed animals were having a babbling conversation. The babysitter was curled up in an armchair with a romance novel. Ford sat down on the overstuffed coffee-colored couch next to the boys. "I'm Ford. What are y'all's names?"

"I'm James and this is Luke," the older boy said.

"Whatcha watching?"

"Baby cartoons," James said. "Mom won't let us watch *Spider-Man* because it's too scary for Luke. But I get to put it on after he goes to bed."

"I like this show. This is *Phineas and Ferb*," Luke said.

"My daughter, Nelly, likes this show. I don't understand it. Why don't those boys ever go to school?" Ford said.

"Because it's summer," James said.

"It's always summer?"

James shrugged.

"I like summer," Luke said. "We go to camp and there's no homework."

Ava came back with a pair of white socks. "Is that all I need?"

"Yeah. Hey, I'm thinking about buying some paintings to hang in the café. Where'd you get that one over there?" Ford said, pointing at the farm scene.

"My ex bought it for me from an artist in New Orleans. I'd just give it to you, but it might be worth some money and I'm thinking about selling it."

"It's nice. You should keep it."

"I don't know. It reminds me of him." Ava looked at the boys on the couch.

Ford could tell what she was thinking—she didn't want to say bad things about their father in front of them. He'd been there himself. "We can talk about it later," he said.

"See you all in a few hours. Be good for Ms. Sandy." Ava ruffled Luke's hair.

"Okay," James said.

The babysitter glanced up from her book. The cover had a picture of two impossibly perfect-looking teenagers holding hands. "Have fun."

Ford parked the truck in front of the roller rink. The warehouse-like building was decorated with a purple-and-orange mural of stick figure skaters. He passed it on the highway every time he took Nelly to New Orleans. Sometimes he didn't notice it and other times the rink made him think about high school and how things could have turned out differently.

"Wow, I didn't know there were any of these left," Ava said.

Ford couldn't tell whether she liked the idea or thought he was crazy. "We'll be the oldest people in there. We can do something else if you want."

"Nope. This is going to be fun." Ava got out of the truck and walked toward the building.

Ford shrugged and followed. So far, so good.

He hadn't been inside the rink for almost twenty years, and he was momentarily stunned by the force of his memories. He'd snuck his first kiss in a dark corner behind the bank of lockers, but most of the hours were spent admiring girls who had no interest in him and his nerdy friends. He remembered the thrill of hearing one of his favorite songs and standing on the boys' side of the rink, wondering if the girl he wanted to slow-skate with would say yes.

Very little had changed in the world of the roller rink. Miley Cyrus was playing on the sound system instead of Madonna, but the air still smelled like dirty socks and churros. The wood-paneled walls remained the same, darkened by the sweat of thousands of leaning teenagers. The lockers had also endured through another generation, losing most of their paint in the process.

A gum-chewing teenager with a shaggy boy-band haircut presided over the skate rentals behind a wooden Dutch door. When Ava and Ford asked for their sizes, the kid just barely managed to keep his expression neutral.

Ford imagined his tweet: "Couple old weirdos rented skates. Call ambulance."

After locking up their shoes and Ava's little red purse, they sat on the bench and put on the skates.

"This is one of my only happy memories of junior high. My friends and I would go to the roller rink and skate for hours," Ava said, putting on her socks and then the brown skates the rink provided.

"Yeah. I came to this very rink. It hasn't changed a whole lot."

"Really? I can't imagine what you would have been like as a teenager."

"You don't want to. I was way too skinny and I had this skater cut that I thought was really cool, but it just meant my hair was always in my eyes."

"Oh yeah? I can beat that. I used to rat my hair and hair spray it out into this giant puffball. It could hardly fit through doorways."

A teenage girl with saucer-sized hoop earrings and her sullen-faced boyfriend skated over and opened lockers. They paid no attention to Ford and Ava.

"As much as I miss my high school buddies, I'm glad to be here with you." Ford stood up and offered Ava his hand.

"What happened to them?" she asked as they half walked, half skated through the hallway leading to the rink.

"Most of them went to college and moved away. One died in a car crash. My friend Robert works at a hospital in New Orleans, but I don't see him much anymore." Ford didn't want to tell her that Robert had introduced him to Marion. He'd lost that friend in the divorce. It was too bad, since he and Robert had been close since junior high. When girls rejected them, they'd always had each other. Until they both got married. Robert's marriage lasted and Ford's didn't. Robert bought Marion's line that Ford was unambitious and a jerk, probably because his wife was also friends with her. Since then, Ford just had his brother, his mom, and Nelly.

The cinnamon scent of churros intensified as Ford and Ava approached the snack bar next to the rink. Red-shaded lamps dangling from the ceiling cast a scarlet glow over the teenagers eating and making out in the booths. The kid texting behind the snack bar counter raised his eyebrows as

Ford and Ava passed by. When Ford saluted, the boy reddened and disappeared behind the soft pretzel display.

They skated to the rink entrance. Some of the kids were holding on to the wall, inching along. Others glided with varying amounts of skill and confidence. All of the teenagers wore identical uniforms of jeans and T-shirts—tight for the girls and looser for the boys. Ford remembered stepping out onto the rink in his Rollerblades, confident in the one sport he was actually good at. He'd dressed pretty much the same as now in a black T-shirt and jeans, but in the old days the pants were always threatening to slide down his skinny hips.

Ava skated to the center of the rink. She turned around and stopped, holding her hands out. Ford felt a little silly, but he glided out to meet her. He was surprised that his body remembered the feel of the skates and how to move in them. He took her hands and skated with a reasonable amount of grace. She slowly moved backward while he continued forward. Then she let go of his left hand and turned around. They sped up and skated side by side. Ford had to dodge the slower teens, but he didn't want to look away from Ava's beautiful smile. He'd forgotten how much fun it was to speed around the rink. Even when he'd been desperately in love with a girl who didn't care about him or fed up with school or his stubbornly skinny body, skating had always made him feel better.

The DJ switched to a slow song and turned on the disco ball. For a second, Ford was nervous, just like that teenage boy asking a girl to skate with him. But he wasn't an awkward teenager anymore, and Ava wasn't going to say no. She slowed down and he put his arm around her. He felt like a dork, but so what? He had taken a risk and it had paid off. He'd made Ava smile. Really smile. One important goal, accomplished.

She was still smiling when they sat down later in the booth at Rosie's.

"Are you sure you don't mind eating here? I'm kind of short on cash," Ford said.

"Me too." Ava's expression became serious. "I'm applying for a scholarship for Sadie, but it might be too late for this year. And James needs new shoes."

Todd brought over glasses of water. "Boss, you really should get out more."

"Todd, this is Ava. Todd here is trying to get himself fired," Ford said.

Todd grinned. "What would y'all like?"

"Everything we make is good, but the omelets are my favorite," Ford said to Ava.

"Well, since I can't have one of your special po'boys, I'll settle for a veggie omelet," Ava said.

Ford ordered the Western and Todd mercifully left without saying anything else.

"He's a good kid, but he likes to mess with me," Ford said, draining his water glass. He'd forgotten how much exercise roller skating was.

"That was fun. Thanks," Ava said. "You made me feel like a teenager again. In a good way."

"I never had that much fun as a teenager," Ford said.

"Me neither. It was always about being cool and fitting in. Do you have the right clothes? Is your hairdo exactly right? Exhausting." Ava laughed. "I'll bet those kids thought we were crazy."

Ford felt a stupid grin stretch his face. He wanted Ava to smile at him forever. "That's one of the great things about being grown-up. I don't care what people think anymore. Life is too short for that."

"I wish I could explain that to my kids. They are going

to take all the stupid junior high and high school stuff too seriously and there's nothing I can do about it."

"Sometimes I want to take Nelly and raise her by myself on a farm somewhere. Just skip all the drama," Ford said.

"I've considered that too. Especially when I'm forcing them to do some dumb homework assignment or trying to sell yet another tub of frozen cookie dough," Ava said.

Todd brought the omelets. They were perfect: fluffy and creamy with just enough butter and salt. The trick was to make sure the egg was cooked through but not browned. Fitzgerald was starting to get his act together. Which meant he'd probably get a better job. The bad ones stayed; the good ones left. Ford and Bobby Joe paid as well as they could and tried to be flexible, but in a small operation there was only so much money to go around.

Ava finished half her omelet and put her fork down. "This is really good, but I can't eat any more of it."

"Yeah, they're pretty big." Ford scooped up a few hash browns. "I guess I should take you home."

"I love my kids a lot, but I don't want to go home right now. I want to keep pretending that neither of us has any baggage. That we're both free."

"Everyone has baggage. And kids are a pretty good kind to have. For one thing, they eventually grow up and let you get back to your own life."

"Sometimes I'm not sure I can wait that long." Ava reached over the table and put her hand on his.

"Then we'll have to make it work right now. I have some ideas."

CHAPTER 10

As they got closer to her house, Ava felt more and more like a jittery teenager. Would Ford kiss her in the truck when they stopped? Would he ask her to go steady? She giggled, something she couldn't remember doing since high school. Ford glanced over at her and smiled.

He stopped the truck in front of the house and put it in Park. Instead of kissing her, though, he got out and opened her door. "I want to see you again—and not just when we're dropping our kids off at day care."

"Me too," Ava said.

"Good. I'm glad I didn't scare you away with my mad skating skills."

"I like a man who's suave on wheels," she said, stepping down from the truck.

"You've got one. Though, I don't think anyone's ever called me 'suave' before," he said.

"I guess I should relieve the babysitter." Ava didn't want to leave Ford standing on the sidewalk. She would rather bring him inside and offer him a glass of wine. They could sit on the couch together and watch TV or just talk. She enjoyed the fantasy for the few seconds it took to reach the front porch. Then she looked back. He was leaning against the truck, hands in his pockets. She waved, turned quickly, and went inside, not waiting to see whether he waved back.

Sandy was curled up in the armchair again, reading her novel while James watched TV. The babysitter was responsible, but Ava sometimes wondered if she had any life outside of her books. She was the only teen Ava knew who didn't constantly check her smartphone. Sandy tucked her novel into her backpack. "How was your date?"

"Fine. Great, actually. Thanks, Sandy." Ava counted out the money she owed her.

Sandy took the bills and shoved them into her jeans pocket. "The kids were good. Luke and Sadie are asleep."

"Let me walk you out to your car," Ava said. She had another crazy fantasy—that Ford would still be there—but of course the truck was gone. Sandy got into her car, a sedan she either owned or borrowed from her parents. Ava stood there a moment after she drove away, feeling the warm night air on her bare shoulders and wondering what Ford was doing. Was he thinking about her as he drove home? Did he really want to see her again, or had he just said that to be polite?

Back inside, she turned off the TV.

"Hey!" James said. "I was watching that."

"It's time for bed. You can watch the rest of *Spider-Man* tomorrow." Ava poured herself a glass of wine. She wanted to sit on the couch and relive the evening.

"Okay, fine. What did you do?" James got up and put the remote on top of the TV.

"We went roller-skating."

"I want to go roller-skating."

"We'll do it sometime. I promise. Did you have a good time with Sandy?"

"Yeah, it was fine." James gave her a long-suffering look

before going into the bathroom and shutting the door. Ava set the wineglass on the end table and put her feet up on the couch. She could still sense the place on her back where Ford had touched her when they were skating together. Even if she never saw him again, the evening was worth it. She felt like having her own life was possible again. She took a sip of wine.

"Mommy!" Sadie yelled from her room.

Ava swung her feet to the floor. Back to mom duty.

Ava felt guilty about how happy she was to be in the familiar *Gazette* lobby. She even nodded a one-sided greeting to the morning show hosts talking about fall fashions on the TV in the lobby.

Usually, she enjoyed weekends with the kids, but aside from the date with Ford, the most recent one had her counting the hours until Monday. At the YMCA, Sadie refused to get into the pool until only ten minutes were left in her swim lesson. Then she cried when it was time to leave. While Ava threatened to take away all her toys if she didn't get out, Luke found a dumbbell somewhere and dropped it into the hot tub. He and James did better with their lesson, but getting Luke and Sadie dressed afterward took twenty minutes. They were more interested in trying to open the locks on the lockers than putting on their underwear.

After the gym, they went to the grocery store, where Luke and James fought about which was the superior brand of Popsicles and Sadie insisted that her tummy needed cupcakes. Luke wanted to push the cart and Sadie screamed every time he touched the handles. James tried to intervene and he and Luke began hitting each other. By the time they got to the checkout, everyone was in tears. Sunday had been more of the same.

Ava got on the elevator and enjoyed the silence. She

thought back to the good moments from the weekend: Sadie singing a song and making up the words; Luke telling her that he wanted to use his Spider-Man powers to become a Lego person and live in Legoland. James had played along, maybe wanting to believe it could work. The younger children sometimes drew the older, practical boy back into the magic of childhood. Occasionally, even Ava found herself thinking that the impossible just might happen.

The elevator stopped on her floor and Ava went straight to the office kitchen. She shoved her lunch into the sour-smelling refrigerator and took a newspaper. On the way to her desk, she passed Rocky heading the other way with his coffee cup. He turned around and fell into step with her.

"What are you doing? Don't you want your coffee?" Ava asked.

"Not as much as I want to see your face when you get a look at your desk. Some big blond guy was here earlier and dropped off some stuff. I don't know how he got past security." Ava stumbled a little and Rocky reached for her elbow. "Hey, it's all good."

"I'm okay. Just a little nervous," Ava said.

"Why? Is he a stalker? Or some crazed fan?"

"No, we had a date on Friday."

"A date? Good for you!" Rocky said.

"Yeah, it was pretty great."

Rocky stopped at their row of cubicles and motioned her to go ahead. When she rounded the corner, Ava spotted flowers poking out of the top of her cubicle. The vase of wildflowers was accompanied by a shoe box of homemade truffles, a bag of cookies, and a sandwich wrapped in waxed paper. Ava sat down before reading the card. *Thinking about you. A lot. Ford.*

"I think he likes you," Rocky said. "Who is this guy?"

Ava drew in a deep breath. "The father of one of the kids Sadie goes to school with. He owns that café near A&M."

"Rosie's? You're dating Bobby Joe?"

"No, his brother. Ford."

"I should have known. Only a café owner would bring a girl a sandwich as a token of love," Rocky said. "I'm going to get my coffee now. Unless you care to share those truffles."

"Go ahead," Ava said

Rocky selected a chocolate from the box. Ford had dusted the truffles with cocoa powder and nestled them in pink paper. Ava popped one in her mouth and it exploded in a rush of soft, rich chocolate.

"These are incredible." Rocky shook his head. "If you don't marry this guy, I will."

"I don't think you're his type."

"I'm too short, huh? I get that all the time."

"Too much hair on your chest." Ava reached into the box again.

"Picky, picky. Can I have another truffle?"

"Only if you keep them a secret. If Marilyn and Norma hear I have chocolate, there will be a stampede," Ava said.

Rocky took one more truffle. "Don't worry. Your secret is safe with me. Shoot, if you're not careful, they'll try to steal your boyfriend too."

"He's not my boyfriend."

"I'm serious, Ava, don't let this one go."

"What do you mean?"

"Come on, I remember that guy in Sports who liked you."

"He wrote about football."

"So what?"

"So, I don't know anything about football," Ava said, knowing the excuse sounded lame.

"He was a nice guy. He brought you flowers every day for a week. You didn't give him a chance," Rocky said.

"It wasn't a good time for me. Luke was getting in trouble in school, Sadie was keeping me up half the night with nightmares, James kept asking me where Daddy was. I couldn't deal with dating."

"And then he moved to St. Louis," Rocky said, crossing his arms across his chest.

"He didn't move away because of me."

"He was pretty upset."

Ava hid the truffles in her desk drawer. "It's complicated to date when you have kids. You should know that."

"Not really. I have no intention of dating. I was married for years to the love of my life. That's enough for me. Believe me, Ava, it's worth making the effort to find the right person." Rocky walked away toward the kitchen.

Ava touched the flowers. She was happy, but worried at the same time. She hadn't thought about Jeff for a while. He had been a nice guy, but she'd convinced herself that he was wrong for her. Why? Because it was easier. Dating had seemed like just another thing to worry about and she'd been scared. Afraid it wouldn't work out. That Jeff would get to know her better and conclude the same thing as Jared—that she was too boring, too much of a mom. And now she was taking the chance with Ford. Would he get her hopes up only to send them crashing down?

She pushed the button to start up her computer.

Two hours later, she took a break from typing events into the calendar and leaned back in her chair to admire the vase of flowers. Ford had called while he was closing down the café Sunday night. Their conversation was a welcome visit to the adult world. Sometimes she felt like all she talked about was homework, runny noses, and other kid problems. They hadn't really discussed anything romantic—mostly just their childhoods, divorces, and jobs—but it didn't matter. Somehow they connected in a way that she hadn't with anyone for a very long time. She couldn't wait to see him again. In fact, she was considering stopping by the café on the way to pick up the kids from school, just to thank him for the sandwich, which she planned to eat slowly, savoring every bite.

The sight of Rocky striding toward her cubicle brought her back to reality. She was still working on her story for the week, so she knew that Judith couldn't have done a hack job on it, at least not yet. This had to be brand-new bad news.

As Rocky got closer, she realized that whatever it was had to be worse, much worse than Judith turning her after-school fun article into a cute-fest. Her boss looked shocked, like the thing he was about to tell her was simply unbelievable.

"What is it?" she said.

Rocky pulled over a chair from the next cubicle. The desk had belonged to Lynn until the former *Bon Temps* editor was laid off. He'd lasted six months in retirement before dying of a heart attack. The chair was too high for Rocky; his feet didn't reach the floor, but he didn't appear to notice.

"They sent me downstairs to Marketing. I was given an offer I couldn't refuse. I can't quit—I have Mike to support. What could I do? I had to take the job," he said.

"They're demoting you? After all these years?" Ava's whole body felt numb. This couldn't be happening. Rocky had hired her, given her stories to write that fit around her children's school schedules, bought her lunch on her birthday. He was more than a boss; he was a friend.

"Yeah, apparently experience means nothing now. Judith will be the editor of *Bon Temps* and *Sunday Features*, effective next week. I'm going to put out this weekend's sections and then I'm done."

"I'm going to be under Judith? She's twenty-three!"

"I think she's twenty-five, actually. Anyway, you're only twenty-nine, right? Wink, wink," Rocky said.

"I wish. Sometimes I feel like I'm forty-five, instead of thirty-five," Ava said. "Geez, this is just . . . wrong."

"I'll be okay. I'm lucky not to get the boot like everyone else. I'll still be writing. Sure, it'll be promotional sections for our advertisers, but it beats digging ditches."

"Yeah, I'll bet doing stories about furniture and whatever is going to be a blast. I never even look at those special sections." Ava drank some coffee from her travel mug, trying to focus her mind on the terrible news.

"I don't read the marketing sections either, so I went to the newspaper morgue and found some. They do something on football every year, one about health, and a few others. Basically spotlights on our advertisers. Exciting stuff. If you'll excuse me, I have to figure out what to do with all the books on my desk and write e-mails referring all my contacts to Ms. Judith." He returned Lynn's chair and walked back to his cubicle.

Ava turned back to her computer and stared blankly at the screen. With Rocky gone, she might quit. What was the last job ad Marilyn had sent her? Assistant editor at the weekly *Saint Jude Social*? She hated the idea of working for a society magazine, writing puff pieces about charity organizations and art shows. But it seemed the *Gazette* was collapsing. She'd thought the Great Purge was over, but apparently, Purge Part Two was just beginning. She and Rocky would have shared a grim laugh over it if he wasn't on the chopping block. She wondered about the bureau in New Orleans. Were they cutting staff in Saint Jude to free up money to start the new operation, or was the expansion just a rumor?

Rocky swiveled around in his chair and called out, "I forgot to warn you, we've stopped running TV listings every day, so all the nursing home residents in town are calling to complain."

Ava was glad to talk about anything but Purge Part Two. "Whenever we change anything, people completely lose it. Remember when we switched fonts from Times to whatever it was?"

"They were right about that. No one over fifty could read it. I speak from experience," Rocky said. "We had to backtrack on that one. But this thing with the TV listings is final. It's about saving pages. There aren't enough ads in the section to support it."

Ava's desk phone rang.

"That's probably a complaint now. Good luck." Rocky turned toward his computer.

She picked up the receiver. "Entertainment department. This is Ava."

"Hello? This is Elspeth Hoffweiser. I've been subscribing to the paper for forty years, but now I'm going to cancel. First, you stopped running *Li'l Abner*. Now no more TV listings? I can't leave this darned old folks home they put me in. My son says it's good for me, but the food is bad and I had to get rid of all my stuff. I lived in that house for forty years. It's gone, all gone. My shows are all I've got."

Ava heard sniffling on the other end. She lowered her voice and tried to sound soothing. "I'm sorry. It wasn't my decision."

Elspeth blew her nose audibly. "It's okay, honey. I'm sorry to be a bother."

"You can save the full guide that runs on Fridays."

"I know. It's just hard when everything changes all the time. Do you know what I mean, dear?"

"Yes, I do," Ava said. *Tell me about it. My boss, who is also one of my favorite human beings, is going to become some kind of salesman. And I have to answer to a snot-nosed brat barely out of college. Not to mention that someone in charge might decide I'm old and obsolete too.*

"I guess I'll just have to adapt. I'm not really going to stop subscribing. Don't you worry about that," Elspeth said.

"Good. Just don't forget to save the Friday section and you'll be fine."

"Thanks for your help, honey." The old lady hung up.

Ava picked up her mug and went to the kitchen. Rocky was leaning against the vending machine, waiting for the coffee to brew. "Who was on the phone?"

"Someone complaining about the TV section."

"Told you." He closed the lid of the vacuum container that kept the coffee somewhat warm and filled his mug. "Look, I really will be okay. Now that I don't have to read so many books, maybe I'll finish writing my novel."

"You should. I'm sure it'll be great," Ava said.

"Yeah, well, critics are the worst authors. But I'm going to try. If Mike will leave me alone long enough to write a sentence."

Ava doubted Rocky would ever actually complete his novel. It was easy to let life fill up with little things—running errands, cooking dinner, working, cleaning. She was guilty of it herself. She hadn't written a short story since Luke was born. Writing required thinking time, and Ava could barely concentrate enough to compose a grocery list.

She filled her cup and started back to the cubicle maze with her boss. She wanted to tell Rocky how much his friendship meant to her, but he wasn't the sappy type. Besides, how could she explain that the job had given her back some self-worth? He'd helped her return to journalism, and now he was being forced out the door. It made a sour taste rise in her mouth.

"Are they doing a country kitchen for you?" she asked.

Usually, when someone retired or left, the paper held a party with food brought in by the staff and set up buffet-style. For some obscure reason, the event was always called a "country kitchen." During the worst period of layoffs, however, the custom had disappeared. No one wanted to bring in a casserole or fried chicken every day. In the last year, only three people had left, so someone had revived the practice.

"I don't want anything. Besides, I'm not leaving the company, I'm just moving. You can stop in anytime you want," Rocky said.

"I will. But it won't be the same," Ava said.

"I know. Things change. We have to roll with the punches." Despite his short stature, Rocky matched Ava's stride as they walked together.

"I'm waiting to be punched. I think I'm next," she said.

"Whatever happens, make sure you get up again and keep fighting."

"I have to."

They arrived back at their area, and Ava went into her cubicle. She drank some coffee, but the sour taste in her mouth would not go away.

After staring at the screen for another hour, she dragged herself back to the office kitchen for one last cup of coffee to drink with her lunch.

Judith was standing by the microwave waiting for something to heat. It smelled like overripe garlic and canned tomatoes.

Ava swallowed hard and put on her best polite voice. "Hello, Judith. What's for lunch?"

"I made my lasagna last night. It's even better the next day. Hillary loves it. She's such an adventurous eater."

"That's nice." Of course the new boss cooked and her angel child ate her food instead of demanding sugary cereal like Ava's kids. Judith was going to be unbearable, clearly the type to casually mention that at age three Hillary already knew her alphabet and could count to ten.

"So, Rocky told you that I'm taking over *Bon Temps* and *Sunday Features*, right?" Judith said.

"Yes." Ava knew she should congratulate Judith, but she couldn't bring herself to say the words.

"We're going to shake things up around here. It's time for a serious update, don't you think? The fuddy-duddies in Entertainment have been doing the same things forever. Same format, same name, same stories. If we want new readers, we have to make things interesting. We're talking about using colored type, more pictures, graphs, links to extra content on our Web site. It's going to be hip and interactive. Relevant. Nobody wants to just read a newspaper anymore."

Judith sounded like she was reciting from a generic pamphlet called something like "Making Your Media Appeal to the Younger Generation." The problem was that the sections really could use an overhaul and they were losing readers. But the "fuddy-duddies" actually did know what they were doing and Judith didn't. She had no idea how much work it took to put out the weekly sections. She seemed to somehow think they could just change the layouts of *Bon Temps* and *Sunday Features* and still make the deadlines. Ava wasn't going to be the one to tell her that she needed to take it slow. "Um, yeah. That all sounds great."

The microwave dinged, and Judith took out her lunch. Once it was free of the oven, the lasagna stunk even more. She swaddled the plastic container in paper towels and strode out of the kitchen area.

Back at her desk, Ava ate her sandwich. Ford had done a simple ham and cheese, but he'd used a sauce with a combination of sweet and spicy that complemented the smoky ham in just the right way. Homemade pickles gave it a little sour crunch. The sandwich and thoughts of Ford distracted her a little from Rocky's demotion. At two o'clock, she went to his cubicle. "I'm going to take off a little bit early if you think you can handle the disgruntled old people."

Rocky pushed his chair away from his computer. "Yeah, that's fine. I think most of them are napping by now anyway."

"Or watching the afternoon soaps. See you later," Ava said.

She didn't want to walk by Judith's desk, but she had no choice. The soon-to-be-editor's cubicle was near the wall on the way to the elevators. Before she even got close enough to catch the scent of overripe tomatoes that still hung in the air, she could hear Judith yelling into her phone.

"I asked for one simple thing and he screwed it up. I wanted a photo of Mr. Banks with one of his toy trains. *One!* The article was about how his dad skipped lunch at work for a week so he could buy his son a train." Judith paused and blew air through her nose. "Yes, I know he makes toy trains now and donates them to Toys for Tots. But having him hold one train is symbolic of that first train he ever owned. Can't you see that?"

Judith paused again, glanced at Ava walking by, and didn't bother to wave. "I know he doesn't have the original train anymore. It's *symbolic*, I said. Germain Gilcrest is a dumbass. I don't care if he's a good photographer. How hard is it to be a photographer, anyway? You point a camera at something and push a button. He needs to learn to do what he's told. He's not supposed to be making artistic decisions. You're the head of Photography. You have to say something to him." Judith slammed the phone down on its cradle.

Ava doubled her walking speed and got out of Judith's sight as quickly as possible.

* * *

When Ava walked into Rosie's Café, the only customers were a few students studying at a table in the corner and two old men drinking coffee on counter stools. Ford was scraping down the grill, but he turned around when the bell on the door tinkled.

"I just came to thank you for the sandwich and those amazing truffles." Ava sat at the stool in front of Ford.

"You're welcome. Do you want a cup of coffee? Iced tea?" he asked.

"Tea, sure."

Ford poured her a glass and started wiping down the sandwich board. "I hope your boss didn't eat all the truffles. He had his eye on them."

"I gave him two," Ava said. "They were incredible. I thought you said all you knew how to cook was hamburgers and breakfast food."

"I made truffles for my ex-wife for our first anniversary. She ate half of one and the rest ended up in a drawer. I chucked them in the trash a month later. Now I just make them for my mom for Christmas."

"No offense, but there's something wrong with your ex-wife."

Ford shrugged. "She doesn't like food very much."

"I guess my ex-husband is the same way, now that I think about it. He was always happy eating a sandwich for dinner or canned spaghetti," Ava said.

"To each his own, I guess."

"I promise to eat the truffles. I plan to hide them from the kids and have one every night after they go to bed."

"Hiding candy from the children. You are a cruel mom." Ford finished with the sandwich board, got out an industrial tub of mustard, and began refilling the squeeze bottles.

"I admit it. I hide the good chocolate. I don't let Sadie

play with my few pieces of nice jewelry either. I have to keep some things for myself."

"I know what you mean. Sometimes I feel like everything is Nelly's, but I won't let her play with my guitar."

"See, you're cruel too," Ava said.

"Not according to Marion. My ex-wife says I'm spoiling her. She thinks the kid should clean her room every night and know all her addition and subtraction tables by age four." Ford put the top back on the squeeze bottle and thumped it against the sandwich board.

"I guess I should be glad that my ex has no interest in his children."

"A man who doesn't want to know his kids? No offense, but there's something wrong with your ex too."

"No argument here." Ava finished her tea. At that moment, it seemed like the best thing she'd ever tasted. "So, speaking of my boss, he was demoted to Marketing. And, since that's not depressing enough, the new *Bon Temps* editor is this young kid with a big attitude and lots of ideas about how the paper can be more hip and modern."

"They should have made you editor," Ford said.

"Me? Yeah, right." Ava laughed.

"Why not? You're smart and you've been working there for a long time, right?"

"That's the point. Judith is right out of school. They want younger people with fresh ideas, who, incidentally, they can also pay less. It also doesn't hurt that she's related to the publisher."

"Ava, you're not old."

"I *feel* old. I use social media because I have to for my job and I do my best with it, but younger people have an advantage. Judith is comfortable with technology in a way I'll never be. Those ten years between us make a huge difference. She doesn't remember a time when not everyone had Internet access. My first computer was an Apple IIGS hooked up to a floppy disk drive with disks that actually flopped."

"None of that matters. What's important is giving people the news they want and need," Ford said.

Ava rested her elbows on the counter. "Not really. It's about making the cheapest product that people will still buy. They are making the calculation that readers won't notice that there is less content as long as there are a lot of flashy graphics and that firing the older staff will save a lot of money without sacrificing enough quality to lose the few subscribers and advertisers we have left. Also, they're starting a bureau in New Orleans, and so they're cutting operations here as much as they can to free up money to expand there." For a second, Ava considered telling Ford that Rocky thought she should apply for a job in New Orleans. But there was no point. She wasn't going to do it anyway. "I guess I'd better go. I have to pick up the boys from school."

"Wait a second. I'll walk you out. It's time to get Nelly anyway," Ford said. He untied his apron and hung it on the wall. "Bobby Joe! I'm taking off."

"Yeah, okay," a voice from the back room answered.

Ford came out from behind the counter. He put his hand on Ava's back as they walked toward the front door. The fabric of her dress felt as thin as a butterfly's wing and she imagined she could feel his rough skin through it.

They reached the van and before Ava knew what was happening, Ford's surprisingly soft lips were pressed against hers. She closed her eyes and wrapped her arms around his neck. He pulled away, too soon.

"I want to see you again," he said.

"Me too, but I can't afford the babysitter every week."

Ford took her hands. His fingers felt strong. "Can you get away when the kids are in school? Fridays? Just for a couple of hours after we drop off Sadie and Nelly?" he asked.

"I think so. I'll check with my boss. My lovely new boss," Ava said.

"It's a date then." Ford kissed her one more time. Then, he was gone, walking quickly around the café building.

Ava got into the van and sat for a moment, waiting for her heartbeat to return to normal.

CHAPTER 11

The next morning, Ford chopped a bell pepper and put it in a prep pan, his hands moving on their own while he thought about Friday. The idea made him a little nervous, but excited at the same time. He was taking a big chance, like he had with the roller skating. Ava might think he was nuts, or she might like it.

"Ford! That's enough peppers. Don't chop up the whole box!" Bobby Joe said, pulling a tray of biscuits out of the oven.

"Sure." Ford hadn't noticed that his prep pan was overflowing. He set it aside and started on the onions.

"Good thing I didn't let you bake this morning. You'd have burned all the biscuits. I'm not going to give you Friday mornings off anymore if you're gonna dream through every breakfast service."

"Sorry, boss." Ford drank some coffee from his travel mug. Bobby Joe was right. He had to wake up. But he didn't want to. All he wanted to do was think about was Ava.

"Yeah, yeah." Bobby Joe broke open a biscuit and took a bite. He slid the tray into an empty slot on the kitchen cart. "I'm going to open the door, lover boy. I hope you're ready."

"Yup." Ford gathered up the prep pans and followed his brother.

Fitzgerald was behind the grill, preheating it and arranging all the ingredients they would need within easy reach. When Ford first met him, he'd thought the cook was a drug addict because he was so pale and skinny. But Fitzgerald was just built like a scarecrow and subsisted mostly on cigarettes and fried eggs. His personal life was a mystery. Ford suspected he might be gay, but he'd never asked. Fitzgerald came to work, complained about the customers, the weather, or feeling tired, and then went home. Wherever home was.

A line of regulars already stood outside the door. An English professor in a ratty tweed jacket was first in line, followed by a businessman reading the newspaper. Ford recognized most of the rest of the customers. He was continually amazed that people came to eat the modest food he and his brother made.

Todd and Annie, their other server, tied on their aprons.

"Let's rock," Todd said.

Bobby Joe opened the door, and within five minutes all the tables were full. Ford fried eggs, cooked bacon, and stirred grits. The world shrank to food, order tickets, his brother, and Fitzgerald.

"I got the pancakes for table four if you can do the omelet," Bobby Joe said.

"Got it." Ford whisked eggs and poured them on the griddle next to the strips of bacon and hash browns. He still felt light on his feet. Only three more days before he saw Ava again. Maybe he'd even get to say hi to her today when he picked up Nelly.

"You're driving me crazy with that singing," Bobby Joe said.

"Was I singing?" Ford flipped the eggs.

"Yes. I haven't seen you act like this since that girl Wendy agreed to go out with you in high school."

"You were jealous."

"Yeah, what happened to her?" Bobby Joe put pancakes on a plate and slid them under the warmer.

"She was in a big hurry to have kids. Married Larry right after we graduated because I told her I wanted to go to college first," Ford said.

"Your loss."

"I used to think so. What you got next?"

"Ham and cheese omelet, pancakes, biscuits and gravy. I got the biscuits. You do the omelet." Bobby Joe plated two of the biscuits from the tray and went to the back for gravy.

Ford grabbed three more eggs. Biscuits and gravy had become one of the signature items on their menu. The biscuits were good, but the gravy made them really special. The recipe used by Rosie's previous owner had been bland and heavy. Ford lightened it up by reducing the ridiculous amount of sausage it called for and added mustard and hot sauce for a little zing. They got requests for the recipe at least once a month.

Bobby Joe returned with the plate of biscuits and gravy, and Ford finished his omelet at the same time. The rest of the breakfast rush went just as smoothly. The brothers worked the tickets together, coordinating so that each table got all their food at the same time. Fitzgerald cooked some, but mostly he fetched things from the back and hauled dirty dishes out of the way.

Three hours later, the rush was over and Fitzgerald went to the dining room to help Todd bus tables. Business wouldn't pick up again until around noon, when the lunch crowd came in.

"I'm going to do a few dishes and then add up the receipts," Bobby Joe said.

"Sure." Ford examined the few waiting orders. He could cook by himself until lunch.

The bearded graduate student whom Ford had seen before sat down at the counter, ordered black coffee, and opened Kant's *Critique of Judgment*.

Ford stirred the hash browns on the grill and glanced over at the student. He hunched over the page, brow furrowed. Ford spoke without thinking. "You want something to eat?" He didn't know why he bothered to ask. The guy never ate anything.

The student closed the book and rested his elbow on it. "Can't. All I got is my grad school stipend. I can spend five bucks a day, tops."

Ford flipped two pancakes. "Let me make you something I'm experimenting with. You can tell me whether it's any good. That way we both win—you get a free meal and I get an honest opinion."

"Fair enough. My name's Pete, by the way."

"Nice to meet you. I'm Ford."

"Yeah, I know," Pete said.

Ford plated the pancakes with the hash browns and slid them under the warmer. "Order up!" He put some butter in the microwave and mixed flour, milk, an egg, and water to make a thin batter. When the butter was melted, he added it in and stirred. He squirted a little oil on the flat top grill and poured on some batter. The crêpe only needed to cook for a few seconds. He flipped it and sprinkled grated cheese on top. He lifted the thin pancake off the grill and onto a plate, and put a slice of ham and a squirt of mustard on top before rolling it up.

"You have to imagine that it has prosciutto and Gruyere instead of cheddar and deli ham," Ford said, putting the plate in front of Pete.

The student took a bite and he stared at Ford with a comically surprised expression. "Dude, I don't have to. This is awesome. Crêpes, who knew? Why don't you put them on the menu?"

"My brother thinks they're too fancy. Bobby Joe doesn't like anything with a French name."

"Crawfish étouffée? What about beignets?" Pete said, his mouth full.

"He makes exceptions for Cajun French. I have some more batter left. How about a sweet one?" Ford spooned some sugar into the batter and stirred.

"You're the boss, man. You make 'em, I'll eat 'em."

Ford put sliced strawberries and some orange juice into a saucepan and let the mixture boil a little. In a bowl, he whisked cream cheese and folded in some of the berry mixture. This time he made two crêpes. He rolled the cream cheese filling inside and topped them with more berries and a dusting of powdered sugar.

Pete reached over the counter for the plate. "Amazing. You could totally sell these."

Bobby Joe came in from the back. "Why does it smell like Strawberry Shortcake took a dump in here?"

"Dude," Pete said. "You should try one of these crêpe things."

"No way. This is a simple café, not some fancy French place. Professor Frenchy French doesn't come here because it reminds him of home. He's here for an authentic American experience. We can't go mucking up our menu with snails and lobster. We're about breakfast all day and down home cooking. You want to do fancy, you have to get a liquor license and stop making pancakes." Bobby Joe poured himself a cup of coffee and slurped from it loudly.

"Your loss." Pete ate the second crêpe and looked at Ford like he expected another one.

"We don't have to change the whole menu, just add a few

new things," Ford said, pouring the last of the batter in two circles on the grill.

"Come on, we talked about this before. Menus are expensive to print, we'd have to buy different food, and probably no one would order it. We've got people who have been coming in here since Rosie was around. They know what they want, and we do a really good business. If we change stuff, we might lose customers," Bobby Joe said.

"Also, some people are afraid of change. Like a certain brother of mine, who has bought the same brand of shoes for twenty years." Ford flipped the crêpes over, let them cook a few more seconds, and topped them with the rest of the strawberries. "You sure you don't want this?"

"Looks like girly food," Bobby Joe said dismissively.

Pete snatched the plate. "More for me, then."

"I am not afraid of change. I switched our brand of napkins, didn't I?" Bobby Joe said.

"Only because the company we were using went out of business. This is the kid who insisted on wearing the same shirt to school every day in the fifth grade," Ford said to Pete.

"I never understood why Mom threw it away. There was nothing wrong with it," Bobby Joe said.

"No, except that it was worn so thin that everyone could see your belly button," Ford said.

"You could have a list of specials. Then you wouldn't have to reprint the menu," Pete said.

"You start doing that, and then people expect it every day. We have enough to worry about with our regular menu," Bobby Joe said, drinking the rest of his coffee.

Pete put his hands in the air. "I give up, dude."

"I told you, my brother's as stubborn as a mule. And almost as ugly as one too," Ford said.

"Oh yeah? Your mug could stop a train." Bobby Joe

grabbed Ford's crêpe bowl and saucepan and headed for the back.

"You could start your own restaurant, you know," Pete said.

"Without Bobby Joe? Nah. He might be pigheaded, but he's my brother."

CHAPTER 12

Ava was at her desk trying to write an article, but she couldn't stop eavesdropping as Rocky explained to Judith how the *Bon Temps* and *Sunday Features* sections were laid out. He'd finished the sections for the upcoming weekend the previous afternoon, and now he had two days to show her how to do it before going to the Marketing department. Things had moved fast—Rocky had found out about his reassignment on Monday and by Friday he'd be gone. Ava hadn't had time to even get used to the idea.

"The templates are here and you just open them and plug in the stories. If one runs long, you can do a jump, but only if it's the center page story," Rocky said.

"Yeah, I know that," Judith said.

Ava turned partway around and looked over at Rocky's desk. Judith was sitting in a chair behind him, leaning back with her arms crossed over her chest like a bored teenager.

"You might want to take notes on this. You'll be on your own next week, and no one else knows how to do this anymore," Rocky said, clearly fighting for patience.

"I'll remember it. Besides, we're going to change all this stuff anyway," Judith said.

"You'll be surprised how quick that deadline comes up. You have to edit all the content too, write the cutlines for the photos, compile the best-selling books list, and get any Associated Press stories you want to use. It's a lot."

"I work fast. I can edit a twenty-inch story in fifteen minutes. I'll have the sections finished in half the time it takes you."

"I need a cup of coffee," Rocky said. "Do you want one?"

"I only drink organic green tea," Judith said.

"I don't think they have that in the kitchen. Why don't you sit at my computer and look at all the layouts while I'm gone. See if you have any questions." Rocky stood up and grabbed his coffee cup.

"Okay, but I'm sure I won't."

Rocky walked over to Ava's desk. "Please kill me now," he whispered.

"I can't do that, but I'll go get coffee with you. I'm afraid I'm fresh out of organic green tea," Ava said, slipping her shoes on and getting her coffee mug.

"Should I just give up and let her sink?" Rocky asked as they walked through the cubicle forest.

"You might not have any choice. She doesn't seem to be listening to a word you're saying," Ava said.

"I forgot how annoying teenagers are."

"Especially twenty-five-year-old ones."

"I'm going to miss you, Ava. I went downstairs and met the Marketing people earlier. None of them have a sense of humor. I told one of my Boudreaux and Thibodeaux jokes and they all looked at me like I was speaking a foreign language."

Ava didn't know what to say. It wasn't like Rocky to be pessimistic. Or for him to talk about their friendship. "I'm going to miss you too."

"Ah, but you will have the charming Judith McCoy to keep you entertained."

They reached the kitchen and got their coffee. It wasn't very hot anymore, but Ava didn't care. She'd come for the company, not the beverage.

Slowly, they started back to their cubicles.

"I'll visit you as often as I can," Ava said. "I'm not letting those two floors get in the way of our friendship."

"I appreciate that. I'd come up here, but I'm afraid the sight of Judith sitting at my desk might be too much for my delicate constitution," Rocky said.

"Mine too," Ava said. For a brief moment, she thought she might start crying. Then Judith came into view, occupying Rocky's chair. Ava gripped her coffee cup handle tightly. This was wrong. Very wrong.

"Wish me luck," Rocky said.

"I know she's big, but you can take her," Ava said.

Rocky gave her a grim smile and went back to his desk.

Ava sat down and tried to concentrate on her story about the upcoming Scottish festival. Soon she put in her earbuds and turned on some loud rock music. She just couldn't listen to Judith's voice anymore.

CHAPTER 13

The night before his second date with Ava, Ford wanted to clean the apartment, but Nelly had other ideas.

First, she came into the bathroom wearing Hello Kitty rain boots and a tutu. "Where Pony?"

"I don't know," Ford said, scrubbing at the sink with a sponge. "Maybe she's in your room."

"Not in my room."

Ford washed and dried his hands. He found the purple pony in the middle of her bed, sitting with a group of stuffed pigs and a half-dressed doll. "Here's Pony."

"Want Pony comb."

"I don't know where the comb is."

Nelly threw herself full-length on top of her pink princess comforter, scattering the stuffed animals, and pounded her fists. "Where Pony comb? Where Pony comb?" After a few repetitions, the words were lost in a garble of hysterical crying.

Ford yanked open drawers, dug through piles of toys, and checked under the couch. He found the comb in the play refrigerator and brought it to her. "Here it is."

"Thank you, Daddy." Nelly sat up, instantly mollified, brushed the hair out of her eyes, and picked up Pony.

Ford went back in the bathroom and finished cleaning the sink. He had just gotten out the toilet brush when Nelly screamed, "I no can do it!"

Ford continued cleaning the toilet, hoping she would figure out whatever it was by herself.

Instead, her voice rose a few decibels. "I no can do it!"

"I'm coming." Ford put away the brush and washed his hands again. Nelly was sprawled out on the bed, the pony and comb lying next to her. "What are you trying to do?"

"I no can do it!" Her face was blotchy from crying, and her hair was a tangled mess.

He sat down next to her and picked up the comb. He wasn't going to make Nelly miserable for the sake of a clean house. His daughter clearly wanted his attention right now. Ava would understand.

The next morning, Ford stood in front of his closet, debating. He hated dress shirts. The collars constricted his neck and the fabric was scratchy. He'd rather just wear T-shirts all the time. But this date was special, so maybe he should try to dress up for a change.

Nelly came into the room toting a baby doll covered with a pink hand towel. "What doing, Daddy?"

"Trying to decide what to wear."

Nelly examined the shirts. She shook her head, went over to his dresser, and dug through his T-shirts and polos until she came up with a shirt advertising a local brand of potato chips. A big red crawfish adorned the front. "This one."

"I don't know, honey."

Nelly shoved the shirt into his hands. "Get dressed.

Time for school." She walked purposefully out of the room, her doll tucked under her arm.

Ford put on the shirt and a pair of jeans. He hesitated for a moment before grabbing his work boots. Nelly was right. He should just be himself.

When Ford and Nelly arrived at the day care, Ava was standing near the big tree on the playground. She wore a black-and-white flower-patterned dress and platform heels. Ford wanted to pull her close and see if she smelled as good as she looked.

"So what are we doing?" she asked.

"It's a secret," Ford said.

"I like surprises as long as they don't involve kids sneaking my favorite lipstick to decorate the bathroom." Ava looped her arm around his. She smelled like oranges and flowers.

"You'll have to drive your own car this time."

"Mysterious."

"I'm a man of mystery," Ford said, hoping he wasn't overselling his idea. He'd asked her to take extra time off, and he didn't want her to be disappointed when she found out why.

At Ford's apartment building, they parked next to each other and climbed the outside stairs to his metal balcony. He'd squeezed two chairs onto the tiny space so that he and Nelly could sit and watch the sunset while they ate their bedtime ice cream. It was his favorite time of day.

As he unlocked the door and let Ava inside, Ford felt like a schoolboy whose homework might not measure up. His apartment was a bachelor pad in the strictest sense of the word. Only he, Nelly, and Bobby Joe had ever been inside. Even Marion had never set a dainty foot on the carpet. Ford had thought it would remain that way for the foreseeable future. Now Ava would see his grape juice–stained couch, the broken top of the toilet tank that he'd mended with duct tape until Bobby Joe could find him a new one, and Nelly's pink-decorated, pony-filled room.

While Ava took off her shoes, Ford glanced around quickly, making sure he hadn't missed any candy wrappers or half-filled juice cups. He'd ended up doing most of his date preparations during a thirty-minute episode of Nelly's favorite morning cartoon. He'd closed the blinds and put out candles on the white tablecloth–covered kitchen table, which he'd set with wineglasses, a bottle of decent red along with a corkscrew, and white cloth napkins that Marion had forgotten to take in the divorce. The warm smell of beef stew and apple pie made the modest apartment seem like a charming bistro—or at least he hoped it did.

"I thought since we couldn't have a real evening date, we'd pretend," he said, taking the stew out of the oven.

"Whatever you have cooking smells great," Ava said as she sat down at the table.

"Beef stew. I wanted something I could make in advance. Besides, we don't serve it at the restaurant, so I haven't eaten it eighty-five times in the last month." Ford set the pot on the stove and tasted the stew. He sprinkled in some salt and tried it again. Pretty good. He'd kept it simple, just a few carrots, potatoes, onions, and garlic. The secret was getting a good sear on the cubes of meat and then letting everything cook for a long time.

Ava worked the corkscrew into the bottle of wine. "I wish I could make something like that."

"It's easy. I could teach you," he said.

She laughed, Ford's new favorite sound. "You'd be surprised."

"It's just a matter of spending the time to learn. I taught myself when I was a teenager, because I got tired of eating the canned gumbo and Hamburger Helper my mom made." He reached into the cabinet and brought down two cereal bowls. He didn't have any fancy china; Marion had remembered to take that. Ford didn't care. He had argued against registering for the fragile, flower-patterned plates anyway. He'd rather have a few good pans and some chef-quality knives.

"I wouldn't even know where to start learning to cook. And I don't have time," Ava said.

"It helps if it's your job. You learn really fast. I had trial by fire. I didn't know how to make much more than hamburgers when we bought the place. The previous owner left a book of mediocre recipes and I started from there. Now I can make pretty much any type of sandwich or breakfast food. Sometimes I make fancier stuff at home, just for fun."

"I leave the cooking to the experts," Ava said, pouring the wine.

"I'm hardly an expert," Ford replied.

"What do you mean? You run a restaurant. I have to look up a recipe to boil eggs at Easter."

"I've never been to culinary school. I'm not a chef, just a cook."

"So what?"

"You seriously don't mind dating a guy who slings burgers for a living?" Ford tried to sound like he was joking, not asking a serious question.

"Why would I?" Ava asked.

"I don't know. Marion thinks I'm unambitious. She's a doctor, and I'm just a fry cook. She said she didn't mind, but I think it started to get to her after a while. Like, she could do better."

"That's crazy. I think I might have mentioned before that there is something wrong with your ex."

"You did." Ford brought the bowls of stew to the table.

"I actually made this last night after Nelly went to bed. It improves with age."

"This is like a real fancy date. Better even. I don't think I've ever had a man cook for me before. Do you want me to bring anything else over?" Ava asked, standing up.

"You can get the salads. You're okay with eating dinner at eight thirty in the morning?"

"I love it. I forgot to eat breakfast again."

Ford got the French bread, while Ava brought the salad plates. They sat down together and he looked at her in the candlelight. She was more beautiful than anyone he'd ever seen. Wispy red curls framed her face, giving it a hint of softness. He wanted to reach out and touch her pale, almost translucent skin. Instead, he put the napkin in his lap and picked up a fork.

Ava took a bite of stew and closed her eyes for a moment. "Wow. I always thought beef stew was that stuff in the can."

"Dinty Moore? That's basically dog food for people."

"Yeah. This is . . . wow."

"It's nice to have someone appreciate my cooking," Ford said. "Nelly would rather eat chicken nuggets and donuts."

"My kids too. Maybe that's part of the reason I never bothered to learn to cook. And my ex . . ." Ava waved a hand dismissively and took another bite.

"Do you still see him?" Ford asked.

"He lives in Chicago and seems to have no interest in the kids. Takes them to Disneyland once a year and that's it. At least he sends the child support." Ava drank some wine and cut a piece of bread from the long loaf.

"If Marion wanted to move to Chicago, I'd pay for the bus ticket."

"Yeah, it has its advantages. But sometimes it would be nice to have help. It gets overwhelming. My parents are still in Wisconsin and Jared's live in California. It seems like both sets of parents have sort of given up on us. Jared's parents have other children with kids who live nearby, so they're not starved for grandparent action. Mostly they just send birthday cards and a check once in a while. My parents do visit sometimes, and I usually just wish they wouldn't. They manage to criticize everything I'm doing without actually helping."

"How could you not be interested in your kids or grandkids?" Ford said.

"I don't know. I swear, I didn't know Jared was such a putz when I married him." Even in the candlelight, the dark circles under Ava's eyes were visible. She rested her head on her hand and looked at him. "I hate the nights when I just wish the kids would go to bed because everyone's asking me for something at the same time. Then, when they are sleeping, I feel so alone. It's crazy stupid."

Ford mopped his bowl with a piece of bread. "I know the feeling. When Nelly is with me, I get overwhelmed sometimes by all the things I have to do for her. But when she's at her mother's, the apartment seems too empty. I spend most of my time at the café, not just because Bobby Joe needs me, but because I don't want to be home alone."

"I know. This is what I miss—being with another adult besides just at work," Ava said. "You have to tell me why we're eating dinner so early. What's next?"

"Well, if this was an evening date, we'd watch a movie, right?" Ford gathered the plates and glasses. "First, though, we have to stop drinking wine."

"Okay." Ava sounded chastened.

"You can't drink red wine with apple pie." He brought the dishes into the kitchen and poured two snifters of calvados.

Ava accepted a glass and held it up to the light. "What's this?"

"Apple brandy."

"Mmm."

"It'll be better with the pie." The pastry was perfectly flaky and golden. Ford wasn't much of a baker, but he might have gotten it right this time. He cut two slices, topped them with homemade whipped cream, and brought the plates to the table.

Ava cut off the tip of her pie. Ford watched her taste it before trying his own. When she closed her eyes again, he knew he'd hit another home run.

CHAPTER 14

Ava woke up confused. She was lying under an unraveling quilt in a room that smelled faintly of Old Spice. Her phone was chirping on the nightstand. She grabbed it and answered. "Hello?"

"It's Ford. I just wanted to make sure you got up in time to pick up your kids."

Ava heard banging pots and voices in the background and guessed he was at work. The pieces started to come back together. They'd had dinner for breakfast and then watched a romantic comedy. She thought that she'd kissed him, but it might have been a dream. Then he'd led her to his bed and left for work.

She'd slept by herself. She didn't know if that was a relief or a disappointment. "Um, thanks. For everything."

"Yep. I had a great time. Sorry to cut it short, but I have to get back to flipping burgers. See you later," he said, hanging up.

Ava got up and tried to smooth out her sundress. She picked up her phone and looked at it. She'd slept for over three hours, and she felt rested for the first time in weeks.

Ford had lined her shoes up neatly next to the bed and she put them on.

She smiled as she closed and locked the apartment door behind her. He'd given her the perfect gift, something only a parent of young children could understand the value of: adult time and a nap free from interruptions. Some people would see it as unromantic, but they had never struggled to stay awake through a long afternoon of homework and squabbling children and then endured a night of soothing kids back to sleep after bad dreams.

When she got into the van, Jared's phone number appeared on her phone's screen. Typical of him to call right when she was leaving to pick up the kids from school. Of course, he wouldn't know that. She answered it, curious as to why he was calling.

"Ava, I wanted to talk to you right after I heard the news, but I've been really busy on a big story," he said.

"What news?" Ava asked, her brain still muddled from sleep.

"The *Times-Picayune*. I can't believe it's only going to be published three days a week."

"I know. It's unbelievable. All told, sixty people were laid off."

"What does this mean for you? I mean, is the *Gazette* okay? What's happening there?" Jared sounded genuinely concerned.

"Well, there's no reason to think our paper will get shut down, at least not right now. But they did push Rocky to Marketing."

"Rocky? What?"

"He's being replaced by the publisher's niece."

"Do you think it's going to be just him?" he asked. "Or is there going to be another round of layoffs?"

"No one knows. But there are rumors that we might open a bureau in New Orleans," Ava said.

"I never thought I'd see the day. I mean, I knew the industry was in trouble, but to see the *Picayune* practically gone and the *Gazette* moving into their territory. It's just weird. What are we going to do, Ava?" he said.

"You still have your job, right?"

"For now. But with all the changes in the industry, I'm not confident that I'll be here until I retire. If the *Pic* can be gutted, who's to say the *Tribune* can't be?"

Ava started the van and turned on the air-conditioning. She felt too hot all of a sudden. "I don't know, Jared."

"Nobody knows, that's the problem. Look, even here, people are leaving to take jobs in public relations. They're scared of the future, and they want out."

"I don't."

"I don't either," Jared said. "I have to go. Take care of yourself. Oh, and the kids. I forgot to ask how they're doing."

"Fine. I have to go pick them up from school."

"Okay. I'm going to figure out a way to see them soon. I promise."

"Sure." Ava hung up. All the warm feelings from her date with Ford were gone.

CHAPTER 15

After working the lunch shift at Rosie's, Ford drove to Metairie with Nelly. The date with Ava had been perfect: the meal, the movie, and mostly just sitting on the couch with her, talking. He'd hated to leave her alone, but he'd promised to work the lunch rush. Besides, by eleven o'clock, she'd been dozing during the movie. Clearly, she was sleep-deprived. He knew what that was like. Marion had never been one for getting up in the middle of the night with Nelly. She'd shove her earplugs in farther and remind him that she had to wake up early for her shift at the hospital.

Metairie was a collection of fast-food chains, nondescript houses, and strip malls that almost could have been anywhere in the country except for the canals that ran parallel to the streets. Ford had grown up in Lutcher, a small town where his mother taught at the junior high school. After retiring, she'd moved back to the suburb of her home city of New Orleans. She'd wanted Ford to move there too, but Marion had been offered a better position at Saint Mary's Hospital in Saint Jude. His mother always complained about not seeing Ford and Bobby Joe often enough, but she refused to sell her house and relocate. She had the typical New Orleanian disdain for less cosmopolitan Saint Jude.

Ford turned by a po'boy shack topped with a sandwich-shaped sign and drove onto his mother's street. Her house was the smallest in the neighborhood. It was painted yellow and the front yard featured a garden with a brick walkway that Bobby Joe had installed. Before he even put the pickup in Park, Ford made a mental list of things to do. The porch light was burned out, the lawn needed mowing, and the skirting below the porch was coming loose. He let Nelly out of her car seat and retrieved his toolbox from the back of the truck.

His mother opened the door and held out her arms to Nelly. "Hi, sweetheart. Maw-Maw has some cookies for you."

"Mom, she had a snack at school." Ford took out a hammer and reattached the wooden skirting. It probably kept coming loose because a raccoon or possum was living under the house.

"A little cookie and a glass of lemonade never hurt anyone," she said.

Ford straightened up and put the hammer back in the box. His mother's puffball of artificially blond hair gave her two inches of extra height, but she still barely reached his shoulder. She was wearing a neon-pink T-shirt and white capri pants, a pretty standard outfit for her. Ford followed her and Nelly into the house.

In her beige-tiled kitchen, she poured a glass of lemonade from the 1980s-era harvest-gold refrigerator. She refused to let Ford get her a new one even though she'd make the money back on energy costs in less than a year. "Would you like an M&M cookie or a peanut butter one?" she asked Nelly.

"M&M," Nelly said, climbing onto one of the chairs around the kitchen table.

"Ford, darling?"

"No, thanks," Ford said.

"Sit down. Let me get you some iced tea." His mother went back to the refrigerator.

Ford put his toolbox on the floor and straddled one of the cane-bottomed chairs. "Your lawn needs mowing."

She set a glass of tea in front of him and sat down. "There's plenty of time for that."

"No, there isn't. I promised Marion I'd have Nelly there by six o'clock." Ford looked over the table at his mother. There was something different about her. Her eyes seemed to be sitting too deep in the sockets. "Are you okay?"

"Yes. Well, no. There's something I need to tell you. I don't want you and Bobby Joe to worry. Bobby Joe, especially. That boy always took things hard."

"What is it, Mom? Come on."

"I haven't been feeling too well lately. Tired, and you know I'm never like that. I finally went to the doctor and had some tests. Turns out I have breast cancer."

"Are you serious?"

"Don't look at me like that. It'll be okay. I'm getting a mastectomy and then chemotherapy. It's stage-one."

"Why didn't you tell me? When *were* you going to tell me?" Ford's brain didn't want to process the information. His mom had cancer and she might die. He repeated it to himself, trying to make sense of the words. He felt like he was falling, even though the chair remained solid under him.

She got up and poured another glass of iced tea from her daisy-decorated pitcher. "Right now. I was going to tell you right now. Bernice will take me to the surgery and treatment, don't worry. The doctors wanted me to go to Houston, but I told them I'm too old for that. If they can't do it right here, then I'm not getting it done."

"God, Mom." Ford covered his face with his hands.

"My surgery is scheduled for October twenty-ninth. They're going to remove my left breast and then do chemotherapy after I've recovered," she said.

"That's over a month away," Ford said. "Can't they do it now? So you can start the chemo as soon as possible?"

"It takes a long time to schedule surgery. The doctor said I was lucky to get in that soon. Anyway, I would like you to help me start going through some of my things and get everything straight, just in case."

"Come on, you're not going to die."

"Someday I will." She sipped her tea. "And I don't want to leave a big mess for y'all to clean up."

Nelly got down from her chair and began rearranging the refrigerator magnets. Ford's mother had owned the same few magnets for as long as he could remember—a Louisiana A&M crawfish, a blue map of the state, a few pieces of rubber food, and one with a picture of Bobby Joe, Ford, and her on a long-ago vacation to Florida.

"Yeah, I'll help you," he said.

"There's something I want you to take right now." She walked down the hall in the direction of her bedroom. Age hadn't slowed her down much. At seventy, her pace still outstripped Ford's own. How such a small woman could move so fast was a mystery to him. Ford was more of an ambler than a speed-walker.

Nelly was busily grouping the magnets into categories— food, places, photographs. She was an arranger for sure. She must have gotten that from Marion. Ford's mother had never been that way. Life was too short to worry about things not being exactly right, she always said. Maybe that attitude had helped her deal with her diagnosis. Still, she might have spent days crying for all Ford knew. He didn't spend enough time with his mother. Sure, he dropped by almost every week, either when he picked up Nelly or before dropping her off at Marion's. But he could never stay long. There was always a dance lesson, an errand, and the café to run. There wasn't enough time and now it was running out.

She returned to the kitchen and sat down. His mother wasn't walking any slower, but her breath came out in short bursts. The sight made Ford's own throat constrict.

She studied him for a moment, her blue eyes searching for something. Then she opened her hand. "I want you to have this."

He drew back. Her wedding and engagement rings. "I can't. What about Bobby Joe?"

"Your brother's wife already has a ring," she said.

"What makes you think I'll get married again?"

She took his hand and dropped the rings into his palm. The engagement ring had one small diamond in a plain setting, and the wedding ring was a thin band of gold. Neither was worth much, but that didn't diminish the significance of the gift. He put the rings in his pocket. It felt like his mother was giving part of herself away. Ford didn't want her to do it. He wanted her to continue to be whole forever.

"I know you will find someone else." She closed her eyes for a moment.

"There isn't anyone else."

His mother opened her eyes. "Isn't there?"

"No." Ford didn't know why he was afraid to tell his mother about Ava. He knew she would like her. Maybe it was something else—an old superstition that if you told someone your wishes they wouldn't come true.

"Well, there will be. I'm sure of it."

"Okay, Mom." Ford drank his iced tea in two gulps. "I'm

going to fix your porch light, and then I have to take Nelly to her mother's. I'm so sorry about all this. I'll call you later today, okay?"

"I'll be all right," she said.

"I love you, Maw-Maw," Nelly said.

Ford's mother drew the girl to her and hugged her until Nelly started to squirm. He turned away so that his mother wouldn't see the tears in his eyes.

When he got back to the café after dropping Nelly off at Marion's, Ford immediately told his brother about their mother's cancer. Bobby Joe was not taking it well. For three solid minutes, he had been stomping around like an angry bear. Ford was seriously considering closing the restaurant and taking his brother out for a beer, just to calm him down.

Bobby Joe slammed yet another armload of prep pans into the stainless-steel industrial sink. "Aunt Bernice is going to drive her to chemo? Jesus, I didn't realize she still had a driver's license."

"Come on, Bobby Joe. Of course she does. She visits Mom every Thursday and drives her to church, you know that," Ford said.

The dinner rush was over, but instead of going home, Bobby Joe had decided to stay and help Ford clean up. He probably couldn't face telling Jeanie the news. Bobby Joe's wife had always been close to her mother-in-law.

"She shouldn't have one. She was never a good driver, and now she's half-blind," Bobby Joe said.

"She taught you how to drive, as I recall." Ford filled a clean bottle with mayonnaise from the industrial tub. "Not much of an endorsement."

Bobby Joe squirted dish soap into the sink and turned on the water. "Mom taught you and look how well that turned out."

"Everyone knows she's a lousy driver. The only reason she hasn't wrecked her Olds is because she keeps it under fifteen miles per hour. I'm thinking about buying her one of those three-wheeled bikes."

"Ha! Our mother would never ride a tricycle."

"She would if it was her only mode of transportation," Ford said.

"Good luck with all that." Bobby Joe snorted. "Remember the time you tried to convince her to sell the house and move into a condo?"

"She'll never let me forget that. At least she finally got a smaller place."

Bobby Joe started scrubbing the pot they used to make grits. "Waited for a year just to spite you, though."

"And she still refused to move to Saint Jude." Ford grabbed the tub of mustard and filled another bottle. Even from the back, he could tell that his brother was a little less tense. His shoulders had relaxed, and he was washing the dishes rather than banging them around.

Ford carried the bottles up front to the sandwich station. Fitzgerald was dumping frozen fries into a basket. He lowered it into the fryer. "Hey, man. Sorry to hear about your mom."

Ford lined up the mustard, mayonnaise, and ketchup bottles. He took the empty lettuce and tomato prep pans. "It's rough."

Pete was sitting alone at the counter. He glanced up from Descartes's *Meditations*. "What's going on with your mom?"

"Cancer," Ford said.

"Dude, that sucks. Where does she live?"

"Metairie."

"Oh yeah? My buddy runs a café down there. Place is filled with all this weird art. Totally trippy, man." The student sipped his coffee. "Anyway, good luck to your mom."

"Yeah." Ford turned to Fitzgerald and lowered his voice. "Make the kid an egg or something. He still looks like he's starving."

Fitzgerald shook his head. "You can't give away food."

"Couple of eggs isn't going to break the bank."

"You're the boss." The cook cracked two onto the grill and added a slice of bread.

Ford took the pans to the back and dropped them in Bobby Joe's wash sink. "Hey, I'm going to see Mom tomorrow, if it makes you feel any better. I already got a reservation at that crappy motel by the railroad tracks."

Bobby Joe rinsed the soapy grits pot and transferred it to the sanitizing sink. "You ought to spring for a decent place. Mom would give you the money."

"I like that dump. I have a thing for scratchy towels and dribbling showers. Besides, it's got one of those vibrating beds." Ford sliced some tomatoes and stacked them in a prep pan.

"Does this mean I'm flying solo?"

"I'm leaving tomorrow, after the lunch rush. Can you handle it?"

"I guess so. I can always get Fitzgerald to come in. Tell her I'll call her tomorrow night," Bobby Joe said.

Ford filled another pan with lettuce. "Will do. Why don't you go home? I can handle it from here."

"Okay. Thanks." Bobby Joe placed the grits pot next to the sink to dry and took off his apron.

When he was gone, Ford got out his cell and called Ava.

"Hey, Ford. I wanted to call and thank you for the date, but I figured you were at work," she said.

"I am, so I can't talk long. I had a good time too. I just wish I'd packed up some stew for you to take home. I always make too much food."

"Maybe I'll have to stop by and pick some up."

Ford started washing the dishes Bobby Joe had left in the sink. "I wish I could invite you to, but I have to go visit my mom in Metairie tomorrow. She just told me she has cancer."

"I'm sorry, Ford. What kind?"

"Stage-one breast cancer. She tells me she's going to be okay, but I'm worried."

"I'm sure you are. Is there anything I can do?" Ava asked.

"No, but I'd still like to see you next Friday," Ford said.

"Definitely. Let me know how she's doing, okay?"

"I will, Ava, thanks." Ford felt a little better after hanging up. His mother would like Ava, he was sure. He had to make sure they met soon. Seeing him with her would make his mother happy.

CHAPTER 16

Ford tossed his duffel bag on top of the paisley motel bed-spread. He really did like the Stardust Inn. The owner, a Pakistani guy named Ralph, always gave him the same room near the ice machine. The familiar chipped sink and washed-out painting of the French Quarter made him feel at home. Besides, Ford was more comfortable around the clientele of truck drivers and small-time salesmen than he would have been with the executive-types in the fancy chain hotels.

He turned on the TV, stretched out on the bed, and flipped through the four channels. He wanted a few minutes to himself before going to see his mother. He'd even set his phone to silent and left it in the car, a risky move with Nelly at Marion's, but his ex was capable of handling anything that might happen. He didn't love Marion anymore, but he trusted her.

He bunched up some of the flat pillows against his head so he could see the TV. An advertisement for a Metairie restaurant came on. The place specialized in disgusting hubcap-sized hamburgers. Amazing that the owner could keep a place like that in business, let alone afford TV advertising. Hadn't Pete said something about a café in Metairie? He was sure it wasn't the same place, but the ad still made him think. Would he ever consider buying another café and running it himself? Sure, it would be nice to do things his own way—put new items on the menu once in a while, for example, but he loved working with Bobby Joe. Besides, his brother had taken care of a lot of the difficult details—getting the small business loan, dealing with licenses and health inspectors, and figuring out where to get food and supplies. If he was on his own, it would be all up to him. The prospect was more than a little daunting. He'd always had Bobby Joe as his safety net. Maybe it was time to break free.

Ford turned off the TV and stared at the ceiling.

He woke up on top of the bedspread. He didn't remember going to sleep, but now it was five o'clock in the morning. Great, his mother had been expecting him. If she was really worried, though, she would have called Bobby Joe and his brother knew where to find him. Ford hadn't realized how tired he'd been. Thinking about his mother's illness was sapping his energy. He felt like he'd fallen into a deep hole and he couldn't even summon the will to try clawing his way out.

He thought he wanted to lie down a little longer, but he couldn't go back to sleep, so he got up, showered, and shaved. Afterward, he turned on the TV and turned it off again. It was too early to go to his mother's house, but he didn't want to sit around the motel. He went outside.

The morning air was chilly, but damp like it always was in Louisiana. He got in his truck and sat behind the wheel. There was nowhere he wanted to go; nothing he wanted to do. He started the truck and drove toward his mother's neighborhood. None of the businesses he passed were open, and the empty streets made him feel even more alone. He knew he should call Ava again later, but the task seemed too great. He didn't feel like talking to anyone, not even her. His brother called it "shutting down," when Ford refused to discuss something that was bothering him. Bobby Joe never shut down. He'd yell, swear, even throw things, and then he'd be okay. Ford just felt frozen. Anything he thought about seemed impossible, so he tried not to think at all.

The light was on in the kitchen when he got to his mother's house. Knowing her, that meant she'd been awake all night. Ford cut the truck's engine and walked up to the door. She answered before he had a chance to knock.

She didn't have her makeup on. Ford could count on one hand the times he'd seen her without it. Even before he got inside, he smelled the cigarette smoke. Bobby Joe had done a report in fifth grade about the health effects of smoking and very seriously told his mother that he didn't want her to die. That was all it took. She quit and hadn't touched a cigarette since, as far as Ford knew.

"Sorry, Mom. I fell asleep as soon as I got to the motel," he said.

"It's okay. I figured you got busy at the café or something. Would you like some coffee?"

"Sure."

She led the way to the kitchen and started the drip machine she'd had as long as Ford could remember. The house looked the same as always. He had been irritated with her for refusing to move into a condo, but he had to admit that the bungalow suited her. She'd scaled down when she relocated to the smaller house. Her living room furniture consisted of a love seat and a petite armchair. Everything was woman-size. There was nowhere for Ford to sit comfortably, let alone sleep, which was why he'd become a regular at the Stardust. The lack of accommodation for her large sons was no accident. His mother had always been independent. She loved her children, but the house was her domain.

Ford sat at the kitchen table and removed his hat. His mother took a tube of cinnamon rolls from the refrigerator, popped it open, and began arranging blobs of dough on a sheet pan.

"Just because I'm sick, doesn't mean you have to spend every weekend here. I know you and Bobby Joe have a café to run," she said.

Ford poured himself a cup of coffee and sat back down. "I wish I could be here all the time."

"No, you don't. Men are no good with sick people. Once you ran out of things to fix, you'd go crazy and drive me crazy while you were at it. Bernice will take care of me. It'll give her something to do besides stare at that old TV of hers all day long." She put the rolls in the oven and joined him at the table. "You can't stop your life because I'm getting old."

Ford didn't want to talk about his mother aging. "You were right, Mom. I did meet someone."

"That's great! What's her name?"

"Ava."

"Lovely." Doris started to stand up.

"What do you need, Mom?"

"Oh, I was going to get some coffee."

"Let me do it," Ford said, getting up before she could protest and finding her favorite *#1 Mom* mug. He'd given her the silly gift when he was ten years old. It was chipped and stained, but she still used it.

"So, tell me about Ava," she said.

Ford set the coffee in front of her. "She works for the *Saint Jude Gazette* part-time and she has three kids. One is a friend of Nelly's."

"Divorced?"

"Yes, her ex-husband lives in Chicago."

"Next time you come, bring her with you." She sipped her coffee.

"I will, Mom. What do you want me to do?"

"I have a few boxes to go to charity. I don't want to make Bernice lift them."

"Is that all?" Ford said.

"Well, you didn't get to mow the lawn last time and that skirting below the porch is loose again. The gutters could use cleaning, and the bushes should be trimmed. You should leave some of the work for Bobby Joe whenever he comes down," she said.

"I'm sure he'll come soon, but I'll go ahead and do everything. There'll be plenty for him to do, anyway. There's always something with these old houses."

"Old? Do you realize that this house is younger than you?"

"Yeah, but I'm not too young either." Ford finished his coffee and went to the sink to wash his mug.

"You just want something to do. You don't want to sit all day and chat with an old lady."

"Do you want me to stay inside and talk to you, Mom?"

"No, go do your work."

Ford shook his head and went outside.

At five o'clock, he went to pick up Nelly. It was a relief to be getting back to his normal life. Taking care of his daughter would force him to think about her and not about his mother. One thing he'd realized after Marion left was that kids left little time and energy for reflection. That was a good thing when dealing with something like a divorce—or an illness.

"We were just going to eat dinner," Marion said when she answered the door.

Nelly ran past her mother. "Daddy!"

Ford knelt down to hug his daughter. "Sorry. I guess I'm a little early. I had a rough weekend. I just found out that my mother has cancer."

"I'm sorry." Marion walked toward the kitchen. "What kind?"

"Breast. Stage-one."

"That's not good at her age." Marion took a cooked chicken breast out of a pan and began slicing it.

"Yeah, thanks. I know."

"I'm sorry, Ford. Truly. You know I love your mother. Do you want to stay for dinner?"

Marion's cooking was aggressively bland. Nothing she made had any seasoning or fat in it. Besides, he didn't want to talk about his mother. He felt wrung out. "I'm tired," he said, unable to come up with a more elaborate excuse not to stay.

"Sit down. I have an extra chicken breast," Marion said.

"Daddy, let's go." Nelly wrapped her arms around Ford's leg.

"Don't you want to eat the dinner your mom cooked?" he said.

"I no like chicken."

"Of course you do, honey. You eat it all the time."

"No like. Want to go home."

Marion turned around, hurt in her hazel eyes.

"This is your home too, sweetheart," Ford said.

"Daddy's is home," Nelly insisted.

"Fine, take her. She doesn't want to be here," Marion said.

"You can't take this stuff personally," Ford said. "She tells me that she hates me practically every day."

"You shouldn't let her do that."

"She's three. That's what three-year-olds do."

"Just go. Please." Marion leaned over the sink, head down.

Ford thought she was crying, but he wasn't sure. He didn't know what to do. Did she expect him to stay and comfort her, or did she really want him to leave? "I'm sorry, Marion," he said.

"Daddy, let's go," Nelly said.

"Your mom's upset."

Nelly ran to Marion and hugged her leg. "It's okay, Mommy."

Marion didn't react. Ford felt sorry for his ex-wife, but sometimes her expectations were unreasonable. She'd wanted him to be something he wasn't too. Besides, Nelly loved her mom; she just thought Ford would let her have fast food for dinner. Which, in his current state, he probably would. "Come on, Nelly."

"'Bye, Mommy." Nelly picked up her pony from the floor and took Ford's hand. He'd missed her little fingers curled around his. He lifted her hand to his lips and kissed it.

CHAPTER 17

Ava couldn't help grinning when Ford showed up at her door dressed as a cowboy, complete with boots and a felt hat. After a month of Friday dates and many late-night phone conversations, they'd finally decided to do something together with their kids. They'd agreed not to make a big announcement to the children—at least not yet, but to present themselves as friends. Ava was still a little bit nervous about the idea, but seeing Ford's outfit somehow made her feel more comfortable. This was a man who was not afraid to look silly for his daughter. Obviously, he realized that the children had to come first.

Sadie had picked out a dress for Ava to wear and lent her one of her many tiaras, so she had a costume too, sort of. She lifted the edges of the skirt and curtsied.

"My lady," Ford said, bowing. "You look stunning. I especially love the crown and sneakers."

"Even princesses don't wear heels to parades, but I promise to put them on for the grand ball this evening," Ava answered.

Nelly wore a cowboy hat too, and she dragged a purple pony by its mane. She didn't wait to be invited in, but rushed past Ava to find Sadie. Ford shrugged apologetically.

"Come in, cattle rustler," Ava said. "We're almost ready to go."

"Whoa," Ford said as he came into the living room. "Who are these two tough characters?"

James, who had protested that he was too old to dress up, but had finally put on his costume anyway, smiled when he saw Ford. "I'm Han Solo."

Luke thrust out his Captain America shield. "Are you a good guy or a bad guy?"

Ford held up his hands. "A good guy, I swear."

"You'd better be," Luke said, lowering the shield. "We're keeping an eye on you, right, James?"

"Mr. Ford is a good guy," Sadie said. Her Rapunzel gown was almost too small, but she'd insisted on wearing it anyway. Ava had managed to talk her out of the matching shoes, though, which would slide off halfway to the parade.

"I just need to grab some plastic bags and we'll be ready to go," Ava said, reaching under the sink and getting a handful of bags for stowing parade throws.

"Are you a cowgirl?" Sadie asked Nelly.

"Yup. This is my horse."

"What's her name?"

Nelly shrugged. "Pony."

Ava herded the girls out the door as they continued their discussion about whether the plush horse needed a real name. The boys followed, sticking close to Ford. Even though the parade route was only a few blocks away, Ava had the wagon out for Sadie and Nelly to ride in. They'd need a place to put their parade loot, anyway. Sadie climbed into the wagon and motioned for her friend to follow.

"I've never been to the Halloween parade before," Ford said.

"We always go. It gives the kids another excuse to wear their costumes. Anyway, we're practically on the parade route," Ava said.

"Honestly, parades have always seemed like too much work to me—finding parking, pushing through the crowds, and all that. Besides, I'm always worried that Nelly will run in front of a float."

"She's three now and she's a smart girl, right, Nelly?" Ava said.

"Don't go in front of floats," Sadie said.

"Okay," Nelly answered.

"They'll be fine." Ava put her arm around Ford's waist. "We'll all watch her."

"Don't worry, Mr. Ford," James said.

"Okay, I won't."

Ava took the handle of the wagon and began to pull it across the lawn toward the street.

"Let me do that," Ford said. "Those girls are heavy."

"Okay." Ava felt warm and happy, basking in the October sun and seeing their families finally together. James and Luke walked next to Ford, talking over each other in their eagerness to tell him some story. Sadie and Nelly played with the stuffed pony and discussed the loot they were expecting to catch. Ava walked a little faster to catch up to Ford and heard Luke telling him that Captain America could break a brick wall with his fist.

They turned the corner and walked one more block to the parade route. The Halloween parade in Saint Jude was still fairly new, so it wasn't as crowded as the St. Patrick's Day or Mardi Gras ones. For some parade-goers, the events were like a tailgate party, where eating, drinking, and socializing began hours before the first float came by and continued into the night. They claimed a spot on the sidewalk near a family with a dog, two ice chests, and four children wearing superhero costumes.

"This is the hardest part," Ava told Ford. "Before the parade comes."

Luke and James bounced up and down, watching the street impatiently.

"Let's play a game," Ford said. "Try to guess what everyone's costume is. I see a mailman over there."

"Where?" James said.

"Oh wait, maybe it was just a guy with a blue shirt."

"I see Superman!" Luke said.

"Batman!" James yelled.

Ava was grateful to Ford for entertaining her sons, and, amazingly, Nelly and Sadie seemed happy to stay in the wagon together. Perhaps this time, for once, there would be no meltdowns before the parade arrived.

A few minutes later, the grand marshal and the first marching band came down the street. Nelly covered her ears when the drums got too close, but recovered as soon as the floats began to roll by and she caught her first beads.

Since it was an afternoon kids' parade, the floats were more funny than scary. Most were homemade, using vehicles ranging from flatbed trailers pulled by trucks, to four-wheelers and ordinary cars. Orange and black beads zinged through the air, almost too fast to catch. The kids danced to the music blaring from speakers on the floats and waved their hands, begging for throws. Ava stood near the back, watching and tossing anything good she found into the wagon. Ford hovered near the street, keeping Nelly and Sadie away from the floats. He really was being overly cautious about their safety—after all, the floats' top speed was five miles per hour—but Ava found it endearing.

By the time the last float rolled by, all the kids wore thick collars of beaded necklaces and the wagon was full of cups, footballs, stuffed animals, and flying disks.

"It's nap time!" Ford announced as he turned the wagon around and started back to the house.

"We're too old for naps!" James said.

"I'm not," Ford said.

"Me neither, and that sounds pretty good right now, even though I know it's not going to happen," Ava said. "How about if I make some coffee and lunch?"

"That sounds wonderful."

"This is the best day ever!" Sadie yelled.

"It is," Ava said.

Monday morning, Ava walked into the office dreading spending another workday without Rocky. She knew that he was still in the building, just in a new cubicle, but she felt like he was halfway across the world. She didn't really talk to anyone else in the Entertainment department, except to exchange pleasantries. Rocky was her best friend at the paper, and now he was replaced by the self-absorbed Judith.

Ava couldn't even look at Rocky's empty cube as she walked by. She sat down at her desk and drank coffee while she waited for her computer to boot up. As she opened the Monday paper, she heard a rustling noise from behind the cubicle wall. The cubicles on the other side—the opposite direction from Rocky's former desk—had been empty since she started working in Entertainment. The few reporters and editors remaining after Purge Part One had clustered together in groups with Rocky and her in one corner and the others, most of whom worked for the daily *Life and Leisure* section, nearer to the elevators. The exception was Judith, who sat closer to the *Life and Leisure* side, though she mostly wrote for *Bon Temps*. Ava was afraid that she knew who was moving in on the other side of the wall.

She got up and went around the corner. She'd expected to find Judith putting up pictures of her perfect child, but she was somewhat surprised to be greeted by her new boss's ample posterior as she plugged in computer cords under her desk. Ava looked away, embarrassed to see her in such an unprofessional position. Judith stood up, seemingly unperturbed, and adjusted her computer monitor. "I decided to move my cubicle closer to the action. No reason for me to be stuck all the way over by the elevators. Besides, here I can keep my eye on you." She laughed, but Ava had a feeling Judith was not joking.

"Um, okay," Ava said. The idea of Judith constantly watching her work made her feel like she was back in middle school, cringing under the gaze of a demanding and unpredictable teacher. Now that she thought about it, Judith did remind her of Ms. Humphries, who had smirked while giving pop quizzes on obscure topics in the history of western literature.

Judith sat down in her office chair and moved the monitor a few inches to the right. "Anyway, I'm glad you came over, Ava, because I wanted to tell you that I had to perform major surgery on your article." She reached into a cooler bag on her desk, extracted a baby carrot, and bit off the end with a snapping sound.

Ava took a step back and willed herself to ignore the wet smacking and crunching coming from between Judith's lips. "My Sugarcane Festival story? Why? What was wrong with it?"

"Ava, I know you started out stringing for the *Metro* section, but this is Entertainment. We are supposed to entertain. You need to jazz it up a little. Hook the reader. What you wrote was dullsville." Judith got another carrot stick.

"I've been writing for Entertainment for over a year now. Rocky did very little editing on my stories," Ava said.

"Well, I do things differently than he did. You can have a look at it. After you finish the calendars, that is."

Ava clenched her hands into fists. "Yes, of course."

"Speaking of which, we're dropping the dining guide as of next week." Judith paused to munch more carrot.

Finally, some good news. The dining guide had made sense before the Internet, but with the same information easily available online, it had outlived its usefulness.

"You will need something else to do on Fridays or whenever you have extra time," Judith continued. "I talked to Rochelle in the library, and since Henrietta was laid off, they could use some extra help. I told her you could go there for at least two hours a week. They mostly need help with filing of back issues, that kind of thing."

Ava was too shocked to answer. Working on the dining guide and the calendars was boring, but bearable since her efforts at least appeared in the newspaper. Filing was a job for a college student or an intern, not a reporter. It was a demotion, and her new boss knew it. Ava rehearsed a few responses in her mind, most of them centering on the theme of Judith's inexperience and the blatant nepotism that had gotten her the job. The even less-appropriate rejoinders included references to her new boss's toxic attitude and possibly non-human origins. Ava couldn't answer. She went back to her cubicle.

"Ava? Did you hear what I said? Why are you walking away?" Judith sounded disgustingly pleased.

Ava stood in her cubicle and focused on her breathing. She could not work for Judith. She knew what she had to do, but she needed a few seconds to gather her thoughts.

"Ava? I forgot to tell you that I decided the Sugarcane Festival story doesn't need to be on the cover of *Bon Temps* next week. I'm going to replace it with my story about the video gamers' convention. The Sugarcane Festival is old news," Judith said.

Ava forgot about yoga breathing, left her cubicle, and went to find the managing editor.

Mann's office was only a few feet away from the cubicles, but it seemed to be on an elevated plane. Instead of fluorescent lights, the room was lit by the soft glow of a standing lamp. His door-size desk was positioned on a red-and-brown rug with a paisley design. Soft music played from sleek black speakers, and a miniature fountain bubbled on the windowsill.

Mann stood and motioned for her to sit in the black leather chair in front of his desk. The editor was one of the few people who literally looked down on Ava. He was at least six feet, seven inches tall and trim without being skinny. His shaved head was as smooth as glass and as dark as black coffee. He wore his usual shirt and tie with stiffly starched pants. "Good morning," he said, sitting back down.

Ava drew in some of the faintly floral-scented air through her nose and lowered herself into the chair. "I heard we might be opening a bureau in New Orleans."

Mann gazed at her, his face unreadable. "Yes. We're just beginning to work out the details. John Cutter from the *Picayune* will run the Friday section down there. We're going to call it *Les Arts*."

"Are you . . . um, I mean, would you consider hiring me?" Ava asked.

"I might. Why should I?"

"Well, sir, I've been working here a long time, as you know, and I think I've done a good job. I know the *Bon Temps* and *Sunday Features* sections, but I've also written news articles. I mean, before Jared left." Ava mentally kicked herself. Mentioning her ex-husband was not going to get her the job. Mann didn't need to think of her as the inferior partner, which was too often how she thought of herself. She was more than Jared's ex-wife. She needed to prove that to the paper and to herself. "What I mean to say is that I'm flexible. I've written a lot of different kinds of articles. I can do whatever needs to be done."

"Maybe so." Mann's expression remained unchanged.

Ava's burst of adrenaline began to dissipate, leaving her wondering what she was doing. Did she really want to relocate her family to New Orleans just to get away from Judith? But it wasn't only that. Not by a long shot. She wanted to be a real reporter, not just a stringer or a half-time data entry clerk. If moving eighty miles away was the only way to do that, then she was ready. She sat up straighter and dug her heels into the rug.

"I've read all of your articles, of course, since I read everything that goes in the paper. I think you write well, Ava. You have an understated style that I like, and you always manage to get to the meat of the story quickly. You were our most reliable stringer, and now you're equally competent in Entertainment," he said.

"Thank you, sir. I do my best," Ava said.

"But I'm confused by this story about after-school activities. It doesn't seem to be your style. In fact, I almost sent the article back to have you rewrite it," Mann said, folding his hands on the desk.

Ava spoke without thinking. "I didn't write it."

"Your byline was on the story. I distinctly remember."

"Yes, sir, but Judith McCoy rewrote it for some reason. By the time she was done, I barely recognized any of it."

"I see," Mann said.

"It was complete crap. Awful and embarrassing. Judith

told me today that my style lacks 'jazz' or something. But that was just bad writing. I'm sorry." She slid back down in the slick leather chair, wishing she could take back the words. Insulting the publisher's niece was not going to get her a job. Making a disparaging comment about Mann's mother would have been worse, but not much.

Mann raised his thick black eyebrows. "What do you think about her becoming the new editor?"

Ava considered. There was no taking back what she'd said, so she might as well tell the truth. "She has a lot of big ideas, but I don't think she really knows what she's doing. Rocky had done things the same way for a long time. I know that. He knows how to put out the sections, though, and Judith doesn't. It's not clear to me that she even has a handle on how to do the formatting. She says she'll figure it out, but we have to put out a newspaper."

"Thank you for being frank with me," Mann said. "Not a lot of people would sit here and say that."

"Yes, sir," Ava said.

"So, I will match your honesty. Judith's uncle pushed us to give her a more prestigious position, and I didn't fight it. I knew that if she was made editor, she would most likely mess things up badly enough that I would be able to fire her, or at least inflict her on Online or some other department. I was hoping to bring Rocky back in a few months," Mann said.

Ava wanted to tell him that she hoped it happened sooner rather than later, but she decided she'd said enough.

"In any case, I would like to give you a chance. Not only do you write well, but you have guts coming in here and telling me what you really think about Judith. Good reporting takes courage. There are too many wishy-washy people out there in the newsroom. Like I said, it's possible that I'll be able to bring Rocky back, but I have to be honest—you will have better opportunities in New Orleans. We're expanding down there, as you know. If we are going to really cover that city, we're going to need a lot more people, more than we already have. Right now, I have one position still open under Cutter in *Les Arts*. Of course, since you are part-time now, you'd make considerably more money. I can give you an exact figure later. Do you want it?" Mann said.

Ava hesitated. She'd love to work for Rocky again, but it sounded like Mann was telling her that the best she could expect was her old position back. She wanted more than that. There were the kids to think of, though, as well as her relationship with Ford. But she remembered what Marilyn had said, children adapt. And she didn't think Ford would let the distance get in the way, at least she hoped not. "Yes, thank you, sir." Ava got up and reached across the desk to shake the editor's hand.

"I expect to have the bureau up and running in the next few weeks, so you'll need to start making plans," he said.

Ava passed by Judith's new cubicle on the way back to her desk, but her new boss was not at home. Ava guessed she was getting organic green tea from the kitchen or hauling more boxes from her old cubicle. She sat down at her own desk quickly, picked up the phone, and dialed Rocky's new extension.

"Good for you," he said when she told him the news. "You'll kill 'em down there in the Big Easy."

"What about you?" Ava said.

Rocky lowered his voice. "I'm not going to wait around for Mann to beg me to come back. I'm not sure I'd even take the job if he offered it to me. I'm applying for positions at other papers. I know it's a long shot with the number of gray hairs I have, but I do have some dignity left."

"I hope you find something." Ava stood up partway and

peeked over her cubicle wall. "I'd better go. The hall monitor is coming."

"Judith?" Rocky said.

"Yeah."

"Tell her to go jump in a lake for me."

"Will do."

CHAPTER 18

Ava hefted the slow cooker onto the counter and read the recipe again, making sure she had all the ingredients for the Mexican chicken soup. Since Ford had done the last dinner-for-breakfast date, it was her turn. She also planned to tell him about her new job. She had no doubt that their relationship would survive the move. After all, Ford's mother and his ex-wife lived in Metairie, so he was there every weekend anyway. It wouldn't be ideal, but it wouldn't be impossible either.

In fact, Ava was more nervous about her cooking skills than telling Ford about the job. She'd picked the easiest recipe she could find. It could cook on low for most of the night and then the Crock-Pot would switch automatically to "keep warm." The pot was a wedding gift from her ever-practical mother. She'd used it once to make a chicken dish that Jared hated enough to actually go into the kitchen and fix himself a ham sandwich.

"Whatcha doing?" James stood in the doorway of the kitchen, slouching in his big-kid pajamas—baggy T-shirt and flannel pants. It seemed like yesterday when her oldest child had worn the tight-fitting cotton dog-patterned ones. In less than three years, he'd be a teenager in jeans and whatever sneakers were the current fashion. Sadie and Luke were in bed already, but Ava decided not to send him back to his room.

"Making lunch for tomorrow. Ford is coming over," Ava said, getting the chicken from the refrigerator.

James edged up next to her and read over her shoulder. "I think we have all this stuff. Can we start putting it in?"

"You can go ahead and open the cans if you want." Ava had already heated up a pan for the chicken. She put it in and then cut the top off the onion and peeled it. She sliced it into rings and tried to chop up the circles into pieces that were roughly the same size. There had to be an easier way to do it. Maybe Ford would give her cooking lessons. She liked the idea of him wrapping his strong fingers around hers to demonstrate the proper way to hold a knife.

"Mom, your chicken is smoking," James said.

"Crap." Ava grabbed the pan from the stove. The chicken breasts were completely black on one side.

"Just cut that part off," said James.

"I'm a terrible cook."

"You just need to practice. That's what you always tell me. Practice makes perfect, right?" James opened the can of corn and emptied it into the slow cooker.

"I guess so," Ava said. Even a burned chicken breast couldn't ruin her good mood. Cooking with her son was nice, even if she wasn't very good at it. She never seemed to have enough time to spend with the kids one-on-one. James had snapped out of his usually sullen mood, at least for the moment, and was back to being a curious, optimistic boy.

"Is Ford gonna replace Daddy?"

Ava ran water in the pan and squeezed in some dish soap. "No one will replace your daddy, honey."

"It doesn't matter. He's not like a real dad. We never see him except when we go to Disneyland," James said.

"He's still your dad and he loves you." Ava cut the burned part off the chicken and washed the pan. This time, she had to watch the chicken cook, not try to do something else at the same time. If she burned it again, there wouldn't be enough left for the soup.

"Mom?"

Ava braced herself for another question about Ford or more observations about Jared. The children usually didn't mention their father's absence. They seemed to take it for granted that he wasn't going to be a part of their lives, which made her sad. She hadn't been very close to her own father either, but she saw other dads at the playground or going to school activities and wished her children had that. She woke up in the middle of the night wondering whether she could have made it work with Jared. Perhaps she could have been more involved in his career and lowered her expectations about how much he should help with the children. But, in the end, it was all just a mistake. Jared didn't want to be a father. He wanted the freedom to go to bars every night and spend the rest of his time writing the kind of big stories that earned Pulitzer prizes. She blamed herself for not realizing that when they got married.

James opened the can of Ro-Tel tomatoes and put the contents into the pot. "I think this is going to be good. Ford will like it."

Ava turned the chicken with a spatula. It had stuck to the pan a little bit. "It's important for me to have . . . friends. You get that, right? You know I still love you?"

"Sure, Mom. I think it's cool. Anyway, Ford is nice."

James had always been the most thoughtful of the three kids. The divorce had hurt him the most, not just because he was the oldest. He tried to organize and understand the world and his parents breaking up didn't fit, so he pretended his father was just gone. Ava didn't like it, but given that Jared seldom made the effort to see the children, it was probably unavoidable. A positive male role model in their lives would have been helpful, but Ava had never had time to search for one. Someone like Ford would be a great positive influence in their lives. At least, she hoped so.

Ava put the chicken in the slow cooker and buried it under the tomato and corn mixture. She placed the lid on and set the timer.

"So, that's it?" James said. "What about dessert?"

"We're already stretching my cooking abilities," Ava said.

"Don't we have a brownie mix or something?"

"I don't know. You're taking this pretty seriously."

"I wish I could skip school and hang out with him. Maybe he'd play my *Star Wars* game with me. Or do that really big puzzle I got for Christmas," James said.

Ava went over to the pantry and got out a box of brownie mix. She couldn't let James see her cry. She swallowed hard and opened the fridge to look for eggs. If she'd known James was so starved for male attention, she'd have tried to arrange something. Sure, they had soccer and swimming lessons, but the coaches and teachers didn't seem like the mentoring types.

Oblivious, James sprayed Pam on the brownie pan. "Maybe next time he can come over after school. Do you think so, Mom?"

"I'll ask him, I promise." Ava turned away and wiped her eyes with her sleeve.

Ford arrived bearing a box of homemade truffles and a bottle of wine. "Whatever you have cooking smells great," he said, following Ava into the kitchen.

"Thanks. I'm hoping for edible," she said.

Ford set the bag down on the counter and slipped an arm around her waist. He smelled like aftershave and something vaguely spicy. Warmth flowed through her whole body. She pulled him close, enjoying the feeling of his hand pressed into her hip.

"I have something I need to tell you," she said, her breathing ragged. She didn't want to interrupt the moment, but if she didn't tell him about the job, she'd be too distracted to enjoy their date.

He stepped back, looking apprehensive. "Not bad news, I hope."

"I made margaritas," she said, taking a pitcher out of the refrigerator. The expression on his face made her anxious. But that was crazy. He didn't know what she was going to say, so he had reason to be wary. She filled two glasses with ice and poured in some of the homemade mixture.

"I had to let go of you for that?" He half smiled as he accepted a glass.

Ava took a sip of her margarita. The drink made her feel light, like she could float on air. She set it down on the counter. "The *Gazette* is starting a New Orleans edition and the managing editor gave me a job there, writing for the Entertainment section."

Ford set his drink down on the kitchen table. "Wow, I mean, um, when do you start?"

"A few weeks. I need to find an apartment soon," Ava said. "We can still see each other, right?"

"Yes. I mean, I want to, but . . . I don't know."

"You go down there every weekend."

"Yeah, but I don't stay. I see Mom, drop off Nelly, and drive right back up here to work another shift at the café," Ford said.

Ava clutched the counter behind her. She hadn't touched

her drink since the first sip, but she was worried she might fall down. "What are you saying?"

"Nothing. I'm just not sure this is going to work. I went through the same thing when Marion left for New Orleans."

"That was different," Ava said. "You told me the marriage was already falling apart."

"Yeah, but we're just beginning. How easy would it be for you to get wrapped up in your life there and forget about me? You and I both have kids and jobs. It's hard enough for us to find time to do the things we need to, let alone see each other."

"People make time to do the things they really want to," Ava said.

"We don't always get to do what we want. You know that. You told me you like writing fiction, but you can't find time for that anymore."

"Are you breaking up with me?"

Ford sat down at the table and stared at his untouched drink. "I don't want to at all. I like you a lot."

"So rearrange your schedule. Talk to your brother. I'm sure he'd understand if you stopped working Friday nights. I could get a babysitter and we could go out after you dropped off Nelly. And we can talk on the phone."

"I've always worked Friday nights. They're busy. I have enough trouble getting in hours at the café as it is. Plus, if I stayed overnight in New Orleans, I'd miss part of the Saturday breakfast shift, which is really busy," Ford said.

"This is crazy. I can't believe it. I can't believe you are just giving up."

"I'm telling you, I tried this before and it didn't work. I don't see how it can."

"You didn't really try with Marion, did you?" Ava said.

"I did. She didn't. She decided it was over. That's why she didn't think twice about moving there."

"That's not what I'm doing."

"I know you believe that," Ford said.

"Fine. Call me when you figure it out. Or don't call, if that's too much trouble," Ava said.

Ford stood up. "Are you asking me to leave?"

"I'm telling you that if you think this is the end of our relationship, then you might as well go." Ava pushed away from the counter and crossed her arms over her chest.

"I feel like you're abandoning me just like Marion did. Her job was always more important than I was. Nelly and I got shoved to the side every day, even before she decided to move."

"I'm not Marion. I *want* to make time to see you. You're the one saying it's impossible."

"I'm not saying it's impossible. I just don't want us to make a mistake. Our intentions might be good, but we'll end up hurting each other," Ford said.

"Let's try and see."

"I don't know, Ava. I need to think about it."

"I don't really feel like eating right now," Ava said, picking up her drink and downing most of it in one gulp.

"I guess I'll get back to the café, then," Ford said. He walked out of the kitchen and toward the front door, moving as though he was in slow motion.

Ava tried to think of something to say that would bring him back, but she'd already said everything she could. She sat down at the kitchen table. She felt nauseated, and not just because of the tequila.

CHAPTER 19

Ford cursed as he got back into his truck. He rested his head against the steering wheel, unable to summon the will to turn the key and start the engine. He felt like screaming, "It's not fair!" the way Nelly did when things didn't go her way. He'd thought Ava was the one, and then, boom, she was leaving. This couldn't be happening. He was already devastated by his mother's diagnosis and now this. Maybe he was being unfair, but it felt exactly like a rerun of Marion. His ex-wife hadn't hesitated for a moment when she got the offer from Oshner Medical Center in New Orleans, even though she knew that Ford wouldn't abandon his brother and the café.

He turned the key and drove toward Rosie's.

"What are you doing here?" Bobby Joe said when he walked in. It was the after-breakfast, before-lunch lull, and his brother was adding up receipts at a table by the door.

Ford sat down across from him and took off his hat. "Ava is moving to New Orleans."

"Oh yeah? She get a job down there or what?" Bobby Joe continued tapping on the calculator.

"The *Gazette* is going to start a New Orleans edition."

"Good thing it's there and not Lafayette or something. I mean, what the heck, you're in Metairie every week anyway," Bobby Joe said.

"It's not that simple. I don't have time to do anything when I go there. I drop off Nelly, see Mom, and that's it."

"Ford, I'm a big boy. You know I can handle things here if you're gone a few extra hours a week. What's your problem?" Bobby Joe shoved the receipts aside.

"It's like Marion all over again. She's leaving me," Ford said, hating the whining tone of his voice.

"She is not. She didn't take that job to get away from you. Reporter jobs are tough to get, right?"

"Marion's career always came first. It was always me who had to take off work to do whatever needed to be done for Nelly, or just for us to have some time together. She never respected my job, never thought it was important. Her job was her life, and there wasn't any room for me," Ford said.

"Yeah, yeah. I know. But Ava's not like that. She took off Fridays for y'all to have your dates."

"But she's moving eighty miles away. We won't be able to do that anymore."

"So, you'll figure something else out," Bobby Joe said.

"I don't think so. She'll be working full-time now and she has three kids. There's no way she'll find time for me," Ford said.

"Give her a chance."

"No, it's better to end it before she moves. I don't want to be strung along. I can't go through that again. I just can't."

Bobby Joe pulled the pile of receipts toward him again. "Fine. Have it your way. But if you think someone like her is going to come into your life again, you got another think coming. And if you're just going to hang around here and mope, you might as well get to work."

Ford stood up and went into the kitchen, feeling like a zombie. He tied on an apron and joined Fitzgerald on the line. The cook gave him a sidelong glance, but said nothing.

CHAPTER 20

Ava parked the van in front of a brick apartment building. Air-conditioning units hung out of the windows and dripped onto the sidewalk below. The green paint on the apartment doors was peeling, and go cups and fast-food wrappers littered the parking lot. She hesitated for just a moment before pulling out her cell phone and canceling the appointment with the landlord. It wasn't worth looking inside. She didn't want to live in a place with old roach traps in the cabinets and rats patrolling the walls at night.

Rocky had given her a list of landlords in Metairie and she was working from that. So far, she wasn't doing too well. The first two places she'd looked at were a baby step above crack houses. Time was running out. She would start her job at the New Orleans office in less than two weeks.

Since the apartment search had hit a dead end of moldy showers and dog-scented carpet, she decided to visit her new office. She drove out onto the main drag of Metairie, a street lined with po'boy shops, gas stations, and hotels. The New Orleans bureau of the *Gazette* operated out of a two-story building with tinted windows and dark brown trim. She parked the van and went inside, where she was greeted by an empty receptionist desk. She walked around it and back to the office area. Instead of a maze of cubicles, there was a narrow hallway with actual offices on each side. Everyone she'd talked to had warned her that the arrangement might not be permanent. The bigwigs at the paper had their collective eyes on a much larger building in the business district that would almost certainly have cubicles. But it would be a mark of success if they could eventually afford to upgrade to a characterless office like the Saint Jude location. No one knew yet whether the New Orleans venture would really work. The fact that the *Times-Picayune* was being published only three days a week left an opening for another paper to step in, but if the great *Pic* couldn't make it in the Big Easy anymore, the *Gazette* might not be able to either.

The first office belonged to Baxter Hebert. A transplant from Saint Jude, he'd previously covered the court system. Someone had decided to move him to *Les Arts*; Ava didn't know why. She knew him by sight, but they'd only spoken a few times. He sat in front of a laptop computer set on a stand that raised it a few inches above his bare beige desk. From the back, his bald spot and slumped posture were all too evident. The hair that remained on his head was a nondescript brownish-black. The hair loss and the blocky orthopedic shoes he always wore made him look older than Ava, though she was pretty sure he was her age. He turned and took off his black-framed glasses. "Hey, Ava. I thought you weren't going to be here for a week or so."

"I'm looking for an apartment. It's not going so well."

"How about a house? You have kids, right?" he asked.

"Three. I'd love to rent a house, but I haven't seen any available so far."

"My landlord has one she's trying to rent. She showed it to me, but it was way too big for a bachelor pad. Let me find her number." Baxter pulled a card from his wallet and reached for the black phone on his desk.

Ava sat in the extra plastic chair. Baxter's office was decorated with a framed poster for the previous year's New Orleans Jazz and Heritage Festival. Four boxes lined up against the wall probably contained his things from his Saint Jude cubicle. A bobblehead doll of a New Orleans Saints football player stood on one of the boxes.

He dialed the number and picked at his fingernail while he talked. "Ms. Sarah? Are you still trying to rent that house? Good. I have someone here who might be interested. Fifteen minutes? Great. 'Bye." He hung up the phone. "You're going to like this house. It's smallish, but the neighborhood is nice."

"I'm ready to go if you are," Ava said.

"Yeah, I need a break."

As Baxter led the way back down the hall, Ava asked him how he'd ended up working in the *Les Arts* section.

"I started out covering plays and stuff for the *Lafayette Advertiser* after college. I got stuck with the court beat because I wanted to move to the *Gazette* and that was the only opening. It'll be nice to spend time in theaters again instead of courtrooms." He opened the glass door for her and they went outside.

"We can take my van since this is my errand," Ava said. As they got in, she hoped Baxter didn't notice the crushed Cheerios and faint odor of fermented apple juice rising from the carpet. There was never enough time to vacuum the inside of the car. Some of her first paycheck should go for a professional wash. On the other hand, Luke's shoes were falling apart again and she still hadn't bought the uniforms the kids would need for their new school. The van would have to remain a rolling crumb depository a little longer.

Baxter directed her off the main drag, and the landscape

immediately became suburban. Oak trees stretched their thick branches over the streets, shading the sidewalks and front lawns. The houses were mostly two-story colonials with a few smaller bungalows made of brick or wood.

"I had no idea this was back here," Ava said. "It's nice, but also close to the office."

"Yeah, my apartment building is a few streets over. It's convenient to work and everything really. I was surprised to find it. You don't think of New Orleans as having nice little neighborhoods like this," Baxter said. "Turn here."

Ava took a right and came to a dead end street. She wanted to buy instead of rent. She might have enough money with the new job, but she couldn't take the risk, at least not until the house in Saint Jude sold. Jared had agreed to let her use the proceeds from the sale for a new house, as long as his name was on the title. It would be nice to be independent from him, but that wasn't going to happen anytime soon.

"Right there," Baxter said.

The one-story brick house had no window units, which meant central air-conditioning. A good sign. The grass and bushes were trimmed, and the sidewalk leading from the street to the porch had been swept clean. They got out and Ava searched for red flags: neighbors with neglected dogs, discarded cigarette butts, toilets repurposed as flowerpots. Nothing.

Baxter knocked on the door, and a woman with curlers in her thick black hair answered. "Hello, Mr. Baxter."

"Ms. Sarah, this is Ava. She works with me at the *Gazette* and has three children."

"Children are fine. No dogs or cats. Can't take the risk what with people being how they are." Ms. Sarah turned and padded into the house. She was wearing a housecoat and slippers. "Excuse my outfit. I stay down the street here, and I just came on over how I am."

The house reeked of floral air freshener, and beige carpet lined the living room floor. "You got three bedrooms down that hallway," Ms. Sarah said. "One bathroom."

Ava walked through the living room and into the kitchen. The yellow stove had a dial to set the temperature and a clock that didn't work. The harvest-gold refrigerator almost matched and looked like it was from the same era. The white linoleum kitchen floor would be impossible to keep clean. But as she went into the bedrooms, pulling open closets and peeking into the tiny, white-tiled bathroom, she could imagine the children's toys on the carpet and their home-work cluttering the kitchen counter. She liked the clean and cozy feel of the little house. She also loved that Jared would have nothing to do with the place. There was no bedroom that used to be cluttered with his computer and piles of pa-pers, no scrape on the side of the kitchen cabinet from the time he'd gotten so mad that he'd thrown a pan across the room. The new house wouldn't have any traces of Ford ei-ther, but she didn't want to think about him. Five days had passed since their aborted date and she was trying to forget. She didn't understand why he just wanted to give up. Maybe he'd been looking for a way out and her moving had pro-vided the excuse. It was humiliating to think she'd been so wrong yet again. She'd thought he really cared about her.

She took a deep breath. It was time to make a new start.

CHAPTER 21

Ford was supposed to be at his daughter's dance recital, but he was on his way back to Saint Jude instead. He'd explained to Nelly that he had to work, and she seemed to understand. Marion was not so easygoing. When he dropped Nelly off for the weekend, she'd given him a lecture about their daughter's development and how important it was for both parents to be invested in her education. Ford didn't bother to remind her that, for one thing, Nelly was three years old and, for another, Marion was the reason they weren't living in the same city anymore.

The visit with his mother hadn't improved his mood any. For the first time, she actually looked her age. He swore her face hadn't had so many wrinkles a month ago and her skin hadn't sagged like it was a size too big. He didn't tell her about Ava moving to New Orleans. She'd probably say the same thing Bobby Joe had—that he was being stupid. Maybe he was. But he didn't want half a relationship with Ava. He wanted all or nothing. He and Marion had run that argument too many times; he would say that she worked too much and didn't care about spending time with him and

Nelly and she shot back that he was a sexist who just wanted her to wash dishes and make beds. That was completely unfair. He had no interest in women like that. Marion's intellectual life was a big part of what had attracted him to her. But what was the point if they never saw each other?

Ford felt guiltily relieved as he drove down the highway toward Saint Jude. He was worn out from dealing with his ex-wife and his mother. All he wanted was to work until he was so tired he could barely stand up. After that, he'd watch some TV and feel sorry for himself.

The pickup seemed to glide through the night. As long as there wasn't too much traffic, he found driving on the highway comforting. He turned on the radio. The classic rock station out of New Orleans was fading, but the Saint Jude one still sounded fuzzy. He drummed his fingers on the steering wheel in time to a staticky Rolling Stones song.

An hour later, he parked the truck behind the café and got out. His brother was in the kitchen, stirring a pot of tomato sauce for the spaghetti and meatballs. Ford had developed the recipe during the first year they'd been in business until he thought it was perfect. Finally, he'd written down the recipe, and now both he and Bobby Joe could make it without a cheat sheet.

Ford tied an apron around his waist. "What do you want me to do?"

Bobby Joe shrugged. "Not much business tonight. I got your noodles ready over there. If you get really bored, you could make me some more biscuit mix for tomorrow."

"Did you send Fitzgerald home yet?"

"I wanted to make sure you showed up first." Bobby Joe stared into the pot of sauce. "I was kind of hoping you wouldn't come back tonight."

"Why wouldn't I?"

"If you made up with Ava."

Ford turned on the wash sink faucet and tossed in some prep pans. "That's not going to happen."

"You're even dumber than you look," Bobby Joe said.

"I don't want to talk about it."

"Okay, fine." Bobby Joe took off his apron and threw it in the laundry basket. "I'm going home."

Once his brother was out the door, Ford stopped washing dishes. He took out his phone and called Ava. As it rang, he thought about what he was doing—making a big mistake, probably. But he couldn't leave her to handle the whole move on her own. His mother had given him the phone number for her real estate agent—a nice lady who had been very helpful in finding her a modest house in a decent neighborhood, not an easy task. Hell, if Ava let him, Ford would load the truck for her. He wasn't trying to have a relationship, or even a friendship. He just cared about her and wanted to help.

"Why are you calling, Ford?" Ava said.

Since he was calling her cell, she would know it was him, but Ford was still taken aback by her abrupt comment. She didn't even bother to say hello. He tucked the phone between his ear and shoulder and began to scrub a frying pan. "My mom has a really nice real estate agent in New Orleans, and I thought she could help you find a place to live there."

"I already have a house to rent. I have to move in next Friday," she said.

"Oh."

"It's been a week since I told you I was taking the job and you haven't called me. What's going on? I mean, I assumed that you dumped me."

"I didn't dump you. I said it might not work to do the long-distance thing," Ford said.

"And then you walk out my door and don't call for a week. What am I supposed to think?" Ava said.

"I don't know. I'm really confused right now. I have a lot going on. I'm really worried about my mom."

"I'm sorry. How is she?"

"Her surgery is scheduled soon. In the meantime, we just wait," Ford said.

"That must be really hard," Ava said.

"Yeah. It's frustrating and depressing. I don't know what to do with myself half the time. I didn't call you last week because I had no idea what to say."

"Look, I'm willing to leave the door open if you think you might be able to start dating again after she feels better. But I can't put my life on hold for you," she said, sounding oddly businesslike.

From her tone, Ford felt like she was already pulling away. Besides, he'd already decided: no half measures. He couldn't stand to watch their relationship die a slow death. He'd been there before, and he couldn't handle that pain again. He dropped the pan in the sink. He was too upset to do dishes. That was a first. "I don't think so. If we're together, I want us to actually be together."

"Clearly, you never cared about me as much as I cared about you. Because I wouldn't have given up if you'd had to move. I guess I was naïve," she said.

"I do care about you. I'm doing what's best for both of us. We deserve to have real relationships. Someone who is there for us, not eighty miles away."

"I'm not going to have this argument again, Ford. I'm done." Ava hung up.

Ford took off his Rosie's cap and threw it across the room. He'd driven Ava out of his life. He could almost hear his brother saying, *"Now, are you happy?"*

No, he wasn't. He was miserable.

CHAPTER 22

Ava cut the engine and got out of the van. Nelly wasn't on the playground, so Ford must have picked her up from day care early. She didn't want his absence to affect her, but she couldn't ignore her disappointment. She wasn't likely to see him again, since they were moving to Metairie right after she picked up Sadie. The thought made her feel lonely and angry at the same time. She'd dared to hope that she wasn't too old, too busy, too tied down for another relationship. Instead, she was destined to raise her children and then spend the rest of her life alone, just like Elspeth, the old TV guide lady.

It was time to end the pity party, as her mother would have said. She had plenty to worry about besides Ford. On Monday, the kids would start their new schools and she would go to work at the New Orleans bureau. In the meantime, they had a lot of unpacking to do. The movers had spent the morning filling their truck with all the things she and the kids had accumulated in the ten years they'd lived in the house. Going through everything, she'd found some of Jared's belongings—an old tie stuffed on the shelf above the closet, a can of shaving cream in the back of the cabinet, a pack of his brand of gum behind the refrigerator. The stuff made her briefly miss him and what they used to have. She threw it all away. There was no going back. He was gone and so was Ford.

She'd stowed the farm scene painting in the van. Though she hadn't yet researched how much it might be worth, she still didn't trust the movers to deliver it safely. The end of her relationship with Ford had cemented her decision to sell the painting. She needed the money and she didn't need the memories. Even though she would earn more at her new job, there were always things she put off doing because of her perpetually stretched finances: getting her hair cut, fixing the broken speaker in the van, taking vacations with the kids. She'd like to use what she got from selling the painting for a beach trip in the spring, maybe to Florida or Alabama. It would be nice for her and the children to relax together for a few days.

She got out of the van and went to retrieve Sadie. Her daughter greeted her with an enthusiastic hug. "We go to the new house today?" she said.

"Yes. Say good-bye to your friends. You start a new school on Monday."

Sadie turned and waved to the remaining kids on the playground. "'Bye!"

Ava wished leaving was that easy for her.

On the way to New Orleans, the kids expressed their agitation over the move by picking at each other. By the time they reached the aboveground cemetery that marked the outskirts of Kenner, the fighting made Ava want to cover her ears or turn on loud music.

"Mom, Sadie's bugging me!" Luke said.

"Sadie, stop bothering your brother." Ava glanced in the rearview mirror. James was staring moodily out the back window. The younger children would adapt easily, but she worried about him. She hadn't told him about the breakup with Ford yet. He'd probably ask soon, and she dreaded delivering another piece of bad news.

"Quit it, Sadie!" Luke yelled.

"What is she doing?" Ava asked.

"She's poking me with her marker."

"Stop, Sadie, or I'm taking away your markers." Ava silently debated with herself. They were less than fifteen minutes from the house. They could stop for dinner or try to make it. She'd rather get to the house, but she knew that fifteen minutes of listening to the kids fight could lead to steering wheel–pounding irritation.

"Sadie! Stop poking me," Luke said.

"God, you two. Just quit it already," James said.

Ava took the exit that led to the airport in Kenner. "Who wants McDonald's?"

"Me, me!" Luke and Sadie cried together. At least they agreed on something.

Ava parked in front of the restaurant and the kids got out and ran to the entrance. Even James shook off his bad mood long enough to join the race.

The kids wanted almost everything on the menu. Ava didn't argue with their choices. The move was hard and they deserved a little treat. She placed the huge order and waited at the counter while James helped the others get straws, napkins, and ketchup.

When the food came, Ava picked at her salad while the kids spread fries, chicken nuggets, cheeseburgers, and toys out on the table.

The strip of businesses where the McDonald's was located could have been anywhere in the country except for a few decorative palm trees and the slight hint of salt water in the air. When they'd first moved to Louisiana, Ava and

Jared had often taken weekend trips to New Orleans. That ended after the kids were born. Aside from her rental house hunting, most of Ava's knowledge of the city consisted of vague memories of the French Quarter. She couldn't decide whether the nondescript street outside the window of the McDonald's was reassuring or disappointing.

James drank the last of his chocolate shake. "I want to go home."

"You know we can't do that," Ava said.

"I want to go home," Luke echoed.

Sadie, as usual, managed to double her brothers' volume. "Wanna go home!"

"We're going to our new home." Ava began gathering the trash from the table.

"Okay, let's go," Sadie said. She jumped down off her chair and headed for the door.

CHAPTER 23

Ford's mother was pulling a casserole out of the oven when he arrived at her house Sunday night. In the nine days since he'd last talked to Ava, Ford had been lost. He'd gone through the motions of working and taking care of Nelly, but his head felt fuzzy, like it was missing some vital piece and wasn't functioning correctly. Seeing his mom woke him up a little. He had to pull it together for her.

"You didn't have to cook dinner. You're having surgery tomorrow. You should take it easy," Ford said, pouring himself a glass of iced tea.

"I'm not dead yet," she said. "What do you want I should do? Sit and watch TV all day?"

"What is it? Smells like Mexican."

"It's a tortilla bake. Bernice gave me the recipe."

Ford had figured as much. His aunt's taste ran toward Velveeta and canned soup. He sat down at the table and sipped his tea. His mother got out two white china plates and spooned Mexi-corn onto each. Ford had never had the heart to tell her that he could barely stand the mix of canned sweet corn and flaccid peppers.

"Your brother liked this last time Bernice made it. He

was down here for the Fourth of July, and I believe you were doing something with Marion's parents," she said.

That wasn't surprising. Bobby Joe would eat almost anything as long as it wasn't burned. Every year, at their annual Thanksgiving feast, he declared their mother's store-bought, precooked turkey to be the best he'd ever had, even though it was so dry that Ford required a full glass of water to get through his plate. What surprised him was that his mother remembered so vividly what they had done on Independence Day two years ago. He sure didn't.

"Bobby Joe wanted to come, but I knew he wouldn't be able to handle seeing you going into surgery," he said.

"I know. He called me and said he'd come down on Saturday instead. That boy acts tough, but he's as soft as they come," she said, adding the casserole to the plates and bringing them to the table.

Ford grimaced. If Bobby Joe had heard that remark, he would have been as angry as he was when he'd caught their former cook stealing cheese from the walk-in cooler. Ford did wish Bobby Joe had been able to accompany their mother to the surgery instead of him. He was happy to be with her, but he didn't like leaving Nelly at Marion's house until Wednesday. From their strained phone conversations, he could tell that Marion was getting frustrated with Nelly, now that they had been together for a few extra days. He hoped his ex might learn something about her daughter from the experience, but it was also possible that they'd just make each other miserable. Plus, he missed Nelly.

"I'll be here tomorrow at ten to take you for the surgery. I already booked my room for tonight at the Starlight. Are you sure it's okay for Bernice to pick you up from the hospital on Wednesday? I can take another day off work," he said.

"Yes. She has a nice air mattress she's going to set up in the living room," she said.

"Wait, she's going to stay here?" Ford put down his fork.

"The doctor says someone has to. Since I'm such an old lady, I guess."

"Geez, Mom. She's older than you."

"Bernice is built like a horse. She'll outlive us all," she said.

Acid rose in Ford's stomach. He didn't know whether he could choke down the casserole, let alone the Mexi-corn. He pictured the two sisters holding each other up like frail trees. He covered his face with his hands.

His mother ate a tiny bite of casserole. "Don't be so dramatic. I'm only seventy. My mother lived to be ninety, you might recall."

Grandma Heloise had power walked every day into her eighties. Ford had always thought her daughter would be just as hearty. He hadn't counted on her getting the big C. He drank some more iced tea and stuck his fork into the canned Ro-Tel tomato, processed cheese, and soggy tortilla mess.

"What I want to know is what happened with Ava. I thought you were serious about that girl, but you haven't brought her around," she said.

"She moved here. To Metairie. She works at the *Gazette*," Ford said.

"Oh yes, they have a New Orleans edition now. So?"

Ford tried the casserole. It tasted exactly like he'd expected—salty tomato and rubbery fake cheese. "I broke it off. It was impossible with the long-distance thing."

"Well, that was stupid," she said.

"Come again?" Ford stopped trying to stab a tomato chunk. His mother never talked like that. He didn't think he'd ever heard her say the "s" word.

"You heard me. Why would you give up on someone you love just because she moved eighty miles away?" She looked down at her plate as though she wasn't sure she could eat any more.

"Because trying to find time to see her would put too much strain on the kids." Even as he said it, Ford realized that it was a stupid excuse.

"Please. Kids can deal with a lot more than that. People act like children are so fragile. I never had that attitude with you boys."

"No, you didn't." Ford remembered his mother explaining that his dad would probably never come back. He'd been ten years old at the time. She'd never minced words with them. Sometimes he'd wished she would.

His mother deliberately ate another bite of casserole. Ford was relieved to see that she had an appetite, or at least that she was trying. His own stomach was calming down. Even though thinking about Ava was painful, it was easier than dwelling on his mother's mortality.

"Look, honey. You have to follow your heart. That's all I'm saying," she said.

"We've only known each other for a couple of months," Ford said.

"That doesn't matter. You know if it's right."

She wasn't the best person to be giving romantic advice. Her own marriage had been a disaster. If they'd had something once, it hadn't lasted. As far as Ford knew, she'd never dated again.

"I know what you're thinking. I'm no example. You're right. But I keep my eyes open and I've seen what I missed. Bernice and Gary were made for each other. I remember the day he came over and washed Dad's car, trying to get on his good side. Scratched the paint, though I can't imagine how. Dad saw him and Bernice together, and he didn't even care about the car. He knew Gary was the one for her." She blinked hard and drank some iced tea. "Mom and Dad, for that matter. She just fell apart when he died. She couldn't live without him."

"How do you know Ava and I are like that? You haven't even met her," Ford said.

"Bernice couldn't stop talking about Gary. That's how I knew with her. You don't talk much, but when you do, I can see it in your eyes. That same look you used to get at five years old when you talked about trucks. With Marion, especially toward the end, you just looked unhappy."

"I don't care much about trucks anymore." Ford pushed the Mexi-corn to the side of his plate.

"You have one," Doris said.

Ford sighed. There was no use arguing with his mother.

The surgery took up most of the next day. Ford hadn't expected all the meetings with doctors and nurses, blood work, and just plain sitting around that had to be done before the surgery could even begin. He was grateful for his aunt Bernice, who asked questions and even wrote the important things down in a little notebook. While his mother was under the knife, Ford and his aunt sipped too-strong coffee in the cafeteria and ate dry sandwiches. Then there were more meetings to talk about how smoothly the surgery had gone, who would care for his mother when she came home, and when she should have a follow-up visit.

It was almost five o'clock by the time Ford patted his sleeping mother's hand and gently told Aunt Bernice they had to leave.

"I hate for her to wake up in this place alone," his aunt said. "She'll be confused and wonder where she is."

"You have to rest," Ford said. "We both do. We'll come back tomorrow, as soon as visiting hours start."

Ford had always known that his mother and her sister were close, but the way Aunt Bernice looked at her lying in the hospital bed made him realize that they were really best friends. Part of the reason, he supposed, was that they only had each other now. His father was gone and Gary was dead. Ford and Bobby Joe were too busy to visit. Just two old ladies left.

Ford took Aunt Bernice to her favorite café and then helped her move what she needed to his mother's house. When he finished carrying in her suitcase of clothes and the air mattress, Aunt Bernice dismissed him. "Go visit your daughter, since you're here," she said.

"Are you sure you're okay, Aunt Bernice?" Ford said.

She bent down and pushed the button that inflated the air mattress. "Yes," she said, over the growling of the motor. "I'm fine. See you tomorrow."

Ford sat in his truck, feeling useless. His aunt clearly didn't want his help, and even though he would like to see Nelly, popping in on Marion was never a good idea. He knew he shouldn't do it, but he found himself looking up the location of the *Gazette* office and driving by. Since it was six o'clock, naturally Ava's van wasn't in the lot. He knew it was her first day of work and he wondered how it had gone. He shook his head as the office receded in his rearview mirror. He had to stop thinking about Ava, but he had no idea how to do it.

CHAPTER 24

On her second day of work at the *New Orleans Gazette*, Ava spent the first three and a half hours typing in events, just like she'd done in Saint Jude. When *Les Arts* editor John Cutter told her that she'd have to compile the weekly events listing, she'd ground her teeth together in frustration. It was just another sign that the powers that be at the newspaper still didn't take her seriously. Her fellow Saint Jude transplant, Baxter, was clearly a rung higher on the ladder. He didn't do any grunt work, as far as she could tell.

The industrial beige carpet and lack of windows in her new office made Ava feel like she was working inside a cardboard box. She'd personalized her space with pictures of the kids and a desk lamp, but there was no changing the off-white walls and steel-gray furniture. She was glad to have an office rather than a cubicle, but she missed the window. More than that, she missed Rocky. He'd written her an e-mail making fun of his sports-obsessed colleagues in Marketing. The workload was light, he said. The supplements came out months apart and there was more than enough time to put them together. He'd started working on his novel during the slow times. "I think of it as the paper unwittingly supporting the arts," he said. Rocky didn't do smiley emoticons, so Ava added it in her head. She wished they still worked in the same building. She really needed a friend. Cutter was fine as an editor, but he wasn't interested in chatting about her children or the latest popular novels.

She checked her in-box. Only thirty minutes had passed, and there were already two new e-mails. The first *New Orleans Gazette* had been printed the day before, and already arts organizations and businesses in the area were contacting her wanting stories, calendar listings, and free publicity. New Orleans was twice the size of Saint Jude and home to hundreds of arts organizations, from back room art galleries to the New Orleans Opera. It was overwhelming.

Virginia approached Ava's open door and knocked on the frame. "Do you want to come with us to lunch?" The young woman had curly blond hair that contrasted sharply with her dark brown skin. Her skirts didn't reach her knees and ranged in color from grape to neon green. The current one was candy-apple red, and she'd paired it with a flowing, white blouse. Despite her eclectic, artistic appearance, though, Virginia was a professional and a very good photographer.

"I brought lunch, thanks. Are you coming to the dress rehearsal for *Grease* this afternoon? I think Cutter wants pictures," Ava said.

"Yeah. Three o'clock. I have to submit the photos from this murder first. I never saw so much crime tape before I moved down here." Virginia leaned against the door frame, balancing on one red ankle boot.

"That's New Orleans for you."

"Come to lunch with us. We're going to celebrate our second day of covering the big city," Virginia said.

Ava glanced at her in-box again. Another e-mail arrived from something called the New Orleans Artist WorkPlay.

"Yeah, okay." She got her purse and followed Virginia's bouncing curls.

Cutter and Baxter read copies of the Tuesday *New Orleans Gazette* as they waited in the three-chair lobby. The receptionist desk was still empty. There had been some debate about a security guard versus a receptionist. Probably they needed both. At the moment, the reporters took turns answering the phone and Cutter had a gun stashed under his desk, just in case.

Cutter saw them and nodded in his usual understated greeting. He had a full head of gray hair and wire-rimmed glasses. He folded his paper in a precise, practiced gesture. Baxter crumpled his and stuffed it into a worn shoulder bag.

"Where are we going?" Ava asked.

"Lou's Café, of course. We can walk," Cutter said.

Outside, they cut across the parking lot of a strip mall containing a dry cleaners, a drive-through daiquiri shop, and a nail salon. Lou's Café was surrounded by cars. Three-dimensional racing stripes ran along the side of the baby-blue building. Faux chrome trim around the windows completed the cheesy doo-wop look. Cutter held open the glass doors and ushered his younger colleagues inside.

As she stepped over the threshold, Ava had a moment of déjà vu so strong that she stumbled a little in her high heels. It was like being back in Rosie's Café: the arrangement of counter stools, the placement of the grill in the dead center of the restaurant, and the Formica tables with vinyl-covered chairs. All it needed was Ford and Bobby Joe behind the counter and the bearded student sitting on one of the stools.

Baxter held out a hand to steady her. "Hey, are you okay?"

Ava nodded. He continued to hold her arm with his clammy fingers for a moment, an expression of concern on his face.

Ava planted her feet on the black-and-white tiled floor. The café seemed less like Rosie's the longer she looked. A neon Coca-Cola clock hung on one of the plain white walls. The vinyl covers of the lunch counter stools were red, not blue, and the solidly built African American man working the grill bore no resemblance to Ford. Once Ava began to count the differences, the dizziness subsided. She reminded herself that her relationship with Ford was over. She was never going to eat a shrimp po'boy at Rosie's again.

"You're not pregnant, are you?" Virginia said. "Because my sister is and she keeps almost fainting."

"No! Just hungry. I forgot to eat breakfast again," Ava said.

"The most important meal of the day," Cutter said. "Let's take my favorite spot." He headed to a table near the window.

Ava sat down next to Virginia and took a laminated menu from the holder. Thankfully, it looked nothing like Bobby Joe's. Even the offerings were different: meat loaf, fried catfish, smothered pork chops, chicken and dumplings. Ava wanted to order something that Rosie's Café didn't offer, but she couldn't shake the idea that what she really wanted was a shrimp po'boy.

"I recommend the po'boys. Also, the meat pies. And the fried catfish. Come to think of it, the meat loaf isn't bad either," Cutter said.

"That's helpful," Baxter said, lowering his menu to give Ava a lopsided smile.

"I aim to please."

Virginia folded her menu and returned it to the holder. "I'm getting a salad."

"A noble choice, but not a wise one. So, what do y'all think of our fair city?" Cutter said.

"I hear the singles scene is better here," Baxter said. "But it seems like it's mostly bars and clubs. I'm too old for that stuff."

"There's way more than that. I mean, there are so many people here. If you have a hobby or something, there's probably a group that does it. I already joined a knitting club," Virginia said.

"Seriously?" Baxter said. "You don't seem like the type really. No offense."

"Plenty of lesbians knit. We like scarves and cute little hats. Well, the butch ones are more into watchman's caps."

"That I did not know," Cutter said. "You learn something new every day."

A young, bald African American man came and took their orders, writing their selections down without raising his eyes from his order pad.

After he left, Baxter tapped his fingers on the table. His nails were bitten down to the quick. "I always wanted to learn to ballroom dance."

"Now, there's a way to meet women. Those chicks can never find any men to dance with," Virginia said.

"There's a group that meets on Thursdays," Ava said. "I put their listing in the calendar this morning."

"Do you want to come with me?" Baxter asked.

"I have two left feet. And three kids and no babysitter."

"Right." Baxter glanced at his hands and hid them under the table.

Virginia gave Ava a half smile. She shook her head in response. She was not going to encourage Baxter. After Ford, she was in no hurry to date.

The waiter brought their food. Ava regretted ordering the shrimp po'boy. Naturally, the shrimp were deep-fried and the sandwich was dressed with the usual mayo, lettuce, and tomato instead of Ford's homemade pickle. All she could think about was how much better his sandwich had tasted. She had to get over him. Fast. Maybe she should try dating Baxter. The reporter was cutting his catfish po'boy into perfect bite-sized pieces. His dark hair was clearly dyed and the way he picked at his fingernails drove her crazy. She had to fight the urge to scold him like one of her children. She imagined Ford's big, rough hands and perpetually messy blond hair. She couldn't help wishing he were sitting across from her instead of Baxter.

Cutter took a bite of his meat loaf and made an *mmm* sound. "This is nothing like the slop my mother used to cook and call food."

"So, what's your advice for fitting into the New Orleans scene?" Baxter asked, forking a mushed-up bit of po'boy into his mouth.

"You won't," Cutter said. "What you have to understand about this place is that if you come from somewhere else, you will never be a New Orleanian. I've lived here for thirty years and people still think of me as a Yank."

"I thought you were from Kentucky," Ava said.

"Kentucky is the Frozen Nawth. People from here don't even consider Texas truly the South. Don't get me wrong. There are advantages to being the outsider. The locals expect me to be uncouth and ask a lot of questions that I shouldn't, so they aren't too scandalized by me. I used to be a society writer before the death of the *Picayune*. I had to deal with all the old money New Orleans types. They didn't like me, but they got used to me after a while."

"You scandalized them? This city is a symbol of debauchery," Baxter said.

"You'd be surprised. Even in the land of Bourbon Street and Mardi Gras, there are rules. Never, ever make fun of debutantes or Mardi Gras krewes, or football, or fraternities, or Catholicism. Don't admit to not liking beignets, crawfish, or gumbo. And I don't even know where to start with the unwritten rules about race," Cutter said.

"You don't have to tell me," Virginia said. "I'm still looking for the bathrooms marked 'colored.'"

"How can you even joke about that?" Baxter asked.

"I can, but you can't, white boy."

The waiter returned to refill their iced tea and water and left without saying a word.

"Anyway, y'all will do fine, I'm sure," Cutter said.

Virginia picked a cherry tomato from her salad and studied it. "I'm not worried. I happen to like gumbo and football."

Ava wasn't sure. She suddenly felt very alone, despite the friendly company. She ate the rest of her sandwich even though every bite made her think of Ford.

When the bill came, Cutter insisted on paying. "This is my gift to y'all. For your birthdays, Christmas, and anniversaries too. Don't say I never gave you anything."

Cutter and Virginia left together, talking about race relations in the South. Ava stayed in her seat for a moment. Maybe it was the memories brought on by her surroundings, but her anger at Ford was fading. He was going through a lot with his mom being sick, and he might not be over his divorce yet. She certainly knew how hard it was to see your marriage collapse. She got up and touched the back of the vinyl-cushioned chair. Except for the color, it was exactly like the ones at Rosie's. She pushed it under the table and followed her coworkers.

Baxter held the door for her. "Are you sure you're okay?"

"I'm fine. It's just a lot. The moving with the kids and everything. New job. New city. I guess I'm tired," she said.

"If I can help with anything, let me know." Baxter took

a card from his pocket. "Here, I wrote my cell number on this for you."

"Thanks." Ava took the card just to be polite and shoved it into the bottom of her purse.

When Ava got home that night, the kids all had crises at the same time. James didn't understand his homework, nothing pleased Sadie for some obscure reason, and Luke went to his and James's room and refused to come out.

Ava gave Sadie a glass of milk, explained the concept of division to James, and went to see Luke.

The room was all boy: Lego creations, toy trucks and cars, Spider-Man sheets. He was curled up on his bed, staring at the wall. James was usually the moody one, but Luke had his moments. "What's wrong?" she asked. The question was useless for the under-six set, but she couldn't think of anything else to say.

"I'm sad," Luke said.

"Why are you sad?"

"I don't like my new school."

Ava sat down on the bed. "Why not?"

"I don't know."

"Do you like the teacher?"

"Yeah."

"Are the other kids mean to you?"

"No."

Ava sighed. "Do you miss your old school?"

"I want to go to school with Joey again."

"We had to move because I got a new job. Joey had to stay in Saint Jude because his parents have jobs there. Do you have a new friend? What about Alexander?" Ava said.

"Alexander is best friends with Jamal," Luke said.

"You can be their friend too."

"No, Alexander is Jamal's friend."

Since she wasn't making any headway, Ava decided to change the subject. "Why don't you come and help me make dinner? We're having spaghetti and ice cream."

Luke sat up. "Okay."

Ava put her hand on the boy's bony shoulder as she led him out to the living room. James was drawing an elaborate picture of Superman in his school notebook, and Sadie had emptied the contents of the pantry onto the kitchen floor. Just another day in paradise.

CHAPTER 25

Once the Friday lunch rush was over, Ford tried to settle into his routine of cleaning and prepping for dinner. But with Bobby Joe doing dishes in the back and no constant flow of orders to distract him, his mind was going to places where he didn't want it to. He was getting tired of his mental stomping ground in the past couple of weeks—mostly worrying about his mother and thinking about Ava. His mother was taking a long time to recover from the surgery, just like the doctors said she would. He'd never seen her so listless and weak. She couldn't start the chemotherapy until she was stronger. She needed to eat, but she had a hard time choking anything down.

The bell over the door rang and Pete walked in. He set his copy of *Kant's Analytic* on the counter and sat down. "How's your mom?" he asked.

"I guess she's doing okay for a seventy-year-old who has cancer." Ford wiped a scattering of lettuce from the sandwich board. He didn't feel like talking to anyone, but he also didn't want to wallow in his thoughts.

"My buddy in Metairie is selling Round the Clock. That's his café. He wants to go to grad school. We're both applying for Tulane," Pete said.

"Why would you transfer?" Ford asked. He got some ground beef and began mixing it with Cajun spice.

"Louisiana A&M doesn't offer a PhD, just a master's. If I want to be a professor, I've got to get a PhD."

"Do you think you'll get in?" Ford formed the meat into a patty and put it on the grill. He seasoned some bell pepper and onion slices and set them next to the burger.

"I hope so. I applied to some other places, but I don't really want to move across the country again. I moved here from Alabama to go to A&M," Pete said.

Ford thought about pointing out that Alabama was hardly across the country, but he didn't want to antagonize the kid. He was young, and to him, home probably seemed like a really long way away.

"Whatcha making?" Pete asked.

Ford turned the burger and toasted a bun on the grill. "A Cajun blackened burger."

"Dude, you can't blacken a burger."

"Don't knock it till you try it."

"You're the cook, man."

Ford got his special burger sauce from the fridge and painted both sides of the bun. He put the meat on and topped it with the vegetables, then placed the plate in front of Pete.

"Dude, there's green stuff on here," Pete said.

"Just try it. If you don't like it, I'll make you a regular hamburger or whatever you want."

"Okay." Pete took a large bite and rolled his eyes. "You're kidding, man. I mean, this is awesome."

Bobby Joe banged through the kitchen door carrying a load of clean plates and began stacking them on the shelf behind the grill. "What the heck is that stuff?"

"My special burger sauce," Ford said.

"We're not changing the menu. You know that, right?"

"I know. We talked about this before. A lot."

"If we talked about it before, why are there still weird sauces in the fridge and ingredients for stuff that's not on the menu?" Bobby Joe slammed his empty bus tray on the counter.

"Come on. What's wrong with a little experimentation?" Ford said.

"What's wrong with it is that I think you're planning to open a café without me and I don't like it," Bobby Joe said.

"Why would I do that?"

"I don't know. So you can use your fancy new recipes, I guess."

"If I was even thinking about opening a restaurant, I'd tell you, I promise."

His brother held him with his gaze, a penetrating look that Ford knew well. "I'm sorry I yelled. I guess I'm just on edge because of Mom," Bobby Joe said.

"Me too." Ford felt like he should hug his brother, but he knew Bobby Joe wouldn't like it, especially in the restaurant. "I'm going to help you clean up some more, but don't forget, I have to go to Nelly's program in an hour."

"Yeah, yeah. And you don't forget that you're on your own tomorrow because I'm going to see Mom," Bobby Joe said as he headed back to the kitchen.

"You sure you're not planning to open your own joint? 'Cause I would totally come eat there if I had any money," Pete said.

"No." Ford pushed the clean plates to the back of the shelf.

"Okay, man." Pete opened his book and started reading.

Ford knew that Ava and Sadie wouldn't be at the Fall Fest program at Nelly's school. Still, he couldn't stop himself from searching for Ava among the parents and grandparents filling the pews. He thought back to the Summer's End program, a couple of months ago now. Being next to her had made him feel like he was about to jump off the high dive. The hurt was so great that sometimes he wished he had never met her. He hadn't necessarily been happy before they dated, but he hadn't been this miserable either.

Nelly missed Sadie almost as much as he missed Ava, it seemed. She'd asked about her friend almost every day in the weeks since they'd moved, and Ford had to explain over and over about Ava taking the job in New Orleans.

"Is this seat taken?" A woman wearing grass-green scrubs pointed to the place next to Ford.

He shook his head and scooted in so that she could sit next to him. He glanced over and it seemed like their eyes almost met. Ford had the irrational feeling that she was single or divorced and that if he asked her out for coffee, she would say yes. He had absolutely no desire to do so. Glancing at her again, he tried to figure out why. There was nothing wrong with the woman. She was about his age and pretty, with soft blue eyes and a nice smile. But he felt nothing. He didn't know if it was because he was still in a funk about his mother. No, the problem was that she wasn't Ava. And he only wanted Ava. He wasn't interested in anyone else.

Nelly and her class filed out from their pew onto the altar. They all wore costumes. Nelly had wanted to be a princess, of course. In fact, most of the girls were dressed as princesses, in puffy blue, yellow, or pink gowns. The boys were mostly superheroes with big fake muscles. Ford wished Nelly had chosen a superhero costume or the cowgirl outfit she'd worn to the parade. He wanted her to be strong and independent, like Ava. He wanted her to think for herself and become something, not just someone's wife. He really was being stupid about Ava, he realized. He was expecting her to change her life for him. But why did it have to be that way? Why couldn't he change his life for her? Maybe he could. He glanced over at the woman next to him again. He noticed that she had on a wedding ring and she wasn't interested in him at all; she was completely focused on the kids singing their pumpkin song.

He hadn't really been paying attention when Pete had mentioned that his friend's café was up for sale, but now that piece of information floated to the top of his brain. And his brother had a point—why *was* he always experimenting with food?

Maybe he was ready to try something different.

CHAPTER 26

Ava entered the last event into the calendar and hit "save." She had been at the *New Orleans Gazette* for two weeks and she was spending on average half of her time preparing the weekly calendars. She couldn't stand it anymore. Mann had believed in her enough to give her a full-time job, but Cutter was still treating her like a data entry clerk who was allowed to write a few short stories about upcoming events.

Cutter's office was empty, so she went to the break room. To Ava, the place was too drab, the fluorescent lights too bright. It reminded her of a doctor's examining room, except that the air smelled like stale coffee rather than medicine. She usually only went in long enough to get her lunch out of the refrigerator. Cutter, however, didn't seem to mind the lack of windows and dingy white counters and walls. He sat at an egg-colored table, drinking coffee and reading the *New York Times*.

"Can I talk to you for a minute?" Ava asked.

"Sure, have a seat," Cutter said and lowered his paper.

Ava sat down in the hard plastic chair. "I know I asked you this before, but I really think we should hire a part-timer to do the calendar. We could even get an intern from Tulane or one of the other schools down here. I don't have time to write a lot of stories I could do, and we're ending up putting too many Associated Press pieces in the section," Ava said.

"But you know how to do the calendars. You did them in Saint Jude," Cutter said.

"Come on, any reasonably intelligent person could be taught to type in the events. I'm no expert."

"It's just not in the budget, Ava. We can't hire anyone else."

"I'll talk to the journalism departments at the local colleges. I'm sure we can get someone cheap," Ava said.

Cutter closed his paper and smoothed it on the table. "You do a good job. Why change anything?"

"Because we could do better coverage if I wasn't wasting my time on the calendars."

"It's not a waste of time, Ava. The calendars are important. People read them to find out what's going on. It's a big part of our section," Cutter said.

"I didn't mean that the calendars aren't important. I meant that I'm a reporter, not a data entry clerk." Ava knew she was crossing a line, but she didn't care. She couldn't stay at the bottom of the ladder anymore. The New Orleans job was supposed to be her chance to finally lose her designation as resident typist, but it wasn't working out that way.

"That's not fair, Ava. We all have to do our share of that kind of work. I spend a lot of time getting the *New York Times* best-seller list and all of the puzzles and columns together to put in the section each week," Cutter said.

"I know. But the calendars take a lot longer than that. Maybe Baxter and I could split it up."

"If you divvy it up, then you have to compare the calendars later to make sure nothing was repeated. Ava, the calendars are your thing. You've always done them. I'm standing firm on this one." Cutter picked up his newspaper again.

Ava stood up and walked back to her cubicle, feeling like a complete failure. Cutter's refusal to split the work between her and Baxter said it all: He saw Baxter as the superior reporter. He wanted him writing stories, not doing calendars. Somehow Ava was going to have to prove that she was as good as the other reporters. If she did that, she was sure Cutter would find the money to hire a calendar clerk. The only problem was, she had no idea how to make it happen.

CHAPTER 27

Friday night, Ford walked into Round the Clock and sat at the counter. He and Bobby Joe had agreed that they would trade off spending Saturdays in Metairie with their mom. During his visit the previous weekend, Bobby Joe had set a trap for the raccoon under the house and arranged for a wildlife expert to pick it up when the critter wandered in. He'd seemed a little more optimistic after the visit, telling Ford that their mother had eaten two small servings of the roasted chicken he made for her.

Ford hadn't told his brother that he planned to stop by Round the Clock. He wasn't trying to hide anything from Bobby Joe; he just wanted to check things out before he said something. Maybe the café wouldn't be worth buying or maybe he'd see it and chicken out. There was no use getting his brother all riled up for nothing.

The café was located near a new condo development on the shore of Lake Ponchartrain. Ford didn't know what had been there before the fancy homes—maybe the area had been devastated by Hurricane Katrina. Now, though, it was a pleasant neighborhood and the café had a good view of the lake. It was the perfect location for an upscale seafood-

192 *Emily Beck Cogburn*

focused restaurant. The only question was whether he could make it work. Even if he managed to get the place in shape, running a restaurant was a twelve-hour day, minimum. He wasn't sure he could do it without Bobby Joe. He shook his head. Too early to think about that.

In contrast to Rosie's, Round the Clock was dark. The mud-brown upholstered booths and matching floors sucked up all the light from the dim overhead fixtures. In the late Reagan era, someone had made the disastrous decision to cover the windows with paisley curtains, hiding the lake view, but the ceiling had old Victorian tiles with raised designs that would give the place a cool vibe if he got them painted.

Pete hadn't been kidding about the art. Paintings covered most of the wall space. Ford was no art expert, but they looked a lot like the farm scene in Ava's house. The style of all of them was similar—he thought it was called Southern primitive, but that might be an old-fashioned term. Ava would probably be interested to see them. When they'd discussed her painting during their roller-skating date, she'd mentioned that some of her reluctance to sell it had to do with her love of this kind of art, whatever it was. He wanted to call her, but he wasn't ready to yet. Not until he was certain what he was going to do.

He could spend all day thinking about Ava, but he had to focus on whether the café would be worth the investment. The waitresses and cooks wore canary-yellow dresses with white aprons. They weren't moving with any particular urgency. New Orleanians ate dinner late. Eight o'clock was the normal time for restaurant reservations. It was almost exactly eight now, though, and only three tables were occupied. Ford was alone at the counter. Even given that cafés did most of their business at breakfast and lunch, the lack of customers was telling.

Ford took a menu from the metal holder. The laminate was disintegrating and coming open at the edges. The breakfast section listed the typical Southern café offerings: grits, eggs, biscuits and gravy. For lunch and dinner, there were seafood po'boys, meat loaf, ravioli, hamburger po'boys, jambalaya, and shrimp Creole. Most of it probably came from a walk-in freezer in back. With a waterfront location, the café should have focused on seafood, but the menu seemed to have no focus at all.

"Sorry, I'm late, honey! I'm Ms. Betty. You must be Ford."

Ford felt a bony hand on his shoulder and turned around. The real estate agent standing behind him could best be described as well-preserved, her tanned skin tight against high cheekbones. Yellow-white curls stood out two inches from her head in every direction, and her perfume was strong enough to make Ford's eyes water. She perched lightly on the stool next to him. "What do you think of the place so far?"

"I don't care much for the décor, but the basics are here. You have to tell me why anyone would have a restaurant with such a great waterfront view and a generic breakfast-all-day menu, though," Ford said.

"I can't speak to that, dear. The place that was here before specialized in seafood, I believe, but the owner retired. Let's take a little tour," she said. "Are you hungry?"

"Not particularly." Ford hadn't eaten much of Bernice's mushy, oversalted shrimp and mirliton casserole, but he had no desire to sample the café's food. Anyway, he could hardly eat and smell Ms. Betty's perfume at the same time. "Show me the kitchen."

She led the way behind the counter. Her cream-colored suit fit so tight that she was forced to walk with small, mincing steps in her three-inch heels. Ford studied the appliances. The grill was the same brand they had at Rosie's and only a little older. But it was filthy. No one had taken the time to scrape the grit from the sides. The vent hood above was caked with grease and dust. The fryer didn't look any cleaner, but like the grill, it wasn't in bad shape. They walked into the back part of the kitchen and Ford went straight to the range. It was older than the one in Rosie's, but each of the burners burst to life when he turned the knobs.

A waitress came to the back and greeted Ms. Betty as she got a stack of plastic cups from the stainless-steel shelf above the sink. Her dress strained at the seams, especially around her ample hips. Her long black braids were piled onto the top of her head in a fat bun. The name tag pinned above her right breast said "Charity."

"Hey, darling. How has your day been?" Ms. Betty asked with evident sincerity.

"The usual. Not busy enough to pay my bus fare," Charity said.

"Don't tell my latest prospective buyer that!"

"Sorry. I just can't live like this, Ms. Betty. I have my child to feed."

"What do you think the problem is?" Ford said. "This is a beautiful location. I'd think you'd do a good business."

"We did when we first opened, but Mr. Kyle started acting weird after a while. I don't know what got into that boy, but he stopped coming to work and just didn't seem to care anymore." Charity hugged the cups to her bosom.

"Kyle is the owner," Ms. Betty said. "His dad bought him this café because he was so interested in cooking. I guess he found something else to get excited about. A girl, maybe."

"Maybe. I best be getting up front before I kill your sale." Charity tucked a sleeve of paper napkins under her arm and left.

"This place just needs a little TLC. The location is good, the equipment is fine. Only thing missing is good management," Ms. Betty said.

"Sure," Ford said, surveying the grimy floor and greasy range. When he and Bobby Joe took over Rosie's, it already had a loyal clientele. This place would be more of a challenge. On the other hand, it was a blank slate, which would give him a chance to start over. There would be only a few longtime customers expecting eggs and grits. And if he changed the name, he could update the whole menu.

"Let me show you the rest of the dining room," Ms. Betty said. "I know you're going to love it."

She opened the back kitchen door and they came out into the part of the dining room near the lake. The restaurant was on the second floor of the building, to protect it from potential high lake water. On his way inside, Ford had noticed that the ground level, under where they were standing, was used for parking. He pushed the blinds on one of the windows aside and looked out. It was too dark for him to see much beyond the lights reflected on the lake, but the view during the daytime would be spectacular.

"As you can see, there's an outside dining area too," Ms. Betty said, holding open the glass door that led to the wooden deck. Wrought-iron railings enclosed the covered dining area. The chairs and tables were ugly, rusting, and outdated, and the harsh lights overhead made the place feel like a cheap bait shop. So much potential, wasted. Ford itched to get in and fix it. Diners should be out here enjoying the view during the day and the play of the lights on the lake at night.

"Can't you just picture this repainted with new tables, and lovely new light fixtures for night dining?" Ms. Betty said.

Ford breathed in the fresh, lake-scented air and refused to admit how much he loved it. "Nice," he said, neutrally.

"It gets better," Ms. Betty said. "You're not going to believe what's up these stairs." She removed a chain from a staircase that Ford hadn't noticed and motioned for him to walk up first.

The lake breeze ruffled his hair like a gentle hand as he ascended and came out on the top of the roof that covered the deck below. While looking at the building from the front, he'd noticed that the third story was smaller than the rest of the structure and he'd expected offices. But the floor-to-ceiling windows he was looking at now were covered with curtains. Ms. Betty opened one of the two blue-painted doors with her key.

"What you have here is two apartments. You could rent them and take in a little extra income or use them for storage, whatever you want. Now, I'm just going to show you one because Kyle is still living in the other, and much as I love the child, he hasn't mastered the art of housecleaning just yet."

"That's fine," Ford said, stepping inside.

He expected a low-ceilinged, beige-carpeted apartment like his Saint Jude place. But the space above Round the Clock had shiny wood floors, a high ceiling, and large, airy windows. He could imagine living in this beautiful apartment with Nelly. He spotted the perfect place for the old couch and her favorite child-size armchair. His four-top kitchen table would just fit in the square of tiled floor in front of the sink, stove, and refrigerator. He walked down the short hallway and found two cozy bedrooms and a bathroom with old-fashioned fixtures like the ones in his mother's house. As he went back to the living room, he reminded himself to keep his poker face. The real estate agent didn't need to know how much he liked the place. Funny, he'd be spending more time in the restaurant than the apartment, but somehow the living space sealed the deal. Maybe he wasn't just looking for a new café, but also a new home.

Ms. Betty squatted down in the corner, near a window. "I can't believe the cleaning crew missed this paint. I'm going to call them up and get them out here to fix this right away."

Ford glanced over and saw a few streaks of red on one of the boards. It was barely visible on the dark wood. "I want to make an offer on the restaurant," he said.

Ms. Betty stood up. "Fantastic! I have all my paperwork right here." She patted her red leather briefcase. "Let's get downstairs and find a comfy booth to talk in."

Ford knew he couldn't sign anything yet. He had to talk to Bobby Joe and get a loan from the bank. But maybe if he let Ms. Betty know he was serious, she wouldn't sell the restaurant to someone else before he could get everything ready to make his offer. He really wanted the place, ugly booths and all.

CHAPTER 28

Ford waited until the breakfast rush was over on Monday morning to tell his brother about Round the Clock.

"I knew you were thinking about getting your own café," Bobby Joe said.

Ford plated the omelet he'd just finished making. "I wasn't until you brought it up. You don't sound too mad. I thought you didn't want me to do it."

"I'd be more upset if you were doing it here in Saint Jude. It kind of makes sense for you to move to New Orleans. Someone needs to take care of Mom, and you have to get your girl back. I guess I can manage without you."

Ford added the toast to the omelet plate. "Order up!"

"I hope your place isn't too fancy-pants, though. Don't do foam or emulsions or whatever, please." Bobby Joe tossed the empty egg carton in the trash and opened a new one.

"I don't even know how to eat that stuff, let alone make it, don't worry." Ford pulled down the omelet ticket and started on the next one, a catfish po'boy with slaw. He didn't tell Bobby Joe that he liked the idea of designing his own menu. His brother had insisted on only having catfish, ham and cheese, and roast beef po'boys on the menu to keep things simple. Ford saw his point, but he loved shrimp po'boys, especially the one he'd made for Ava. He also wanted to serve shrimp Creole, crawfish étouffée, trout almondine, coq au vin, and seafood gumbo. He'd do French and Creole cuisine, but put his own twist on everything.

"How is Mom?" Bobby Joe asked.

Ford guiltily pulled himself out of his food fantasy. "Good. I moved the nicer TV from the bedroom to the living room so she and Aunt Bernice can fight about whether to watch the news or a rerun of a sitcom. I also got to eat Aunt Bernice's awful casserole."

"Mexican or Cajun this time?" Bobby Joe stacked two more bowls into the crammed bus pan.

"Cajun. Shrimp and mirliton," Ford replied. Bad as it was, Aunt Bernice's casserole had inspired him to put the dish on the menu of his new café, at least when the little green mirliton squashes were in season. He'd use less cheese than his aunt did, add more spice and maybe hot sauce, and top it with homemade bread crumbs, not the canned ones his aunt used. He finished making the catfish po'boy and placed it on the hot plate for Todd.

"Mom likes that cheesy glop, so I guess she won't starve." Bobby Joe took the bus pan to the back and returned with an empty one.

When he came back, Ford said, "I thought you liked it too."

"Am I that convincing? No, I mean, I can stomach it better than you, but I do have taste buds."

"Good to know." Ford read the next ticket. Pecan pancakes for Professor Frenchy French.

"Are you sure you're going to buy that place?" Bobby Joe asked.

"If the bank will give me a loan. I have the paperwork, but I haven't filled it out yet," Ford said.

Bobby Joe loaded his bus tub with empty prep pans from the sandwich station. "I'll cosign the loan if that helps, but only if you promise to try to get Ava back."

"Why is that any of your business?" Ford asked.

"Because I like the happy Ford better than the mopey one." Bobby Joe pushed through the back kitchen doors with his dirty dishes.

Ford shook his head as he poured the batter for Frenchy's pancakes on the grill. His mother was right—Bobby Joe was a softie.

ℭHAPTER 29

Ava loaded the dishwasher and poured herself a glass of cheap wine. She sat down in front of her laptop and opened her e-mail. She had to put in an hour or so before bed if she was going to make the next day's deadline. Her advance story on the mirliton festival wasn't done yet, and there were probably last-minute e-mails from arts organizations wanting their events in the calendar. At least she was too busy to think about Ford.

"Mom?" James was standing in the doorway.

Ava's threadbare robe had slipped down on her shoulder. She pulled it up and tried to erase the worry from her face. "Yes, James?"

"I forgot to ask you if I can go to Matt's house after school tomorrow."

"Who's Matt?"

"Just this kid in my class. He has a new video game and he said we could play it. His mom will be home. Please?" James's expression was pleading.

"Sure. Just give me his mother's phone number."

"Thanks, Mom."

The boy slouched back to his room. He was like a male

version of herself at ten years old. Too tall, too thin, too timid. But he had a friend! She wanted to do a victory dance, but James would be mortified if he saw her. Instead she raised her glass in a solitary toast. At least one of them was happy.

Ava eyed Virginia's sports car. It was purple with custom spinning hubcaps. "Do you get a lot of speeding tickets?"

"Sure. What's the fun in driving this baby if you don't let it rip once in a while?" Virginia opened the door and got in. She was wearing a grape juice–colored minidress that reminded Ava of something Sadie had in her closet, and a red cropped jacket.

"It is a nice car." Ava slid into the leather seat and imagined what it would be like to drive a vehicle that wasn't shaped like a box on wheels. The van accelerated, but only in the technical sense of the term. It had the pickup of a wet blanket.

"It's my baby." Virginia patted the dashboard with her orange-tipped fingers.

"So, you know where we can sell this painting?"

"There are a bunch of galleries in the warehouse district. You've seriously never been there?" Virginia said.

"My ex and I used to come to New Orleans sometimes, but we mostly stayed in the French Quarter. Jared likes Southern folk art, but he doesn't do galleries. We went to House of Blues instead."

"I hear they have a huge collection. I studied art in college."

Ava leaned back and the leather seat creaked. "But you became a photographer."

"I was going to paint, but I have absolutely no talent. The profs at Louisiana A&M advised me to become a camera jockey instead. I wanted to switch to fashion design, before I found out the textile people at A&M are all into making art, not clothes that people would actually wear." Virginia fastened her seat belt and pulled out from the curb so quickly that Ava braced herself against the armrest.

She watched out the window as they passed the familiar dry cleaners, chain drugstores, po'boy restaurants, and seafood boiling shacks lining the street near the *Gazette* offices. After a few minutes, the businesses were replaced by a row of white condominiums. Next to the housing there was a white-painted restaurant standing a story off the ground on blue wooden legs. The truck parked right in front reminded her of Ford's notoriously unreliable pickup. Virginia stopped for a red light, and as Ava watched, a tall, muscular man wearing a blue cap got out. Blond curls stuck out from the bottom of the hat. Before she could get a good look, the light turned green and Virginia stomped on the accelerator.

Ford always visited his mother in Metairie on Friday, dropped off Nelly with her mother, and drove back to Saint Jude to work in the café. So, he was unlikely to be at this restaurant in Metairie on a Wednesday afternoon. Still, those shoulders, those curls . . . Why was she even thinking about it, about him? He'd forgotten about her, and she needed to do likewise.

"Hey, are you okay?" Virginia had stopped at another traffic light and she looked over at Ava.

"Huh? Yeah, I was just thinking about something."

"That's some kind of thinking. I've said your name like five times now. I thought I was gonna have to call nine-one-one." The light changed and Virginia punched her foot onto the pedal.

Ava shook her head. "Sorry, I zone out sometimes."

"Yeah, like that time in the café. You thought about seeing a doctor?"

"What? No, it's just that I left someone behind in Saint Jude."

Virginia sped through a yellow light. "A boyfriend? Girl, you never told me you had a boyfriend."

"*Had* is the key word. When he found out I was moving here, he ended it."

"That's messed up."

"We both have kids, so he thought a long-distance relationship would be . . ." Ava didn't know what word to use. Difficult? Inconvenient? No matter how she tried to explain, it sounded lame. Why was she trying to defend him anyway?

"Saint Jude is not that far away. But you know, maybe he was just looking for an excuse, a way to let you down easy," Virginia said.

Ava slumped down into her seat. "Yeah, I've thought of that."

"Get over it. Find a new man. There are plenty of single guys in New Orleans. I think Baxter is sweet on you."

"Maybe. But he's not my type."

Virginia laughed. "Yeah, he's kind of funky-looking. Seems like a decent guy, though, and he isn't a slack-jawed meathead."

"I know. Am I just shallow?" Ava felt guilty that she didn't find Baxter attractive. She kept comparing him to Ford in her mind and Baxter came up short. She couldn't help it. Stupid, because Baxter would probably stick with her through anything, not run off like Ford. Not that she had evidence of that. If he was put in the same situation, maybe the reporter would give up too. He might not even like kids.

"Nah, you can't fake chemistry. You either have it or you

don't. You and Baxter would make a flat soda pop for sure," Virginia said.

"Gee, that makes me feel so much better. It's not my fault, it's my body's fault. Or his body's fault," Ava said.

"What are you gonna do?" Virginia said with a shrug.

Outside the window, Metairie had been replaced by the Warehouse District in downtown New Orleans. Cobblestones and bricks lined the street and sidewalk in front of brightly painted wooden buildings. Cafés and restaurants alternated with art galleries advertised by hand-painted signs. Virginia pulled up to the curb. "This is it. Fergie Gallery."

Ava got the wrapped painting from the backseat. Jared would be mad if he knew she was selling it. He'd given it to her for her thirtieth birthday. But she needed to break with the past and, besides photographs, the painting was one of the last things she owned that reminded her of him. She didn't want it anymore.

Virginia held the door of the gallery open and Ava stepped inside. The colors and frenetic energy of the paintings made the space seem alive. Some of the artists, such as Mose Tolliver and Clementine Hunter, were familiar and others were more obscure. Ava understood why this was Jared's favorite kind of art; it had a playful quality. These artists weren't breaking the rules like Andy Warhol or Marcel Duchamp. They didn't even know the rules and they didn't care. They just created whatever they wanted.

But as she studied them, she noticed something odd about some of artwork. She walked closer to a painting of a watermelon with Mose Tolliver's signature.

"Can I help you?" A young woman with a pierced nose and an armful of tattoos stood up from behind a slick, wooden desk.

"Not me. I'm just along for the ride," Virginia said. "Hey, I love your skirt. Where'd you get that?"

"This? The vintage shop on Chartres. They have the best stuff and they don't charge crazy prices like some secondhand stores. I mean, who's going to pay twenty to fifty bucks for a shirt someone's already worn, even if it is Christian Dior?"

Ava moved to the back of the gallery, studying the paintings as she went. She was grateful for Jared's extensive knowledge of Southern folk art, some of which she'd absorbed during their marriage. She knew, for example, that Mose Tolliver, also known as Mose T, used house paint and recycled boards for his art. She wasn't completely confident in her ability to distinguish between house paint and oil, but she remembered that Jared always said oil took a long time to dry—months in some cases. She glanced toward Virginia. The photographer was effectively blocking the clerk's view of Ava as they discussed their favorite clothing designers. Perfect.

Ava sidled up next to one of the Mose T paintings, a depiction of a roundheaded person with a rectangular nose. At first glance, it seemed to fit the artist's usual style, but the paint seemed too thick and glossy in the wrong way. Ava had just filed and painted her nails, but she held her breath and used one to scrape at the paint. It was just wet enough that a tiny glob stuck to the bottom of her nail. Good thing she'd used Ruby Redalicious polish and not a lighter color.

As she made her way back to the front, Ava looked at the paintings again. Some artists, like Purvis Young, used oils later in their careers, when they could afford it, but Mose Tolliver stuck with house paint and plywood until his death in 2006. Ava didn't touch any of the other paintings. Many looked too clean and new, a telling sign since most of the artists were deceased except for a few like Rosalind Palmer and Bernice Sims. She got out her phone, turned it to silent, and snapped pictures of a few of the paintings. She returned the phone to her purse before approaching the desk.

"Ava, this is Jetson," Virginia said.

"Nice to meet you," Ava said. "Do you sell any of your paintings to restaurants or coffee shops around town? Like House of Blues?"

"Nowhere that big. But Round the Clock has a big collection of folk art. The owner's dad bought most of it here," Jetson said.

"What's Round the Clock?"

"A café in Metairie, right on Lake Ponchartrain."

"Thanks. Well, we should go. We're going to be late for our lunch reservations," Ava said.

Virginia gave her a startled look, but Ava ignored her and walked toward the door.

"Okay, well, see you later. I'm going to check out that vintage shop," Virginia said to Jetson.

They went outside and got in the car. Virginia cut in front of a streetcar as she merged into traffic. "I thought you were gonna sell that painting."

"I changed my mind," Ava said.

"How come? I thought it reminded you of the evil ex and it had to be gone from your sight immediately."

"I wasn't sure we'd get the best price at that gallery. Plus, I haven't really done my homework. I need to find out about how much it's worth before I try to sell it."

"Whatever. At least I got a tip on where to get good deals on clothes in this city. Did you see that girl's skirt? I love stripes. And she only paid seven bucks for it! That's my kind of clothes shopping." Virginia rounded a corner just slow enough to keep all four wheels on the ground.

"Cool," Ava said distractedly.

"Girl, you are zoning out again. I don't think you heard a word I just said."

Ava examined her paint-encrusted nail. She could be looking at a really big story, but she had to be sure before doing anything. "Yeah. Striped skirt, vintage store. I got it."

Virginia parked the car next to Baxter's Camry in the *Gazette* lot and got out. "Sure you do, dream weaver."

CHAPTER 30

Ava didn't have time to think about the paintings again until Friday morning, after the weekly section deadlines had passed. As she drank her scalding coffee and ate one of the beignets Baxter had brought from Café Du Monde's Metairie location, she examined the photos on her phone. It wasn't just the wet paint; she thought the paintings were odd, but she couldn't pin down how. When her computer finished booting up, she typed *"Mose Tolliver"* into the search engine and scrolled through hundreds of photos of his paintings. None of them were the ones from the gallery, but that didn't prove anything. There were plenty of obscure works of art that hadn't been photographed and put online. She focused on paintings with similar themes to the ones from the gallery, those with watermelons and round-headed people, trying to decide how exactly the photos on her phone looked different. The paintings from the gallery had thicker, glossier finishes than the ones on her computer screen, lending credence to her theory that the former had been done with oil paint, though it was difficult to tell from the photographs. The sliced watermelons in the gallery paintings were rounder and the seeds smaller than the ones in the Internet photos. The noses on the people were smaller in the gallery photos and their hands were larger. It wasn't just the proportions either; the styles didn't seem quite the same—like two signatures made by different hands.

After an hour, Ava was convinced that the paintings at the gallery were forgeries. Besides studying the photos, she'd also confirmed that Clementine Hunter had used oil paint to create at least some of her works, but she'd died in 1988. Ava hadn't touched any of the Hunter paintings at the gallery, but she had a feeling at least some of them still had wet paint. She would have to go back and check. But first, she wanted to visit Round the Clock and see the other paintings. At a restaurant, it might be easier to touch the paintings, or at least get close to them without attracting suspicion.

She typed the name of the café into the computer and squinted at the photo that came up. The restaurant had a sign with a fake clock on it that read three p.m. The last time she'd seen that sign, a familiar-looking blond man had been walking toward it. She still didn't know why Ford would be at a café in Metairie in the middle of the afternoon, but she was suddenly positive it had been him. Without taking the time to consider that she might just want it to be him, she picked up her cell phone and dialed his number.

"Ava. I was hoping you'd call."

His voice made a lump form in her throat. Speaking was suddenly difficult. "Yeah," she managed to say.

He plunged on, not seeming to notice how strangled she sounded. "I'm really sorry I gave up on us. I've been meaning to call you, but I've been having a hard time with my mom being sick. Sometimes I feel like I'm just barely holding it together for her and Nelly. Can you please forgive me?"

Ava was stunned into silence. She'd expected an awkward

conversation, but not this kind of awkwardness. He wanted another chance? "Um, I'm sorry. I don't know."

"I'm going to buy a café in Metairie. I need to be close to my mom . . . and you. I'm going to make this work. We can make this work."

"Just like that, you want to try again? I thought it was impossible for you to have a long-distance relationship." Ava's shock was replaced by anger. He couldn't expect her to just start up where they left off. Part of her wanted to, but most of her didn't trust him anymore.

"Yeah, I was an idiot. I know that now," Ford said.

Ava pulled in a deep breath and forced herself to focus. "Were you just at a restaurant? What's it called?"

"That's the one I'm thinking about buying. It's called Round the Clock."

"Does it have a lot of Southern folk art on the walls?" Ava asked.

"Yeah, why?"

"Can you meet me there?"

"Okay, sure. Why?" Ford said.

"I'll explain later." Ava hung up and grabbed her coat from the rack. She told herself that she was excited about finally getting her big story and not about seeing him again.

Ten minutes later, she was clutching the armrest as Virginia tore down the busy main drag of Metairie.

"So, you want me to shoot photos of the paintings at this café because you think they might be fakes?" Virginia said.

"You got it. This could be a big story. Just what we need to show Cutter and the others in the bureau that we have it," Ava said.

"Works for me. Do you know where this place is?" Virginia asked.

"I have the address right here."

"Then lead on, Nancy Drew."

"Not too fast. It's just one more block." The condo block ended, and the café came into view. "Right there. With the big clock on top."

Virginia pulled around to the side of the building and parked underneath. "You didn't tell me it was on the lake. This is nice," she said.

They got out of the car, went to the front of the building, and walked up the steps to the front door. Ava couldn't ignore the part of her that ached to see Ford again. She wanted to believe that he'd just been too busy and overwhelmed to call her, but was picking up the phone so hard?

CHAPTER 31

Ford and Bobby Joe had been walking out of the real estate agent's office when Ava called. Ford hated to admit it, but his brother was a great negotiator. After securing the loan from the bank, they'd met with Ms. Betty and presented their offer. Bobby Joe demanded a deep cleaning, a new range, and all the paintings, which could be worth thousands of dollars. Ford had thought Ms. Betty wouldn't even agree to take the offer to the seller, especially since they'd gone below the asking price. But she actually seemed pleased.

"Was that Ava?" Bobby Joe asked after Ford got off the phone.

"Yeah. It's weird. She wants to meet me at Round the Clock. Something to do with the paintings," Ford said.

"Aha, so you have your in. Don't screw it up, brother. I'm going to see Mom." Bobby Joe jangled his keys as he got into his truck.

"I'll meet you there later," Ford said.

He drove slowly to the café. His brain was clicking double-time. What did Ava want with the paintings? What was he going to say when he saw her? He felt like a kid on his first date. He parked his truck under the building, thinking how close the restaurant was to being his. So much was happening at once that he could hardly keep up. He walked inside and spotted Ava immediately. She and a young woman wearing a purple dress were studying a painting hanging above one of the booths. Ava scraped at the paint with a red fingernail and showed it to the woman.

Ford took off his baseball cap. Ava looked stunning as always in her striped dress, short jacket, and platform shoes. Her red curls skimmed her shoulders and danced as she moved her head. Ford reached them just as Charity, the waitress, approached. "Can I help y'all?" she asked.

"Can we sit here?" Ava said. She'd taken her hand away from the painting just in time.

"Sure, no problem. I'll be right back with some water." Charity went to the kitchen.

Ava turned and met Ford's eyes. For just a moment, he thought he saw a hunger that matched his own. She looked away quickly. "This is my friend Virginia. She's a photographer at the newspaper."

Ford introduced himself and sat down in the booth. Ava and Virginia sat together on the other side. Virginia took a menu from the holder on the table and studied it.

"Tell me everything you know about this café," Ava said.

"Why are you so interested in these paintings?" Ford asked. He watched her for some sign, just another little reassurance that she might be willing to take him back. He wanted her more than anything. Why had he ever let her go? He'd convinced himself that he was doing the right thing and it almost worked, until he'd started to feel like he'd been punched in the gut.

"The paintings are all fakes. Well, most of them anyway. This one over our heads has Mose T's signature, but he only used house paint. This is oil." She held out her finger, which had a glob of paint under the nail. "We want to know whether they were bought at Fergie Gallery."

"I don't know where they are from. The owner is a guy named Kyle Alvarado. His daddy bought the café for him, but the kid is tired of running it, so he's unloading. As you can see, it's not exactly a jumping joint," Ford said.

"It's noon and only three tables are full. This place isn't jumping, it's barely out of bed," Virginia said. "Is it safe to eat here? I mean, we won't get food poisoning, will we?"

"I had a look around, and I didn't see any evidence of bad food handling. Order the fries and maybe a fried po'boy. All that stuff comes out of the freezer, so it can't be too terrible. I'm not saying it'll be haute cuisine, though," Ford said.

"I'm not so hungry anymore," Virginia said, putting down the menu.

"You don't know anything about the paintings?" Ava asked.

"No. We just made an offer on the place today, and my brother asked them to include the paintings because he thought they made the place unique. Of course, Kyle could refuse. Maybe not, though. He's a young guy and I think he just wants out," Ford said.

"We need to find out which paintings were bought at Fergie Gallery and whether they're fakes. This could be a big story and if we break it, we might finally get some respect around the office. I don't know about Virginia, but I feel like I'm still second-class, even though I'm full-time now," Ava said.

"I could definitely go for some more respect," Virginia said. "Also more money."

"I don't know what I can do, but I'll help any way I can," Ford said.

"I'm going out to the car to get my camera. Order me a

Diet Coke if the waitress wanders this way again." Virginia slid out of the booth and left.

Ford folded his hands on the table. "I'm sorry for everything I did to hurt you, Ava. I messed up big time. I want you to give me another chance. Please."

"Why should I? How can I trust you ever again? How do I know you won't find some other excuse tomorrow or two years from now?" Ava said.

"Because I can't imagine my life without you. I thought I was doing the right thing, but then I realized it doesn't matter. My mother might die, and I started thinking that life is short and we have to decide what's really important. I can live here or in Saint Jude. Nelly won't care. Sure, Bobby Joe and I put a lot of work into the café, but he has his own life. It's time I got mine."

"I'm sorry about your mother. How is she?" Ava's voice softened.

"I don't know. Getting those doctors to tell me anything is damn near impossible. She got through the surgery okay, but she's seventy years old," Ford said, staring at his hands on the table.

Virginia returned and set a professional camera on the table. "Ready for action."

A moment later, Charity approached, order pad in hand. "You folks decide what you'd like?"

Ford didn't really want anything, but he ordered fries and a Coke. Ava and Virginia ordered diet sodas.

"Can I take some pictures of the art?" Virginia asked.

"I don't see why not," Charity said. "Especially since Mr. Kyle is going to sell the place. I'll be out of a job soon, so what do I care?"

"Maybe not," Ford said.

"Yeah, sure." The waitress tucked her order pad into her apron and left.

Virginia took the lens cap off her camera and pointed it at the Mose T painting. She got up and circled the room, shooting all the art.

"You're really going to buy this place?" Ava said.

"Someone needs to be down here to take care of my mom, but I can't just sit around. I have to do something. Besides, she wouldn't want me at her bedside all the time. My aunt is doing most of the heavy lifting. I'm helping as much as I can, but there are certain things she doesn't want me to do. Also, I have to be down here a lot if I'm going to convince you to give me another chance. I'm going to bring you flowers and chocolate every day until you agree to go on another date," Ford said.

"Great, so I'll have a stalker."

Ford was stung by her comment. He'd hurt her badly, though. He could see it in her eyes. She'd been more upset by the breakup than he'd realized. Maybe that was good news—it might mean that she felt the same way about him as he did about her. If he could just get her to trust him again. "No, if you want me to leave you alone, I will. I promise."

"I don't know what I want, Ford." A frown creased her face. "Do you know how I found out about this gallery? I was going to sell the painting Jared gave me."

"How come?"

"I need the money. Anyway, it reminds me of him. I'm sick of it. I don't want to think about the days when we had a real relationship. There was a time when we had fun together. He changed; maybe I changed too. Why am I telling you all this?"

"Because I'm a nice guy who made a mistake, but I really do care about you," Ford said. "And maybe you missed me as much as I missed you."

"I shouldn't even be talking to you. I move a few miles away and you cut me loose." Ava stood up and slung her purse over her shoulder. "I don't know why I called you. I can't give you another opportunity to disappear on me again."

Ford watched her leave. Clearly, he'd done something wrong, but he wasn't sure how he could have handled it differently. Would anything make her change her mind? He didn't know, but he had to keep trying. The waitress brought the drinks and left again. Ford drank some Coke, just for something to do.

Virginia came back to the table and snapped a picture of him. "Where's Ava?"

"She walked out on me," Ford said.

"How'd you manage to run her off?" She put the lens cap back on her camera and sat down across from him.

"I told her I was sorry and said I missed her."

"You bonehead," she said.

"What should I have said?"

"Not that, obviously. Anyway, she won't get far. She's wearing three-inch heels and she doesn't have a car."

"Good to know," Ford said.

Virginia drank some soda. "Look, I think Ava really likes you. I don't know what all the drama is about, but you need to work it out."

"I'm not giving up yet."

"Are you moving down here just to be near her? 'Cause that's a big commitment. Kind of romantic really."

"My mom lives in Metairie too. But I probably wouldn't be buying this café if not for Ava."

She shook her head. "Ballsy."

A few minutes later, Ava slid back into the booth. "Can we start over?"

"Fine by me," Ford said. "Hi, my name's Ford."

Ava laughed. "Not that far back."

Charity brought the fries and Ford sampled one. All of

a sudden he was hungry. They were the standard frozen bagged variety, but at least they were hot. "I'll call you if and when the sale goes through. What are y'all going to do about this in the meantime? Don't you need to call the cops?"

"Forgery is a federal crime," Ava said. "We will report it, but I want to find out a few things first."

"Cutter isn't going to let us accuse someone of a crime," Virginia said.

"No, we let the cops do that. But once we call them, we won't have access to anything. We won't be able to take any more pictures, for instance."

"Yeah, but they might accuse us of tampering with evidence."

"Photographing isn't tampering. Neither is talking to people. We do a little digging, call the cops, and when they make an arrest, then we turn in the story. We'll have the scoop," Ava said.

Ford dipped a fry in ketchup. If this was his only way to connect with Ava, he'd take it. Take it and milk it for all it was worth.

Ford couldn't remember the last time he'd sat at his mom's kitchen table with his brother. Easter, maybe. Bobby Joe looked as tired as Ford felt. The day had been one stressful thing after another: the meeting with the real estate agent, seeing Ava again, then coming to his mother's house and finding her pale and sleepy from pain medication.

"I can't believe Aunt Bernice talked me into staying. I should be closing Rosie's tonight," Bobby Joe said.

"You know Aunt Bernice. She gets an idea in her head and you can't stop her. Besides, you were in Metairie anyway," Ford said.

"I know, but now I'll have to listen to Fitzgerald whine all day tomorrow about him having to pick up the extra shift," Bobby Joe said. "Besides, it wasn't exactly a fun time."

Bobby Joe had a point—the evening had been more of a chore than a pleasure. Their aunt had fixed them her cheesy crawfish casserole and they'd all sat around the table, picking at the food. At seven o'clock, their mother had gone to bed and Aunt Bernice switched on the TV. She'd eventually fallen asleep in the recliner and the brothers escaped to the kitchen. Ford didn't care for his aunt's cooking, but he had to admit that she was doing a good job nursing his mom. The house was clean and all her medicine was neatly lined up on the counter. She knew what Bobby Joe and Ford would need too: a six-pack of beer.

"How's the wife?" Ford asked, taking a drink from his half-full beer.

"Jeanie had the late shift tonight at the hospital. I don't know how she thinks she can go to graduate school with the crazy hours nurses have," Bobby Joe said.

"She's still going to get a master's in English?"

Bobby Joe drained his bottle and banged it on the table. "Guess so. She took the GRE and everything. Why she wants to study nineteenth-century British literature, I'll never know."

"Could she apply to schools down here—University of New Orleans or something?"

"I don't know. Why?"

"I was just thinking, maybe you want to let Todd and Fitzgerald run Rosie's and come work here with me at the new café," Ford said.

"Let those two idiots run our restaurant into the ground? No way."

"You could hire someone else."

"It's our place. I can't let someone else take it over," Bobby Joe said.

"Not even to be here, close to Mom? Or maybe you could just come down here until she gets better," Ford said.

Bobby Joe got up to get another beer. When he sat down again, Ford caught a glimpse into his brother's mind. Bobby Joe didn't think their mom was going to get better. He didn't want to give up Rosie's, but he also didn't want to come to New Orleans and watch her slowly die.

"You can't stand to see her like this," Ford said.

"No, I can't. It's tearing me up. Look, this is harder for me. At least you have Nelly." Bobby Joe used his T-shirt to twist the cap off the beer bottle.

"So what? You have Jeanie."

"Maybe not for long." Bobby Joe chugged the beer like a college kid at a frat party.

"Come on," Ford said.

"She's sick of the long hours. Not seeing me on weekends. Says I don't pay enough attention to her. I'm not supportive enough of her dream to go back to school."

"God." Ford put the empty bottles in the recycling can. "You gotta work it out."

"I'm trying to."

"You want another beer? Or whiskey?"

"Mom doesn't keep whiskey." Bobby Joe rested his elbows on the table.

Ford reached into the cabinet above the refrigerator. "Yes, she does. For special occasions." He took out two jelly glasses, filled them with ice, and splashed in some Jack Daniel's.

"Stuff's probably old as the hills, then," Bobby Joe said.

"It doesn't go bad." Ford brought the drinks to the table and sat down.

"I guess." Bobby Joe eyed his glass dubiously and took a sip. "Speaking of women, how goes it with Ava?"

Ford drank some whiskey. He didn't usually mess with

the hard stuff, and it burned going down. "She says she doesn't want to get back together with me, but she wants me to help her with a story she's writing for the newspaper."

"At least she's talking to you about something. Turn on the Ford charm and you'll get her back. What's the article going to be about?"

Ford told him about the forged paintings and the café.

"Sounds like a story to me." Bobby Joe finished his drink and stood up. "I gotta get out of here."

"Neither of us should drive. Let's walk back to the hotel together." Ford put the glasses in the sink.

It was dark outside. The cool air made Ford's head feel clear, even though he'd drunk more whiskey and beer than he usually did in a week. They left the quiet neighborhood and came out onto busy Williams Boulevard. Ford couldn't help looking at the *Gazette* office as they passed. His mother hadn't mentioned Ava again. He still hoped one day soon the two would meet.

"Are you hungry?" he asked Bobby Joe.

"No."

"Well, we should eat anyway."

"Fine."

Stevie's po'boy shack was two blocks from the Starlight. The restaurant really was a shack, not much more than a tiny house with a hand-painted sign tacked to the roof. But Stevie, or whoever actually ran the place, made bread on site and used tomatoes that tasted like they'd come out of someone's garden. Ford ordered oyster po'boys for both of them and vetoed the beer Bobby Joe wanted, getting Cokes instead.

"I don't want to see Mom suffer," Bobby Joe said when they were outside again.

"Neither do I." Ford waited for his brother to say something else.

"God, Ford, she can't die. She was supposed to be a grandma for my kids."

"Are you going to have kids?"

"I don't know. I thought we had plenty of time. But we don't. It's all going to be over before we know it. I'm gonna buy Jeanie some flowers tomorrow. Tell her I want kids now." Bobby Joe swayed a little, nearly bumping into Ford.

Ford smiled in the dark. His brother was being dramatic, as usual. By the time morning came, he'd have forgotten all about his vows and gone back to worrying about whether there were enough French fries for the dinner service. Still, he had a point.

Back in the hotel room, Ford tuned the TV to a reality show and they sat on their beds eating the sloppy sandwiches. During the few road trips they'd taken as kids, they'd stayed in cheap motels like the Starlight. The brothers had shared a bed while their parents chain-smoked together in the other one. The places they visited didn't make much of an impression on Ford, but he remembered watching TV with his brother and eating greasy pepperoni pizza on the bed. Bobby Joe was and always had been his best friend. He was going to miss working with him.

CHAPTER 32

Tuesday morning, Ava and Virginia stood outside Fergie Gallery again.

"We have to get as much information as we can without making Jetson suspicious," Ava said.

"I know, I know," Virginia answered, taking a picture of the gallery sign. "I can be stealthy, don't worry."

Jetson was hunched over her smartphone behind the desk when they entered the gallery. "Hey, you all were in here the other day," she said.

"My wife and I are thinking of buying some paintings for our new house," Virginia said, putting her arm around Ava.

"Oh, you didn't tell me that before. Cool."

"We wanted to look around again and find out a few more things first," Ava said. "Can you tell me who owns the gallery?"

"Mr. Ferguson," Jetson said, looking down at a scratch on the surface of her desk.

"And what's his first name?"

"Richard."

Ava took note of the girl's sudden lack of confidence and

decided to take a stab in the dark. "Are you related to Mr. Ferguson?"

"Yes, he's my father."

"So, your name is Jetson Ferguson?"

"Yeah. Why do you need to know all this stuff anyway?" Jetson asked.

"We just like to know who we're buying from. There are a lot of dishonest people out there," Ava said. "How long has he owned this gallery?"

"Two years. That's when I graduated from UNO. Guess he kind of bought it to give me something to do." She lifted one tattooed shoulder.

"Who does the art buying? You?"

Jetson's eyes widened for a moment, but then she quickly rearranged her face into a neutral expression. "Oh no. I don't do any of that. Dad and his friend Jeb Alvarado are the art experts. Mr. Jeb's son owns the Round the Clock café. To tell you the truth, Jeb buys some of the paintings from Dad, just as a favor to a friend."

Ava looked at the girl hard. Something was not adding up. "Why would Alvarado help your dad find paintings for the gallery and then turn around and buy them? Why not just buy the paintings directly from the artist or whoever?"

"I don't know. Taxes maybe? I'm just a clerk. I sit here all day and read books or play games on my phone. Dad thinks I'm lacking direction, so he set this whole thing up to give me something to do," Jetson said.

"Just like Kyle Alvarado and his café."

"Yeah, but he's getting out. I can't do that. The gallery belongs to Dad. He didn't trust me enough to put it in my name."

"You could quit," Ava said.

"And do what? I don't have any marketable skills. All I

have is a lousy degree in art history." Jetson's phone dinged and she glanced at it.

Virginia came up to the desk. "Is it okay if we take pictures of a few paintings?"

"Gee, I don't know," Jetson said. "My dad told me never to let people do that."

"We just want to decide whether we want to buy them," Ava said.

"Whatever. I don't care."

Virginia quickly took a shot of Jetson and aimed her camera at the gallery wall, clicking the shutter rapidly. "We better get going. We have that appointment," she said.

"Yes, we'll be back. We just need to think about what will go with our furniture," Ava said.

"Sure." Jetson picked up her phone.

When they were outside, Ava said, "So we're married now?"

"Best idea I could come up with. Worked pretty well, if I do say so myself," Virginia said.

"As long as she doesn't get suspicious and start figuring out what we're up to."

"Why would she?"

"I don't know, but we need to work fast before she does. Let's get over to Round the Clock," Ava said.

"I'll drive as fast as I can," Virginia said.

"Please don't. You drive plenty fast enough normally."

"Whatever you say, Mom."

As soon as Ava and Virginia walked in the door of Round the Clock, they were greeted by a woman wearing a mask of makeup and half a bottle of perfume. "Darlings! Ford told me you were coming. I'm Ms. Betty, the real estate agent. He and Bobby Joe just closed on the café. I'm afraid you missed Bobby Joe, though. He had to get back to Saint Jude."

"I'm Ava and this is Virginia," Ava said.

"I know, I know. Come have a seat, dears." Ms. Betty led them to a table.

Ava couldn't guess Ms. Betty's age—she could have been anywhere from forty-five to sixty-five. She wore a tight-fitting pink suit and matching heels that would have been perfect for an Easter brunch.

Ava studied the art on the walls and tried to guess which paintings were fake. The game helped keep her mind off the fact that she was going to see Ford again. She'd get that little burst of electricity coursing through her body when he arrived. All she could do was try to ignore it.

Ms. Betty began gathering up the papers on the table. "My work here is done. Signed, sealed, and delivered. I'm so happy for Ford, getting a new start like this." She turned and glanced toward the kitchen as the door opened. "I'm going to be your first customer."

"Whatever you want. On the house." Ford was dressed in work boots, jeans, and a stained T-shirt. Even though she was trying hard to stay angry, Ava felt sorry for him. His straw-colored curls were wet with sweat, and his red-tinged eyes had dark rings around them.

"Here are the keys," Ms. Betty said, setting a ring on the table and heading for the door. "Enjoy, darling. Call if you need anything."

"Thanks," Ford said.

"How's your mother?" Ava said, after Ms. Betty had sashayed out the door.

"Hanging in there. She starts chemotherapy on Monday." He put a folder on the table and sat down.

"That'll be hard, I bet."

"Yeah. It seems stupid to be buying this café while she's going through this."

"I understand," Ava said. While going through her divorce, she'd focused on the children even more than before. She'd also reorganized the entire house and cleaned like a madwoman. Anything to stay busy and keep her mind off the breakup.

"So here are all the documents I can find," he said, slapping the top of the folder.

"Let me look through them first," Virginia said. "That way I can go ahead and photograph the ones that look important." She grabbed the documents and went to a booth in the corner.

"She's trying to get us alone. She has the crazy idea that we should get back together," Ava said.

"That doesn't seem crazy to me," Ford said.

"I have to figure this out first, and you have to help your mom and get the café going."

Ford shrugged. "I know."

Ava folded her hands on the table and examined the Cotton Candy Pink nail polish Sadie had insisted she wear. "I've hit a dead end with this art fraud thing. Ferguson and Alvarado are clearly in it together, buying the paintings from some forger, but I have no idea how to find out who is actually making the art."

"I don't know either. Why do you think Kyle is selling the café?"

"Could be a coincidence. Maybe the kid is tired of running it. Or his dad might think they're going to get caught for some reason. Maybe we're not the only ones who are suspicious. Another buyer or even a café customer could have caught on and threatened to turn them in. Could be that Alvarado knows about this and Ferguson doesn't, so Alvarado is pulling out. Or maybe the two had a personal spat and Alvarado decided to quit. He tells his son to get rid of the café and the paintings."

"Why not just sell or destroy the paintings instead of dumping the restaurant too?" Ford asked.

"I don't know. Something isn't adding up and I can't figure out what it is." Ava leaned back and stared at the red swirls in the painting above the booth where Virginia was sitting. "All the more reason to give up and call the FBI."

"Not yet. Take a closer look at the documents and think about it some more. You might figure it out," Ford said.

"I've been doing that." Ava rubbed her temples. "I'm all out of ideas."

Virginia brought the folder back to the table and set it down with a slap. "Most of the paintings were recorded as being bought from a gallery called Beemer in the past two years. I checked on my phone and as far as I can tell, Beemer doesn't exist."

"Dead end." Ava opened the folder and closed it again.

"Don't be such a wet blanket. I want to take down the paintings and get good photos of them before we go," Virginia said.

"Okay with me. I'm going to paint the walls anyway," Ford said.

Ford and Ava took the paintings down and Virginia photographed them, carefully positioning the art near the windows to get enough light.

When Ava noticed one by Rosalind Palmer, some of her bad mood lifted. "Can we take this painting with us?"

Ford paused as he took down a Clementine Hunter. "Of course. Take whatever you want."

An hour later, all the paintings were leaning against the wall. Ford dismissed their offer to help him store them. "I'll take care of that later, but before you leave, I want to give you something." He walked quickly to the kitchen.

While he was gone, Ava picked up the Rosalind Palmer

painting. She wasn't sure she wanted a gift from Ford. Despite all his help recently, she still wasn't convinced that she should trust him again. She considered hurrying out the door with Virginia before he came back, but something told her to wait. A little voice in her head, maybe, that still hoped.

Ford returned with a bunch of daisies and a small box. Ava shrugged to indicate that her hands were full, even though she was torn between wanting to run out of the room and rushing forward to embrace him. Virginia took the gifts and whispered something to him.

Ford gave her a small smile in answer. "'Bye, Ava. Good luck with the story."

"See you later," Ava said. As he walked away, she wished she had dropped the painting and run to him.

CHAPTER 33

The next day, Ava scrolled through the contacts on her phone. She tried to go quickly past Ford's name, but it seemed to stand out among all the professional contacts. She stopped on Jared. It was nine o'clock in the morning. Hopefully, he was awake, but still at home. She'd tried to find Rosalind Palmer's address online after getting her painting from Round the Clock the previous day, but the artist kept a low profile and wasn't very well known outside of New Orleans. She could have tried to find another gallery that sold her paintings and tracked down the address that way, but it seemed easier just to call Jared. He should still have the information from when he bought her painting years ago. Her ex was meticulous about paperwork, especially when it came to his art collection.

She leaned back in her office chair and dialed his number. It rang three times and she thought she might have to leave a message. Maybe she could tell him to e-mail her the information so she wouldn't have to talk to him. No such luck; he answered before the end of the fourth ring.

"What's wrong?" he asked immediately. "Are the kids okay?"

Ava was knocked speechless. He was actually worried about the children? She guessed it wasn't an unreasonable assumption since she hadn't called in two years. They were able to do most of their correspondence by e-mail. "They're fine. I just need to ask you something."

"Shoot." Jared's favorite expression. His shorthand way of saying, *Go ahead, I'm listening.* She used to think it was cool. Now it sounded overly breezy, a nearly forty-year-old man trying to be hip, especially if he still did the pretend gun with his finger too. Luckily, she couldn't see that over the phone.

"Do you have Rosalind Palmer's address?" she asked.

"I should. I can look through my papers. Let me check the file cabinet. What's going on?"

"I thought I might buy one of her paintings." The lie didn't flow out as easily as she would have liked, but she couldn't tell Jared the truth. He might steal the story or he might tell her to go to the police.

"I don't buy that," Jared said over the sound of rustling paper. "For one thing, if you'd won the lottery, I think I'd know about it. For another, you would have e-mailed, not called."

Ava blew air into the phone. She should have known that he was too good a reporter to fall for her story. "If I tell you, you can't tell anyone."

"If you don't tell me, I'm not giving you the address. Come on, Ava. I'm dying here."

"There's a gallery in the Warehouse District that I think is selling fakes of her paintings. And of some other artists too," she said.

"Did you go to the FBI?"

"Not yet."

"You know that once you do, you won't have access to

anything," Jared said, his thoughts clearly running along the same lines hers had.

"I know."

"This could be a huge story. Not just locally, but nationally. Art fraud is serious business."

"I know." Ava's palms started to sweat. The phone felt too hot in her hand.

"I won't tell. Good luck. Here's the address. I remember it was in the Lower Ninth Ward."

"I know. I was there too. I just couldn't remember the address and I didn't want to wander around trying to guess. Thanks." Ava picked up her pen and turned to a blank page in her notebook.

Virginia got off I-10 at the Superdome exit and drove toward the French Quarter. "We're going to see the famous Ninth Ward, huh?"

"You haven't been there yet?" Ava said.

"No. Believe it or not, I haven't taken any murder photos or anything else in that area."

"I was there right before Hurricane Katrina and it was pretty run-down. From what I've heard, it's even worse now."

"People are crazy. Why would you move back after that?" Virginia said.

"Some people are really attached to their idea of home. I don't understand it either. I used to think of myself as the girl from Wisconsin, but now I don't so much. It's just a place." As she looked out the window, though, Ava was reminded that New Orleans was more than a place. Following the Mississippi, they passed the T-shirt shops and oyster bars of the French Quarter, and then the artsy bars and ethnic restaurants of the Marigny neighborhood. Even though it was an ordinary weekday, they saw women wearing pink tutus over jeans and T-shirts, school-age boys tap dancing and playing brass instruments, and a man dressed like Uncle Sam walking an imaginary dog. Nothing comparable existed anywhere in the country, or really, the world. Soon, though, they crossed into what Jared had called the "danger zone." Ava didn't know whether it was really dangerous or not, but the area was certainly depressing. The shotgun houses lining the narrow streets had once been painted bright pastel colors. A few were rebuilt and had neatly placed shrubs in front. Others stood empty and gutted, like sightless eye sockets. Some of the abandoned houses still had the spray-painted markings put there by first responders after Katrina. Ava was glad that she didn't remember anymore what most of the symbols meant.

The houses on either side of Rosalind Palmer's had been torn down, leaving only weed-filled lots, fast-food wrappers, and random lumps of concrete foundation. Ava didn't remember the place very well since she and Jared had visited over ten years previously, before James was born. She did know that Palmer had neighbors then and she recalled two ladies in curlers sitting on their porches staring at her and Jared as they got out of the car. She hoped they were doing okay now and had found new homes.

Virginia parked in front and turned off the engine. "Guess she doesn't have to worry about her neighbors having loud parties," she said, the first words she'd spoken since leaving the French Quarter. Virginia had clearly been affected by what they'd just driven through. The story about New Orleans was that it was back and better than ever. But certain things would never be the same. Most of the people from the Ninth Ward lacked the means to really rebuild like others in the city had.

Ava opened the door and put her black high-heeled boots

on the broken sidewalk. She'd called Palmer to let her know they were coming and why. The artist sounded outraged when Ava told her what she thought was going on. "Fergie what? Ain't she some singer or something? I never heard of such a gallery."

Virginia took a photo of the house. "What's an artist doing living in a place like this?"

"Rosalind Palmer's not exactly Norman Rockwell. Just because she sells a few paintings in local galleries doesn't mean she's hit the big time," Ava said.

"I wonder why someone would bother forging her paintings, then."

Ava considered the question as she studied the modest home. The problem had been weighing on her mind. It could be that the forger wanted the paintings at Fergie to reflect a wide range of Southern artists, not just the most famous ones. But then, why not buy real Palmer paintings, since they weren't as expensive as a lot of other folk art? Sometimes the whole forgery operation, to the extent she understood it, made no sense to Ava.

Virginia opened the screen and knocked on the wooden door behind it. Palmer answered the door wearing a floral dress that was big enough to conceal several small children. Her hair was shorn close to her head, and her full lips were painted a deep red. She gestured them inside with a thick arm.

The living room contained a brown vinyl couch and a floral fabric–covered recliner. The wooden floors were scratched and creaked under their feet. Ava thought she remembered shelves of elephant statuettes lining the walls when she and Jared were there, but now there were paintings instead. Some looked like Palmer's and others had a darker style—bold drawings of Satan and black birds with enormous wings.

Ava introduced herself and Virginia.

"May I take a few pictures?" Virginia asked.

"Sure, honey, I don't got nothing to hide and any publicity is good publicity. Now show me that painting," Palmer said.

Ava sat down on the couch and took the painting from its plastic bag. It depicted an African American man sitting in a chair, reading the newspaper. Ava knew Palmer's work well enough to recognize that it was a subject she would paint. However, the colors were too bright, the lines too messy. Palmer snatched it and held it out in front of her as Virginia snapped a picture. Palmer's mouth twisted as she stared at the painting. "Now show me the receipt," she said.

Ava handed over a copy made from Virginia's photograph, wishing the artist would tell them what she was thinking. Was it hers or not?

"I never sold nothing to this character, and I didn't paint this garbage," Palmer said, tossing the canvas onto the couch.

"Is it a copy of something you did paint?" Ava asked.

Instead of answering, Palmer picked up a black book from a table behind the recliner. She flipped through it and then handed the open book to Ava. The page showed a painting of a man in a chair reading the newspaper. He faced the opposite direction and his clothes were a different color, but clearly whoever had painted the picture from Fergie Gallery had seen it.

"Who owns this painting?" Ava said.

"Man name of Ferguson. Lives in the Marigny," Palmer said.

"Fergie," Virginia said, lowering her camera.

Palmer closed the book. "He's a doctor. Owns a lot of my art."

"He owns an art gallery too. The one that sold this paint-

ing to the father of the owner of the Round the Clock café.
We're going to figure out where it came from," Ava said.

"You let me know. 'Cause if someone's putting my name
on some sloppy paintings, I sure want to know who it is."

"We'll be in touch," Ava said.

CHAPTER 34

Nelly ran to Ford as soon as Marion opened the door of her condo. "Daddy!"

Ford bent down and hugged her, glad that he'd come to visit. After spending all day supervising the workers helping him renovate the restaurant and pulling up hundreds of worn-out floor tiles himself, all he'd really wanted to do was drink a beer and watch TV. But Marion had invited him over for dinner, and he'd felt compelled to accept. "It's good to see you, sweetie," he said.

"You been gone forever!" she said.

"Only a week." Ford gently extracted himself from her and went to sit on the couch.

Nelly climbed up next to him. "I have a new school," she said.

Ford glanced at Marion. He'd left finding a day care in Metairie to her, and to her credit, she hadn't argued. She seemed to understand that working on the café and helping Aunt Bernice take care of his mother was draining him. That was exactly how it felt, as though the energy was being slowly sucked out of him.

"It's a good one, I think," Marion said, sitting down in the armchair. "You like it, right, Nelly?"

"Yeah. June is my new friend."

"June is a girl in her class," Marion clarified. "The school goes through kindergarten, so she can stay for two more years if we want her to."

"Thanks for everything. I really appreciate it," Ford said. He couldn't help noticing that the condo was unusually messy—Nelly's pony was on top of a pile of blocks, board books were open on the coffee table, and a sippy cup rested forgotten on the windowsill. He liked the chaos—it made the place seem lived in, but Marion might not feel the same way.

She reached down and picked up a plastic toy ball from the floor, rolling it absently on her palm. "We've had a good time, haven't we, Nelly?"

"Yeah." Nelly got off the couch, took Pony, and began rearranging the blocks.

"Why don't you come and help me in the kitchen?" Marion said, standing up.

Ford was bone-tired. All he wanted to do was sit and watch Nelly play. He felt like they'd been apart for a month rather than a week. But he followed Marion into the kitchen area.

"When do you think you'll be ready to take her back?" Marion asked as she opened the fridge.

Ford sat down on one of the kitchen chairs. "I don't know. I'm sorry, I have a lot going on. I think the café renovations are coming along pretty well—I have the kitchen tile replaced and the old booths hauled away, but there's a lot of work still to be done. And I have to take Mom to at least a few of her chemotherapy appointments and cook her dinner sometimes. Aunt Bernice can't do it all."

"I understand. But it's not good for Nelly to have an un-stable environment," Marion said.

"What do you mean 'unstable'? She's here with you. She has her own room and all her stuff here. That's better than her being at my half-furnished apartment above the restau-rant right now. All I have in there is my bed. I haven't had time to move in anything else yet."

"The sooner she gets into a routine, the better. You know, being with you during the week and me on weekends." Mar-ion dumped some precut, washed salad greens into a bowl.

"Are you having a hard time with her?" Ford asked.

"I love her, you know that."

"Of course you do, she's your daughter."

"But I work really long hours at the hospital and some-times she won't go to bed until ten o'clock, no matter what I do. It's hard to come home after a day of being on my feet and then spend the evening cooking dinner that she doesn't eat, cleaning up messes she makes, playing ponies with her, bathing her, dressing her for bed. She hates baths and hates to brush her teeth. Every night is a battle," Marion said, not meeting Ford's eyes.

"I know," he said. He couldn't blame Marion for being who she was. He'd learned that a long time ago. She had a lot of energy for work, but not as much for family. He wasn't convinced that she was able to change that fact about herself.

"And I have no one to help me," she continued.

"What about Nate?"

"It didn't work out. Besides, he doesn't like kids."

"I'm sorry, Marion. I promise I'll get her stuff from Saint Jude this week," Ford said.

"I feel guilty wanting you to take her back." Marion brought the salad bowl over to the table.

"It sounds like you've done great with her."

"I've tried, Ford, I really have."

"I know. Why don't you let me make dinner? Take a little rest—go read a book or something."

"Are you sure?" Marion said, her face brightening.

"Yes, you deserve a break," Ford said, going back to the living room. "Nelly, do you want to help me make dinner?"

Marion disappeared down the hallway to her bedroom, which Ford had never seen.

Nelly bounded into the kitchen and got on the chair that Ford put near the counter. A half hour later, there were croutons on the floor and Nelly was making her own "salad" with bananas and raisins. Ford's pasta sauce was simmering on the stove while the noodles boiled. He felt some of the anxiety of the past week disappear. He vowed to finish getting his apartment ready right away, even if it meant slowing down the café renovations. He and Nelly needed to go home.

CHAPTER 35

Ava walked into Round the Clock and blinked hard. The café looked completely different. The brownish tiles had been ripped out and some black ones were stacked in the corner, waiting to be installed. The mud-colored booths were also gone, so the only seating was the brown vinyl-covered counter stools.

The restaurant didn't look much like Rosie's, but Ava still couldn't help thinking about the café. She thought back to the first time she'd talked to Ford, after the preschool program. That smile. That po'boy. She shouldn't have come to Round the Clock alone. Virginia's chatter would have been a welcome distraction.

In fact, she didn't know why she was at the café at all, except that she was completely stumped by the art fraud story. It didn't help that her regular duties at the newspaper—compiling the dreaded weekly calendar and writing about plays and festivals—kept her so busy that she barely had time to think about who was forging the Southern folk art. Part of her was ready to simply give up and call the FBI, but she'd allowed herself one more visit to the café first. Besides, something told her that the answer was there, though she admitted that she might just want to see Ford again.

She walked through the deserted dining room toward the kitchen. Music and voices speaking in Spanish drifted out through the swinging doors. She pushed them open.

Ford was rolling blue paint onto the walls while two other men laid black-and-white tiles in the corner. He set down the roller and washed his hands in the sink. "Hey, Ava. I'm glad you called."

Ava wanted to embrace him and tell him that she was ready to try again. She missed their long talks on the phone at night and mornings spent lounging on his couch watching TV. Every time she saw him, she wished things had happened differently. But she just said, "It's good to see you. How are your mother and Nelly?"

"Mom is doing okay. The chemo is rough for her, though. Nelly is living with her mom for now, but I'm hoping to move her into the apartment upstairs with me soon. How are your kids?"

"Fine, the usual dramas," Ava said. "I came to ask you if I could see the paintings again."

"Sure. I put them in the empty apartment." He led her out the back door and up a set of outside stairs. He moved slowly, as though weary all the way to his bones.

"How are *you* doing?" she said.

"Tired," he said.

"I can't imagine dealing with everything you're going through right now." Ava was momentarily distracted by the view as they ascended to the third story of the building. The lake was gorgeous and at the same time, looked slightly dangerous. Another Hurricane Katrina could easily wash everything away again. They walked across the balcony, and Ford opened one of the doors. She followed him into the unfurnished apartment, sunlight coming in through the tall windows and illuminating the dust in the air. The paintings were leaning against the wall and she headed toward them, wondering why she thought seeing the art again would tell her anything.

She knelt on the floor and flipped through the paintings. She didn't know what she was looking for. Some clue, anything. "I've almost given up on solving this riddle."

"What have you found out?" Ford asked.

"I haven't had time to do much, but I did talk to Jeb Alvarado. I didn't tell him what I was doing. I pretended I was just interested in the art here at the café. The weird thing is that he seems to know nothing about art. He claims that he doesn't do any buying for the gallery and he doesn't know who does. He bought the paintings as a favor to his friend Dr. Ferguson. He could be lying, but somehow I don't think so," Ava said.

"So, Jetson was lying. But why?"

"Covering up for her dad?" Ava examined a Purvis Young and tried to decide whether it was a fake. "I called Jetson and she gave me a phone number for him, but it didn't work. I really don't want to call his office, but I might have to. Maybe I'll end up scheduling a plastic surgery appointment."

"Why? You're perfect the way you are," Ford said.

Ava felt her face go hot. "You don't think I could use some enhancements?"

"Don't even joke about that." Ford crossed his arms over his chest. "But you can't give up until you talk to him."

"I feel like giving up. Assuming Ferguson did the buying, which seems like the only answer at this point, he's not going to just tell me who the forger is," Ava said.

"If you don't find out who made the forgeries, you still have a story, but it won't be as good. Besides, it might take the FBI longer than you to figure it out. Do you have any other ideas?"

"Not right now. Who lived in this apartment?" Ava said.

"The owner, Kyle. Jetson had the other one."

Ava replaced the paintings and stood up. "Why would she live here when her rich doctor daddy could get her any place she wanted?"

"I don't know. Maybe she had a thing with Kyle. He gave her the bigger apartment," Ford said. "The waitress, Charity, mentioned once that Kyle used to be really into running the café, but then seemed to lose interest. Ms. Betty suggested maybe he became interested in a girl. Could be that the love interest was Jetson."

"I should probably talk to Kyle too. He might know something, even if his dad doesn't."

"I have his number," Ford said. "Come downstairs and I'll give it to you."

Back in the café, they went into the office and Ford got a slip of paper and an envelope from the drawer. "Here's his phone number, and this is for you. Not what I wanted to give you, but the best I could do on short notice."

Ava slipped the envelope and the paper into her purse. Even though he was sweaty and his jeans and T-shirt were smeared with grease, she wanted to pull Ford close, feel his strong arms around her. But she still felt betrayed. She wasn't ready to trust him.

They walked out to her van together.

"I hope I'll see you again," he said. "At least come to the café when it opens and I'll make you a po'boy."

"I don't know, Ford." Ava wanted to say yes, but she remembered his seemingly cavalier response when she'd taken the job in New Orleans and how he'd disappeared for weeks after that. He'd bought the café in Metairie, but hadn't told her. She'd called him because of the paintings. If she hadn't, would he have taken the first step? She didn't know.

After he said good-bye and went back into the restaurant, she opened the envelope. Inside was a restaurant order ticket. Across the front was written: "This receipt good for one breakfast date with Ford Dupree. No expiration date. Call to redeem."

By the next Tuesday, Ava still hadn't called Dr. Ferguson's office. She'd spent Monday taking care of Sadie, who had the stomach flu. When she'd arrived at work the following morning, she'd had to immediately begin on the events calendar, which was due by five o'clock. Every entry she typed in made her more annoyed. She needed to work on the art fraud story. It was her only chance of being freed from the calendar drudgery.

It was almost noon, and she still had half of the events left to enter when Baxter knocked on the door. "Do you want to go get lunch?"

"I guess I have an hour," Ava said. She didn't want to go out to eat with Baxter, but she couldn't think of a good reason to say no. Except that she really wanted to go to lunch with Ford instead. Somehow she needed to forget about him.

"Good, I'll take you to my favorite po'boy shack," Baxter said.

The air freshener attached to the vent in Baxter's Camry blew vanilla-scented air on her as he drove. Stevie's was only a few blocks from the *Gazette* offices, but Ava had never been there. On the way, Baxter talked in his monotone voice about a play he was going to review at a local theater. Ava couldn't concentrate on what he was saying. She couldn't date him; he was nice, but boring. Virginia was right. The spark was missing.

At the restaurant, Baxter ordered an oyster po'boy to

share. Ava rested her head on the back of the booth. She was tired for no reason, stress maybe. Surprisingly, the kids were adjusting well to their new home. Ava was the one having trouble with the move. She missed Rocky, the old house, and most of all, the Friday dates with Ford. Part of her thought she should give him another chance. Maybe he would be more committed this time. After all, the man had moved to Metairie partly to be near her. His broken marriage was evidence that he was a quitter, but as a fellow divorcée, how could she judge?

Baxter placed Ava's sandwich half on a paper plate and began to cut his portion into bite-sized pieces. The meticulousness of the operation irritated her, and she wanted to throw the plate on the floor. It was unfair. He was a perfectly nice person, but she wasn't attracted to him. Ford would have picked up the sandwich in his strong hands and taken a large bite, not caring if some of the lettuce spilled back onto the plate. He liked to jump into things without hesitation, whether it was food, roller skating, or buying a café. She liked that. He'd looked so tired when she'd seen him at the restaurant, stressed and strung out. She wanted to call him, just as a friend, and offer to help with his mom, but she wasn't sure she could say what she wanted to: *I'm sorry about your mother. I miss you and maybe I was wrong.* She was afraid of opening herself up to hurt again. It was easier to pretend he didn't exist, even though she had his breakfast date coupon in the top drawer of her desk.

"You're not eating. This is an incredible sandwich, you should try it," Baxter said.

Ava took a bite, but she couldn't really taste anything. Her stomach clenched.

Baxter forked up another piece of his dissected po'boy. "It seems like you haven't been around the office much lately. Are you working on a big story or something?"

Ava couldn't answer. All of a sudden, she knew what was happening. She'd caught Sadie's stomach bug. Within an hour, she'd be alternating between the bathroom and the bed. "Baxter, can you please drive me home? I don't feel well."

The hurt in Baxter's eyes was obvious, but there was nothing Ava could do about it. All of her energy was focused on getting into his car without vomiting.

CHAPTER 36

Ford wanted to get to Saint Jude and pick up the rest of his and Nelly's things. Even though he still had a lot to do to get the café ready, he needed his daughter back during the week-days. After spending the morning helping his workers lay tile in the dining room, he climbed in the truck and turned up the music loud, the way Nelly liked it. On the way to the highway, he passed by the *Gazette* office. Before he could talk himself out of it, he made an illegal U-turn and circled back to the lot.

Ava's van was parked near the side door. Ford pulled up next to it and killed the engine. He hesitated. Maybe he should just call her. What if she was busy or on a deadline? No, he'd promised himself to stop making excuses and take charge of his life. He got out of the truck.

He pulled open the glass door and walked into the lobby. Offices made him itchy. They were always too cold and he hated the smell of mildew and cheap carpet. The reception-ist's desk was empty, so he walked down the hall. The first office he passed had a nameplate that said "Baxter Hebert."

"Can I help you?" Baxter rose from behind his desk and came to the door. He was shorter than Ford by nearly a foot and his khaki trousers were wrinkled.

"I'm looking for Ava," Ford said.

"She had to go home. She didn't feel well. It was so weird. I was at lunch with her and she took one bite of her sandwich and asked me to drive her home."

"Is she okay?"

Baxter fiddled with his tie. "I don't know. She wouldn't let me come in."

"Give me her address."

"Who are you?"

"Ford Dupree. Our daughters are friends." Ford thought that sounded innocent enough. It must have worked, because Baxter wrote down the address without another word.

Ava's little bungalow was newly painted, but the lawn needed mowing, just like her yard had in Saint Jude. Gardening was apparently not her forte. Ford rang the doorbell and waited. Nothing. He opened the door and went inside. "Ava? It's Ford."

"Ford? What are you doing here?"

He followed the voice to the bedroom. Ava was in bed with the blankets pulled up to her chin.

"I was worried about you. I went to the office to look for you and Baxter said you were sick. Why'd he just leave you alone?" he said.

"Because I told him to. I didn't want him watching me barf. I don't particularly want you watching either." Ava shifted under the blankets as though she was going to stand up and then fell back against the pillows.

"Get used to it. I'm not going anywhere. Write me a note so I can pick up your kids from school. Unless they take the bus."

"They don't because it's a magnet school across town and they'd have to transfer buses," Ava said.

Ford went to the kitchen and found a reporter's notebook and a pen. He handed them to her.

"I guess I'm not in any shape to get them. Thanks." She wrote on the pad. "Take the carpool number from the fridge. As long as you have that on your dashboard, they'll let you pick them up. I'll have to call Sadie's day care and tell them you're getting her. Why are you doing this for me?"

Because I love you. But he couldn't say that, not yet. "Because that's what friends do."

Ava sank back under the covers. "I appreciate it."

CHAPTER 37

Through her haze of sickness, Ava tried to process what was happening. Ford was in her house. Why, she wasn't sure. He'd said something about being her friend and picking up the kids. Good thing too, because if she stood up, she'd probably vomit some more. She drifted off to sleep again.

She woke up later feeling sweaty and thirsty, but otherwise relatively normal. She took a long, hot shower and changed into clean jeans and a T-shirt. Only after she was completely dressed did she remember to look at the clock. It was ten in the evening.

Ford was loading the dishwasher. He'd obviously cooked dinner, and from the spicy, tomato-y aroma, she guessed spaghetti. Her stomach grumbled. She sat down at the table. "Is there any of that left?"

When he turned around, she couldn't help smiling. He was wearing one of her flower-patterned aprons and he held a dripping plate in his hand. He put the plate in the dishwasher. "Nope, the kids ate it all. But I can make you something if you want to eat. Grilled cheese? Eggs?"

"A grilled cheese sounds good. I hate to cause you any

trouble, though. You've done so much already," Ava said. "Um, what *did* you do?"

"Let's see. I picked up Sadie and the boys at their schools. James and Luke did their homework and helped me make dinner. Sadie had a tea party with her stuffed animals and the boys watched TV. Then I put them to bed."

"God, you might get the stomach flu. I'm so sorry."

Ford spread butter on a piece of bread. "I might. But it was worth it."

"Why are you here?" Ava hated how the question sounded, like she was trying to imply that he had an ulterior motive. Like she didn't trust him.

"I figured you needed help." He shrugged. "Baxter just left you here, and I knew someone had to take care of your kids."

"I haven't been exactly encouraging you to be my friend. I'm sorry."

The butter sizzled as Ford laid the bread in the pan. He sliced two perfect pieces of cheese with Ava's chef's knife and placed them on the sandwich. "You were right. I gave up too quick. You already had an ex-husband who took off, plus you have the kids to think about. You can't be with someone who is going to abandon them. I have to prove to you that I won't." Ford turned the sandwich and spread the other side with butter. "If it's okay with you, I'm planning to drive your kids to school tomorrow and then come back here to make you the best breakfast you've ever had."

"More than okay." Ava's resolve to resist him was fading fast. How could she let go of a man who risked getting the stomach flu to take care of her children? Especially since she wanted to touch him so badly that her fingers ached. She took a bite of the sandwich, savoring the creamy cheese and toasty bread. She was slowly progressing with her cooking skills, but her grilled cheeses often had soggy bread and an unmelted square of cold cheddar in the center. "How's the café renovation going?" she asked.

Ford hung up the apron and sat down across the table from her. "It's almost done. The tile is installed, walls are painted. I'm hiring a crew to clean up the dust and then I'll be ready to train the new workers. I have three cooks and some waiters lined up. It's going to be a completely different menu from Rosie's. I want to take the classics and update them—the shrimp po'boy I made for you, a pan-fried trout almondine with a creamy, spicy sauce, blackened redfish with a Caribbean twist, that kind of thing."

"What are you going to call it?"

"I don't know yet. Not Rosie's Café II, that's for sure. This is going to be a different kind of restaurant. Liquor license and everything."

Ava had been eating the sandwich one small bite at a time, just to make sure her stomach didn't rebel. But it felt fine and she felt more than fine. She finished the last bite and stood up.

"What's wrong?" he said.

"I really want to hug you, but I'm afraid I'll make you sick."

"I'm willing to take that chance." Ford got up and wrapped his arms around her.

CHAPTER 38

Ford and Bobby Joe loaded everything from Ford's Saint Jude apartment into their pickups and a rented trailer. They caravanned to Metairie and parked side by side behind the café. Ford didn't relish spending a day hauling furniture and boxes, but it was a relief to finally be moving the rest of the furniture in and making the place his own.

He got out of his truck and opened the back of the trailer. Moving seemed to multiply the number of his possessions, and even though he'd gotten rid of as much as he could, it still seemed like too much.

Bobby Joe came up beside him, and they both surveyed the load.

"I guess we ought to do the trailer first, since we'll probably have to unhook it to get everything out of your truck," Bobby Joe said.

"Big stuff first. How about the couch?" Ford said.

"As good a place to start as any."

They wrestled the couch up the outside stairs and set it down on the balcony, both of them breathing hard. Ford took his time propping open the apartment door to give them both a break. They picked up the sofa again, rotated it, and maneuvered it through the door.

"What's that red stuff in the corner? No one died in here, I hope," Bobby Joe said.

"Nah, just paint. Let's put the sofa right on top of it." Ford was surprised that the cleaners hadn't removed the spot. They'd done a great job on everything else. He followed his brother back down the stairs.

"Are you back with Ava now?" Bobby Joe asked over his shoulder. "Taking care of her kids while she was sick should have put you in her good graces."

"She felt better yesterday. We had a nice time eating the breakfast I made and watching movies while the kids were at school. She even offered to babysit Nelly some weekend afternoons so I can work," Ford said. A "nice time" was understating it. The day had reminded him of what he loved about Ava—the way they could talk for hours or just sit together and laugh at a movie. It had been even better than their old Friday dates.

"She's a good one, Ford. Don't mess it up again," Bobby Joe said.

"I'm cooking lunch for her tomorrow. I'll try not to poison her. How are things with Jeanie?"

"You know, the two cooks I had to hire when you left are actually making things easier. I'm mostly just doing the business stuff now, and I can take care of some things from home. We're going on dates once a week. Seems to be helping," Bobby Joe said.

"I still find it amusing that you had to hire *two* people to replace me," Ford said.

Bobby Joe rolled his eyes. "You're irreplaceable for sure."

"Let's get Nelly's bed next." Ford grabbed the edge of the mattress and yanked it out of the trailer.

"Once we get you moved in, I want you to show me

everything you've done for the restaurant. I have to make sure you aren't screwing this up," Bobby Joe said.

"Sure, boss man," Ford said, picking up his end of the mattress. His brother never changed. Good thing Saint Jude was eighty miles away.

Ford woke up surrounded by boxes. Morning sunlight shone in from the window, making an elongated rectangle on the cluttered bedroom floor. The list of things he had to do was daunting, but making Ava's lunch was top priority. He found the coffee machine and beans in one of the boxes marked "*kitchen*" and unpacked while it brewed. As soon as the coffee was ready, he drank it down and headed to the grocery store.

An hour later, he was back in the apartment kitchen with the ingredients for his shrimp macaroni and cheese. He wanted to try out what he hoped would be one of the restaurant's signature dishes. His brother would not approve of the mac and cheese he was making. "*Why you gotta use those fancy cheeses? What's wrong with American?*" he'd say. Still, Ford was sure that he'd like it if he tried it. The mac and cheese was really a simple dish—even Nelly would eat it, as long as he left out the shrimp.

He was just taking it out of the oven when he heard the knock. He washed his hands and opened the door. "I hope you're hungry."

Ava shrugged out of her short fake-fur coat and hung it on the hook on the wall. "Of course. You know I never eat breakfast unless you make it for me."

"You're feeling well enough to eat mac and cheese, right?" Ford kissed her lightly on the lips and went back to the counter, feeling like he was floating rather than walking. He tossed the homemade dressing in his mixed green salad.

"Oh, sure. It's been over two days. I'm totally fine now,"

Ava said, sitting at the kitchen table. "I left a message at Dr. Ferguson's office, but I haven't heard anything yet."

"I hope you didn't make an appointment." Ford got out two wide-rimmed white plates.

"I'm not that desperate yet. I keep thinking that this thing has to be simpler. The forger should be local. Someone Dr. Ferguson knows."

"Why?" Ford asked absently, tasting the mac and cheese. He loved the combination of mild and sharp cheddar, Gouda, and a tiny bit of feta. He'd put in just a hint of Cajun seasoning to complement the seafood and some sautéed onions. He wanted to make it with crawfish, but not until they were in season. That would be his spring special.

"I don't know. A hunch, I guess. I feel like the answer is right under my nose and I'm not seeing it." Ava pounded the table with her fist and the wineglasses Ford had put there jumped.

"Hmm." Ford arranged the mac and cheese and salad on the plates. At Rosie's, presentation wasn't very important. Customers wanted the food to taste good, but they didn't expect beauty. If he wanted the new place to be more upscale, though, he was going to have to start thinking about plating. He wasn't going to make polka dots with a squeeze bottle or smear sauce on the rim like some fancy chef, though. He wiped the edges of the plates. Smearing the sauce reminded him of something. What was it?

"It doesn't matter. I don't want to think about the art fraud anymore. It's time to call it quits and let the FBI do its thing," Ava said. "That smells incredible."

"I'm thinking of putting it on the menu, but I want your opinion first," Ford said. "Do you think it's too cold to eat outside?"

"I'm from Wisconsin, remember? We wore shorts if it was above fifty degrees."

"Well, I'm putting on a jacket." Ford got his quilted flannel from the hook next to her furry coat and opened the door. He loved the balcony. It was so much better than the tiny one outside the old apartment where he and Nelly used to eat their ice cream. She was going to love the new place, he was sure. He'd furnished the balcony with two black wrought-iron chairs and a table, but he was ready to buy more chairs if he could convince Ava and her kids to have dinner with them. In fact, he'd almost gone ahead and bought the extras, but superstition had stopped him. He carried the plates out and set them on the table while Ava followed with the wineglasses and flatware. She'd put on her coat too, but she hadn't buttoned it over her black wrap dress.

"This is nice," she said, settling into her chair. "Have you brought Nelly here yet?"

"No, I just got the furniture moved in. Before, I only had my bed and a few clothes. I was so focused on getting the café ready that I put it off. But last time I saw her, it hit me just how much I miss her. Sometimes I feel like every day I don't see her, I'm letting time slip away. She's growing up so fast, and I don't want to miss a moment." Ford examined the plate critically before taking a bite. He could do upscale cuisine. He was going to make this work.

"I know how you feel. I love having a full-time job, but letting the kids go to aftercare and stay at school until five o'clock is hard. I'm so used to picking them up at three thirty and having a long afternoon with them. Now everything feels so rushed. They don't seem to mind, though. We just make sure to relax and do fun things they like on the weekends." Ava tasted the mac and cheese. "This is amazing. Wow. I don't even really like mac and cheese normally."

Ford savored some of the rich, subtly spicy dish. Ava's endorsement sealed it—the mac and cheese was going on the menu. "Thanks. I'm happy you like it."

"'Like' doesn't even begin to describe it." She picked up her wineglass and gazed out over the lake.

Ford hadn't had much time to enjoy the view, but now he watched a bird circle over the still water. It was calming. "Part of the reason I wanted to ask you to try it is because . . . well, I also wanted to ask you what you thought of my idea for a name for the new restaurant."

Ava looked back at him. Her eyes were as green as emeralds, and her beauty almost made him forget what he wanted to ask.

"I want to call it Ava's Place. With your permission, of course."

"Ford, that's . . . wow, I don't know what to say," she said.

"I'm hoping you'll say yes. But if you don't, I understand." Ford picked up his wineglass but didn't drink any.

"Yes. I love it," Ava said. "But you don't expect me to wash dishes or cook, do you? You know I'm no good at that stuff."

"No, but I do need an official food tester." Ford sipped his wine.

"That I can handle. I know it's going to be a lot of work, but I think this is going to be a great restaurant."

"I'm going to try, that's for sure. If it doesn't work out, I don't really have a backup plan. I don't want to move back to Saint Jude."

"I don't want you to either." Ava looked out toward the water again. "I'd want to go with you and I'm starting to feel comfortable with my job here. I just have to figure out what's going on with this art fraud, so the editor will start to take me seriously. But so many things about this forgery bother me. For example, I don't understand why the forger used oils on all the paintings when some of the artists are known for working with house paint," Ava said.

Paint. The smeared sauce had reminded him of paint.

Ford glanced at the red wine in his glass. The red smear of paint in the apartment that wouldn't come off—was it oil? He couldn't tell, but Ava might be able to. "I think I have a clue for you," he said.

"You do? What is it?"

"I'll show you." Ford stood up. He didn't want to interrupt their lunch, but he realized how important the investigation was to Ava.

They went back inside the apartment. He had to move some boxes away before he could shift the couch. Ava helped him without saying anything. A few minutes later, he shoved the end of the sofa until the paint stain was visible. "I think this is oil."

Ava knelt down and scratched at the paint. She brought her fingernail up close to her eye and then sniffed it. "Looks like oil, smells like oil. And it definitely looks like a color that was used on some of the Mose T paintings. But what does it mean?"

Ford shrugged, but she wasn't asking him for an answer; she was staring at the stain, thinking.

"Maybe the forger worked here. Which would mean it was . . ." Ava trailed off.

"Jetson," Ford said.

Ava slapped her forehead and stood up. "Why didn't I see that before? Geez, she was an art student! She acted so innocent. I thought she was too young and incompetent to pull it off. She did it, and her dad probably didn't even know!" She hugged Ford. "Finally, we have the answer!"

Ford squeezed her tightly, not ever wanting to let go. She kissed him and he decided that he didn't care at all if the rest of his mac and cheese got cold.

CHAPTER 39

Ava and Virginia laid out all the documentation on the floor of Ava's office. During the four days since Ford had showed Ava the paint stain, she'd stepped up her efforts to collect evidence. She'd gathered testimonies from three artists saying that the works from the café were not painted by them, documents confirming the identity of the gallery owner, and the receipts for the sales of the paintings. They also had the pictures Virginia had taken at the gallery and some photos of the outside of the building. All they needed was an arrest from the FBI. Ava knew she couldn't interview Jetson or her father before bringing in the Feds. If she found out she was going to be arrested, the girl might flee or destroy evidence.

"Are we ready to do this?" Virginia asked.

"It's time. I think we have as much information as we're going to get." Ava sat down in her office chair and dialed the number from her computer screen. "Yes, I want to report a case of art fraud. Can you meet us at the Fergie Gallery in the Warehouse District?"

Five minutes later, Ava was holding her breath as Virginia drove, or rather, raced, down the brick streets, startling pigeons and tourists. "Aren't you worried you're going to get stopped for speeding?" she asked the photographer.

"You're the one who said the sooner we get there, the more time we have to talk to Jetson before the FBI comes and spoils the party." Virginia jerked the car to a stop in front of the gallery. "I told you, the cops are too worried about protecting drunken tourists from pickpockets to bother with a girl on a mission. And look, no FBI."

Ava took out her pocket recorder and then returned it to her purse. It was going to be hard enough to get Jetson to talk. She didn't want to scare the girl off by asking permission to record her. She'd just have to take notes quickly.

They went inside and found Jetson behind the desk, reading an art magazine. Virginia pointed her camera at her and shot a few pictures. Ava gave Virginia a look and she started taking photos of the paintings instead.

"You all sure are taking a long time to decide which paintings to buy," Jetson said. "In fact, I have a feeling you don't want to buy anything at all."

"No, I'm not in the market for forged paintings. Where did they come from?" Ava asked, putting the thick folder of evidence on the desk and getting out her notebook.

Jetson glanced at the folder and nodded as if she knew what it contained. "I made them. All of them," she blurted out. "I'm sure you figured that out already or you wouldn't be here. I had a studio in the apartment above Round the Clock. Kyle was so infatuated with me that he let me stay there for free."

"But then he decided to sell the café." Ava talked and wrote at the same time, trying to get down every word Jetson was saying.

"He was scared. He thought someone was going to figure out that the paintings were fakes. He asked me to stop and I said no, so he took the easy way out. The jerk didn't even tell me he was putting the café up for sale. Only reason I found out was that I was there one day when he was talking to the old blond real estate chick."

"Why did you use oils? You must know that Mose T and some of the other artists you forged never did," Ava said.

"Because house paint sucks. It's hard to work with, it dries fast, and it looks like crap. Anyway, I'm not some starving artist painting on whatever old board I can find. I have plenty of money to buy supplies." Jetson pulled her top lip back in an unattractive sneer. "I didn't think that bonehead Jeb would know the difference anyway—or the idiot tourists who wander into the shop."

"Didn't you ever think about the artists you were ripping off?"

"Not really. Most of them are dead, anyway."

Ava refrained from rolling her eyes. "Not Rosalind Palmer. She's living in a shack in the Ninth Ward. You were basically taking food out of her mouth, and her paintings don't even sell for that much."

"It wasn't about the money. Can't you see that? I had to prove I was a real artist. No one took me seriously," Jetson said.

"So you decided to prove yourself by copying other people's work. Nice. What about your dad? You basically told me he did it. Did you want to send him to prison?"

"No, of course not." For the first time, the veil slipped and Jetson looked like what she was—a frightened twenty-something kid. "He won't really get locked up, will he?"

"Not if you're honest and say he knew nothing about it," Ava said.

"He didn't have a clue! I swear!" Jetson turned at the sound of a car pulling up.

"Did Jeb know about this?"

"No, just me and Kyle. His dad didn't know. I really didn't think it was that bad. All I did was make a few paintings."

"Forgery is a big deal," Ava said, putting away her notebook.

"I guess." Jetson glanced out the window. Two men in black jackets got out of the car and read the sign over the building.

Ava put her business card on the desk. "Call or e-mail if you want to tell me anything else. Good luck."

"My dad has a good lawyer. I'll be fine," Jetson said, but she still bit her lip as she looked toward the door.

By Friday, Ava and Virginia were ready to turn in the story. Cutter wanted it on the front page of the Sunday paper. Ava read through the article one more time, checking for errors, and then sent the editor an e-mail. It was done. She tapped the Saints bobblehead doll on her desk, and it nodded like a sugar-crazed child. It had been a gift from Cutter. He'd given them to all the Saint Jude transplants as a welcome. She would have preferred a box of pralines or, better yet, some of Ford's truffles. She gave the bobblehead another push and it fell off the desk.

Chapter 40

Ford wasn't sure that his mother was really up to seeing the restaurant, but she insisted. He showed her the nearly finished dining room and kitchen and then helped her up the stairs to his apartment with Nelly following along impatiently.

His mother stopped at the top of the stairs and he guided her to one of the outside chairs. "Lovely view," she said, sounding just a little out of breath.

"It's the lake, Maw-Maw," Nelly said. "I wanna see inside."

Ford's mom stood up slowly and walked the few steps to the apartment door. "Who lives in the other one?" she asked.

"I'm just using it for storage right now," Ford said.

"You could knock down the wall in between and have one big space," she said. "In case your Ava wants to move in with her kids."

Ford had to admit the possibility had occurred to him. But he couldn't seriously think about that yet. "I guess," he said and held the door for his mother and Nelly to enter.

He was happy with how the place had turned out. There

were three small bedrooms, one for him, one for Nelly, and a third that was a playroom for the moment. He'd arranged the living room the same way as his Saint Jude apartment to help Nelly feel at home. His mother sat on one of the armchairs. "Very nice," she said.

"Where's my room?" Nelly asked.

"Down the hall," he said, following her tiny footsteps.

Ford had painted the walls of Nelly's room her new favorite color, lavender, and placed a new stuffed pony on the bed. She climbed on top of her princess comforter and hugged the pony. "I happy to be home," she said.

Ford sat down and put his arms around her. "Me too. I missed you, sweetheart."

Nelly wriggled out of his grasp, jumped off the bed, and began to rearrange her play kitchen.

"I'm going back to the living room," he told her. "I have to get lunch ready. Sadie and her family are coming over."

"Okay," Nelly said.

Ford went back to the kitchen/living room area. His mother was still on the chair, looking out the window. "How are you doing?" he said.

"I feel pretty well today," she answered. "I'm proud of you, son. You did all this by yourself."

"I haven't actually opened the restaurant yet." Ford checked on the mac and cheese baking in the oven. He'd made two pans this time—one with shrimp and one without. He was also roasting a chicken, mostly for his mother, since the chemo sometimes made it hard for her to eat rich food. When he heard the knock on the door, he turned to get it, but his mother was already up.

She let in Ava and her children. The kids didn't hesitate, but immediately rushed into the living room.

"Where's Nelly?" Sadie asked.

Nelly ran out of the bedroom and embraced her friend

while James and Luke began unpacking the toys and games they'd brought.

"Mr. Ford, will you play a game with me?" James said.

"I want to play too," Luke said.

"Sure, set it up," Ford said. He went into the living room. "Mom, this is Ava."

His mother had already sat back down, but she smiled up at Ava. "I'm pleased to meet you. I'd like to say I've heard a lot about you, but my son is not too good at telling me what's going on in his life."

"I've told you about Ava, Mom," Ford said, going back to the kitchen and getting some glasses out of the cabinet.

"Not enough. Sit down and tell me all about yourself," Ford's mother said to Ava.

Ava sat on the armchair next to her. "I'm a reporter for the *Gazette*," she said.

"Yes, I know, dear, I've been reading your stories."

Ford brought the drinks to the table, where James was setting up a board game. Sadie and Nelly had gone to her room and he could hear them talking excitedly. Ford found himself looking at the wall that separated the two apartments. Would Ava and her kids want to live above a restaurant? Would James like helping him in the kitchen? Ava had mentioned once that he seemed interested in cooking. Ford knew he shouldn't, but he allowed himself to fantasize about having the large family he'd always wanted, and a woman he loved more than he'd ever imagined possible. After their lunch together, they'd agreed to resume their dates, on Saturday nights now instead of Friday afternoons. He couldn't wait for the first one, which would take place that very night. They were going to choose one of the famous New Orleans restaurants that he'd never eaten at before. It was going to be a difficult decision.

"Mr. Ford! Let's play!" James said.

"You'll have to teach me," Ford said, taking a place at the table.

"I will," James said.

As James explained the rules, Ford managed to figure out what was going on enough to get through a game. Half of his attention was on Ava and his mother talking, and Nelly and Sadie running into the living room with armfuls of plastic toys. Now the apartment really felt like home.

Chapter 41

Cutter had the *New Orleans Gazette* spread out on his desk when Ava and Virginia walked in on Monday morning.

"I can't stop looking at this article. I mean, I edited it so I've already read it three times, but I can't believe what y'all did here. This is the kind of award-winning journalism we need to get ourselves established in this city. I'm submitting it to the Louisiana Newspaper Association Awards for sure," he said.

"Thanks. We sort of lucked into it," Ava said.

"No luck about it, sister. We worked hard on this, especially you. Don't sell us short," Virginia said.

"I love the part about the father. He's just trying to help out his daughter and she screws things up royally. And the pictures. I'm not going to ask how you got photos of all the receipts and paintings," Cutter said.

"Nothing illegal. We had permission from the café owner and Jetson. Of course, she didn't know that we were going to turn her in to the Feds," Ava said.

"I don't want to know. But I want you two in Metro. We are expanding our New Orleans coverage. If we're going to compete in this city, we have to have reporters on the ground. I want both of you off Entertainment and on news. We can find someone else to compile calendars and write advance stories about plays. What do you say?"

"I'm a photographer. I shoot whatever," Virginia said.

"Yeah, but you should have priority on big stories like this—especially with Ava."

"How about a raise too?" Ava said.

Cutter steepled his fingers. "I'll see what I can do."

Ava felt a little flutter of hope. Finally, no more calendar duty, no more second-class citizenship. All her hard work was paying off at last.

As they left the office, Virginia put her arm around Ava's shoulder. "I like the idea of us as a team," she said.

"Me too," Ava said. "I think we're finally going to get some respect. Maybe some more money too."

Baxter came out of his office. "Y'all's story is off the charts. It's being bounced all over the Internet. People are linking to it, commenting on it."

"We're famous," Virginia said.

"Not y'all, so much, but Jetson."

"Poor kid," Ava said.

"The poor rich girl will land on her feet, don't you worry," Virginia said.

"What makes you say that?" Baxter asked, shoving his hands in his pockets.

"The thing she did was stupid, but it took some brains."

"That makes no sense, but I know exactly what you mean," Ava said.

She excused herself, went into her office, and shut the door. The work didn't stop. For the moment, she still had to compile the calendars and Cutter wanted a follow-up to the art fraud story. She'd start with Palmer. The artist would certainly be willing to discuss the effects of the crime on her sales. The desk phone rang.

"I'm moving to the frozen North. Any advice?" Rocky said by way of greeting.

"Buy a coat and some long underwear. Are you getting into the ski resort business?" Though they corresponded sometimes by e-mail, Ava hadn't talked to her former boss since moving to New Orleans. Calling him was one of the many things that always got shoved to the bottom of her to-do list.

"Nope, got a job at the *Cold Falls Times* in Cold Falls, Minnesota. It has a new owner, and they actually want an old fart to help with the restructuring. They're making me managing editor. It's a small paper in a small town, but, you know, I kind of always wanted to live in the sticks."

"Unbelievable. Good for you," Ava said.

"It's not official yet, but Judith will probably get canned. Her first stab at putting out *Bon Temps* and *Sunday Features* was so bad that they had to call me upstairs to fix it. She had badly edited stories, inconsistent fonts, you name it. Her next couple of weeks weren't much better. I think she's given up. Mann tried to get me to come back, but I said, 'Sorry, Charlie.'"

"I hope you like your new job. I know you'll kick butt up in the Land of Ten Thousand Lakes," Ava said.

"Saw your story. You should get a raise for that," Rocky said.

"I might. Virginia and I just talked to Cutter."

"How are things in the Big Easy?"

Ava tapped a pen against her notebook. "Good. It sounds crazy, Rocky, but I actually feel like I belong here. Even though Cutter says that Yankees can never really be Southerners, it feels right."

"Are you still dating that café owner?"

"Yeah. He bought a café in Metairie and he says he wants to name it after me."

"I told you he was a good one," Rocky said. "I'm really happy for you."

"I guess I should thank Judith for pushing me out of Saint Jude."

"I wouldn't go that far. I'd better get off the phone. I have Mike's five hundred toy cars to pack," Rocky said.

"Good luck. Get yourself an ice scraper and a pair of warm boots."

"Will do."

$\mathcal{C}$HAPTER 42

On Thanksgiving Day, Ford and his brother cooked together again. It had been their mother's idea to hold the feast at the restaurant, a little test run before the grand opening, which would be the week before Christmas. Ford still wasn't used to cooking in the new kitchen. He kept turning to the right when he wanted to put something on the grill instead of to the left, and the sandwich board seemed too far away.

"I hope that oyster dressing is almost done. This fried turkey isn't going to stay crispy forever," Bobby Joe said.

"Yeah, yeah." Ford opened the oven and took out the hotel pan of dressing. For some reason, Bobby Joe had decided to buy himself a turkey fryer kit, maybe because he worried that their mother's days of hosting Thanksgiving were over. Or perhaps he just wanted a new toy to play with. In any case, he'd set up the huge pot and propane-fueled burner outside, which had left Ford alone in the kitchen for most of the feast preparations. He didn't mind that too much. Though it was nice to have Bobby Joe around, he didn't need his brother micromanaging his cooking.

Bobby Joe had made the pies, sweet potato and pecan,

earlier in the day—as well as the cranberry sauce. Ford was responsible for the side dishes, which had always been his favorite part of the meal anyway. He'd made the oyster dressing, dirty rice, sweet potatoes with pecans, and his own homemade version of green bean casserole.

"Looks good," Bobby Joe said, leaning over the pan of dressing. "Have you ever made this before?"

"No," Ford said. Thanksgiving had always been their mother's holiday, even though she didn't cook. Ford had never usurped her place as host before, since Thanksgiving food didn't appeal to him much anyway. But cooking it had been surprisingly fun, maybe because all of his favorite people were in the dining room of his new restaurant, waiting to eat it.

Bobby Joe dipped a spoon into the pan and tasted. "God, big brother. You really can cook."

"Thanks," Ford said. "Let's get this show on the road."

"Roger that." Bobby Joe went outside to get his turkey, while Ford transferred his food into serving bowls borrowed from their mother's house.

He took the dressing and green beans out to the dining room first. Ava, Virginia, Bernice, his mother, Nelly, Pete, and Jeanie all sat together at one of the big tables. Ford thought his mother looked too thin. The chemotherapy made her already small appetite alarmingly tiny, but she was upbeat most of the time. She'd bought a blond wig that was even puffier than her real hair had been, and she still wore her usual brightly colored sweaters and slacks. Aunt Bernice was, as always, more subdued with her gray curls and brown top. Nelly held their attention, probably entertaining them with one of her incoherent stories about school. Pete was also listening, his philosophy books put away for once. Bobby Joe had driven him down for the meal when he'd found out he had no one to spend the holiday with.

Virginia, whom he'd also invited because she had no family in town, stopped talking to Ava when he came in.

"Let me come help you carry the food out," Ava said.

"No, you all sit and visit. Bobby Joe and I have this covered. We run restaurants. We ought to be able to handle Thanksgiving," Ford said.

"That boy just can't stand to sit still," Virginia said.

"He never could," Ford's mother said. "Ava, dear, my granddaughter has been bending my ear this whole time. I'm so sorry we haven't had a chance to talk more."

"That's okay," Ava said. "Virginia and I have been rude, chatting about work. How are you feeling?"

Ford excused himself and went back to the kitchen for the rest of the food, passing Bobby Joe, who was carrying a huge golden-brown turkey.

"Do you really have to lug that thing to the table, or are you just showing off?" Ford asked.

"Hey, it's my first Thanksgiving turkey. Of course I'm going to show it off," Bobby Joe said, placing the bird at the head of the table.

Ford shook his head and went to get the rest of his side dishes. He really didn't mind his brother stealing the glory. He had everything he wanted.

$\mathscr{C}$HAPTER 43

Ava gathered up the children's discarded backpacks and shoes from the front hallway. The afternoon was unusually quiet. Sadie was playing with ponies on the floor while James and Luke sat at the kitchen table doing homework. Ava lined up the shoes and began to sweep the floor. After a lot of hard work, she had her place, the sense of identity she'd been craving. Moving away from the house she'd lived in with Jared had made her feel like she was finally making a life for herself apart from him. It didn't hurt that Cutter had given her a small raise and she no longer felt dependent on the child support. Now Jared's money could be used for music lessons and educational summer camps for the children rather than necessities like school clothes. Though the new job wasn't just about the money. It was also about getting her sense of self-worth back. Everything was coming together, including her relationship with Ford.

There was a knock at the door, and the boys stopped writing on their worksheets.

"Who there?" Sadie called.

Ava looked through the peephole before opening the door to Ford and Nelly.

"Sorry to drop by unannounced, but I had to figure out something to do with this darn thing," he said, gesturing to the huge fir draped across the front steps.

"Big tree!" Nelly said.

"Nelly!" Sadie ran past Ava and hugged her friend. The two girls giggled and embraced like long-lost sisters.

Ford grinned. "I brought pizza too. Just in case y'all haven't had dinner yet."

"Pizza!" Luke dropped his pencil and ran to the door.

"You can help me carry it." Ford left the tree and went back to the truck with Luke. James ran after them.

Together, the boys and Ford unloaded two pizza boxes and a tree stand. "Luke and James, you take the pizza to the table. I'm going to talk to your mom for a minute," Ford said. He took Ava's hand, led her outside, and shut the door.

The tree was still draped across the front porch. Ava looked at it and then at Ford. They'd been dating again for over a month and she felt as comfortable with him as she had before the move to New Orleans. Maybe more. Still, she was nervous about what he wanted to tell her.

Ford reached into the pocket of his jeans and took out a ring box. "My mom gave me this ring when she got her diagnosis. She hadn't even met you yet, and she wanted me to give it to you. Somehow she knew we were right for each other."

Ava took the box. She held it for a moment before raising the lid.

"I want to marry you. If you'll have me," he said.

Ava tried to find any lingering doubts in her mind. Was she worried he'd find an excuse to end their relationship again? No, she wasn't. He'd proved his commitment to her in everything he'd said and done, supporting her work, getting to know her kids, cooking meals for them, taking her out every chance he could, and listening to all her complaints, hopes, and dreams. She couldn't ask for anything more. "Yes," she said. She took out the antique diamond ring and put it on her finger. It was exactly the right size.

"It looks perfect on you," Ford said.

Ava hugged him. "It is perfect. This is perfect."

"I wasn't really worried you'd say no. Well, maybe a little bit."

"I did have to think about it for almost half a second." Ava pulled away. "Let's get this tree inside and tell the kids."

James opened the door and looked out at them. "Um, can we bring the tree in now?"

"Sure, kiddo. I just asked your mom to marry me and she said yes," Ford said.

"Really? That's great." James turned and ran back into the house. "Hey, y'all, Mom and Ford are getting married!"

"I guess he's happy."

"He likes you," Ava said. "In case you can't tell."

"I like him too. Please, help me with this tree, my lovely fiancée," Ford said, reaching down into the branches.

Once they'd set up the tree, Ava got the box of Christmas ornaments from the closet. Watching the kids put up all the paper gingerbread men, clothespin tin soldiers, and salt dough Santa Clauses they'd made over the years, she felt that sense of belonging even stronger than before. She and the children had always been a family, but Ford and Nelly made it seem complete. It felt so good to have another adult by her side to share her life with—someone who would watch the children grow up with her and experience all the moments, good and bad.

For the first time since her childhood, she was excited, rather than just stressed out, about Christmas. She and

Ford together would do the holiday right. They would bake cookies, make crafts with the kids, watch movies, and pick out presents together. She touched the ring on her finger.

She couldn't wait for it all to begin.

ACKNOWLEDGMENTS

First, I need to thank my readers. If you didn't buy, read, pass on, and review my books, there would be no more books, at least in published form. So, I love you all.

Second, thanks to my reporter and editor friends, John Wirt, James Minton, Greg Langley, Vicki Ferstel, Greg Garland, Sandy Davis, Laura Maggi, Judy Bergeron, Charles Lussier, Gene Mearns, Sam Irwin, and any others I forgot, because of my own sieve-like brain. In different ways, all of you have been immensely helpful with my writing, and I couldn't have done it without you.

I also have to once again acknowledge all my help from the publishing world: my agent, Steven Chudney, and Kensington editor Martin Biro, along with all the staff whose hard work made this book.

Last, and most importantly, thanks to my family, and especially Jon. He reads every draft and picks me up when I think I'm just done. Without him, there would be no books.

If you enjoyed *Ava's Place*, be sure not to miss
Emily Beck Cogburn's

LOUISIANA SAVES THE LIBRARY

For Louisiana Richardson, desperate times call for crazy-like-a-fox measures. As the new librarian at Alligator Bayou Parish's struggling library, she's returning to her Southern roots and facing trouble hotter than fresh cornbread out of the oven. Somehow, she's got to draw readers back in and prove the library is still vital—even as domineering parish board head Mrs. Gunderson plans to shut it down for good. If that means Louise has to resort to some unconventional methods—like outrageous inter-library Zumba classes, and forming a book club that's anything but Oprah-approved—well, it wouldn't be the first time she went out on a limb. . . .
Soon Louise is doing everything she can to rally the whole community. Before she knows it, she's sparking welcome changes—and uncovering surprising secrets—throughout her new town. And between glasses of sweet tea, bowls of mouth-watering gumbo, and the warmth of a tantalizing new love, the newly single Southern mom might find a life she never imagined—and a place to finally call home.

Emily Beck Cogburn crafts a novel full of charm, delight, and acres of heart about the enduring joys of storytelling and the ways hope can write life's most extraordinary moments.

Read on for a special excerpt!
A Kensington trade paperback and e-book on sale now.

CHAPTER 1

Louisiana Richardson was tempted to go back to her Cheerio-littered van and find a coffee shop to hide in. Cleaning the house, preparing for the babysitter, and tearing herself from her crying one-and-a-half-year-old daughter, Zoe, had been exhausting. Besides, she was sure that she'd just been invited to the shower so Trish's baby could be outfitted with the latest in high-tech infant gear. A fellow library science professor at Louisiana A&M, Trish had never graced her with more than a terse hello. The transplanted Texan sometimes gave her pitying glances when Louise opened her purse to find a discarded sippy cup or tried in vain to remove a juice spot that made her shirt look like a map of Europe. Trish's wrinkle-free clothes were always color coordinated, and she never accidentally wore one blue and one black shoe.

Louise shifted the gift to her other arm and rang the doorbell. One side of the package bulged with an excess of crumpled-up paper, and the box peeked out on the opposite end. With her children constantly interrupting, she'd barely managed to get the thing wrapped, let alone make it look pretty. The sight would have made Martha Stewart choke on her almond tea biscuit.

When a tall blond woman wearing a cream-colored pantsuit and gold high-heeled sandals answered the door, Louise nearly dropped the gift and ran. But it was too late.

"Hi, I'm Louise," she said, manufacturing an upbeat tone of voice. When she first arrived in Louisiana, she'd considered finally ditching the nickname, but quickly abandoned the idea. "Louisiana" had sounded exotic and interesting to her childhood friends in Minnesota. Here, judging from the incredulous looks she got the first few times she'd introduced herself, it was just too much. There were women in Georgia named Georgia and women in Virginia named Virginia, but apparently no one in the Pelican State shared its name. Except her. So "Louise" it was.

"Alicia. Pleased to meet you." The woman stepped back to let Louise in. Her toenails were not only painted but also professionally manicured. Alicia's hair and makeup were so impeccable that she looked like a living doll—the perfect embodiment of a Southern belle, if such an animal still existed. Once Louise was inside the house, the survival of the species was abundantly evident. Southern belles with blond-highlighted hair, wearing ironed, breezy blouses, sipped champagne by the fireplace. Southern belles in creased slacks balanced tiny plates of bite-size morsels as they admired the gifts piled next to Trish. Southern belles with charm-school posture and blemish-free skin trotted to the kitchen in their strappy, high-heeled sandals to refill drinks.

Louise was a mutt in a room full of purebreds. She hadn't realized that baby showers down South were so formal. In Minnesota, her jeans and plain black T-shirt would have been perfectly acceptable, but they were shabby next to the silk blouses and tailored pantsuits. As usual, her makeup was limited to an indifferent slash of cinnamon lipstick, and her straightish, shoulder-length brown hair wasn't tinted, fluffed, blow-dried, or permed. Louise couldn't afford a manicure or a dye job, and all her clothes were relics of the previous decade. When they were married, her ex-husband had enjoyed buying cute dresses and sexy little tops for her. Shopping for clothes with Brendan had made her feel like a princess. On her own Louise had no motivation to update her wardrobe. Her ex was gone, and chasing after children didn't require cocktail wear.

Louise tried to find a dark corner where she could become invisible, but Alicia's house was maddeningly bright and open. The combination of the ten-bulb chandelier in the living room/kitchen/dining area and the sunlight coming in through the windows lit up every inch of the space. The beige and white decor seemed unnatural—there wasn't a stain or smudge anywhere. It reminded Louise of the magazine-worthy perfection of her former in-laws' mini-mansion with its artfully placed vases of flowers, spotless floors and countertops, and beds piled high with decorative pillows. After the first visit, she'd understood Brendan's periodic comments about her lack of housekeeping skills. He didn't nag her; instead, he'd say something like, "Shouldn't we clean behind the refrigerator once in a while?" "We," of course, meant her. Just like his father, Brendan never did housework. When they were first married, that detail hadn't seemed important. Back then, their relationship was about long, passionate discussions over glasses of wine. The misery, betrayal, and pain came later.

Louise's own modest ranch home looked like a day care gone to seed. The toy-strewn living room was decorated with stickers and marker scribbles. That morning, Zoe had put a blanket on the coffee table and arranged a tea party for her stuffed animals, using every piece of play food she could find. Dinner dishes still in the kitchen sink gave off an odor of curdling milk and stale macaroni and cheese. Paper, crayons, and coloring books covered the kitchen table. Louise had done the dishes and swept the crumbs from under the kitchen table for the babysitter's sake. As she now endured Alicia's appraising gaze, she wished she'd skipped the party, left the housecleaning for later, and snuggled on the couch watching morning cartoons with her kids instead. Zoe was obsessed with Elmo, and her delight at seeing him on the screen was so infectious that it made the puppet's high-decibel voice bearable, even endearing.

Alicia half turned and glanced at the group of elegant women. It was clear that she wanted to join her friends but felt that she had to be polite. "So, do you go to Community?"

"No. What's that? A church?" Louise didn't recognize any of the guests. None of the other library science professors had apparently bothered to come, probably because they knew about the Community clique, whatever it was. Louise was out of the loop, as usual. She felt like a kid during her first day in a new school. She had the wrong clothes, the wrong name, even the wrong accent.

Alicia fluffed her blond mane. "Well, we like to say that life is inspiration." After an awkward pause, she glided back to the living room area, sitting next to another statuesque blonde and laughing about something, most likely Louise's nondescript jeans.

Louise didn't need an instruction manual on Southern manners to know that she'd been snubbed. All the assembled belles focused on Trish, who had draped her pregnant body in a pastel flowered dress and roller-curled her honey-blond hair for the occasion. No one looked at Louise.

She inched around behind the women, skirted the last love seat, and slid her present onto the edge of the pile, backing away slowly. From her perch on a straight-backed chair, Alicia glanced at her and then at the badly wrapped present. Her tight smile was the kind usually reserved for an errant child. Chastened, Louise took another step back.

Trish was busy tearing open a large, professionally wrapped gift. The woman sitting next to her—a sister, maybe—recorded the offerings in a notebook shaped like a baby's bottom. She gave Louise a genuinely friendly smile before her attention was drawn by the exclamations of the observing ladies. "I've seen those diaper pails!" someone squealed. "They use grocery bags so you don't have to buy expensive refills!"

All of the chairs were taken, so Louise stood next to the buffet table and searched for a kindred spirit in the group. But everyone focused on the gift-opening ritual with baffling intensity. The women appeared to be having fun, but maybe it was all pretense. How could anyone get excited about baby clothes, blankets, wipe warmers, pacifier holders, and other assorted infant accessories? When Louise was pregnant for the first time, she'd been new in town—Iowa at the time—and had no friends around to throw her a shower. Even though she could have used the gifts, she didn't miss the party. Big gatherings caused her inner shy child to reappear, making her awkward, bored, and miserable all at once. Feeling that unpleasant mix of feelings begin to churn around in her gut, she decided to leave while the belles were preoccupied.

She retrieved her worn black purse from behind the designer handbags and walked quickly toward the front door. Thankfully, her tennis shoes made no noise on the wood floors. They would be called "sneakers" in Southern speak. In Louisiana, sub sandwiches were po'boys, counties were parishes, minor wounds were bo-bos, lollipops were suckers, pop was . . . well, she hadn't yet figured out that one. Sometimes, she felt like she'd stepped through Alice's looking glass: everything was just a little bit off-kilter.

Opening the front door, she sighed with relief. Free at last. Except that a woman in a peach dress blocked her way. Louise let out a different kind of sigh.

"Lou-Lou! Where do you think you're going?" Sylvia set down a neatly wrapped present on the stoop, the better to adjust her underwear. Even though her pregnant belly strained the front of her dress, she was stunning with her wavy auburn hair, bright green eyes, and naturally pouty lips enhanced by glossy pink lipstick. Sylvia's makeup was always flawless, and she had a seemingly endless wardrobe of fashionable clothes. Despite being nearly six feet tall, she usually wore three-inch heels. The current pair were peach platform sandals that matched her dress exactly. She reminded Louise of a red-haired Barbie, but somehow they were friends anyway.

"I'm escaping the Museum of Southern Perfection," Louise said.

"Shut up! You are not. I just got here."

"Forget it. We aren't part of the Community community."

Sylvia checked her lipstick in a compact mirror. "The coffee shop?"

"No, I think it's a new-wave church. You know, the kind with electric guitars and preachers in headset microphones."

"So what? I'm hungry. Carry this present for me. Come on, I'm pregnant."

"I know, I know." Louise picked up the box. The pink wrapping paper was covered with winged cherubs. "What's with the girly stuff? Isn't she having a boy?"

"I don't know. Is she?" Sylvia stepped inside and speed-walked to the refreshment table, her heels clicking. All the other guests followed her with their eyes. Sylvia waved, taking the attention for granted. Unlike Louise, Sylvia was never ignored. "Hello, ladies. Trish."

"Hi, Sylvia. So glad you could make it." Trish set aside the onesie she'd just unwrapped and beamed, glancing briefly at Louise, almost certainly noticing her for the first time.

"Well, I'm sorry I'm late, but getting the hubs to watch Jimmy is always a challenge. Especially when there's a game on." Sylvia took a baby-blue plate and eyed the selection of refreshments.

Louise delivered the present, and Trish immediately tore off the paper. "Oh, Sylvia. This is lovely."

"Just a little something my friend made," Sylvia said, filling her plate with tiny shrimp quiches. "It's nothing."

Trish held up a baby-size quilt decorated with a boy fishing in a blue denim lake. The assembled ladies made admiring noises.

"Sneak. You knew it was a boy," Louise said, coming up behind Sylvia and also getting a plate.

Sylvia grinned, her mouth full of quiche. "No, I got lucky. My friend Bonnie from high school has a girlfriend who quilts."

"Everyone quilts around here, don't they?"

Sylvia pursed her lips, thinking. "Everyone knows someone who does. I'll say that, Minnesota girl. Do you have homemade quilts for your kids?"

"You can add that to the list of my parenting failures."

"Oh my God. I'll get you some, don't worry. Poor quiltless children."

Louise laughed as she selected some fruit and miniature cheesecakes, feeling at ease for the first time since she'd set foot in Southern-belle land. Even though Sylvia had long legs and a gorgeous smile, something about her was comforting. She could even make Louise stop worrying about the number of calories in each of the deceptively small desserts—at least temporarily.

Trish opened Louise's present next, a starter kit of baby bottles that she had picked from the registry. The gift seemed to sum up Louise's entire persona: safe, boring, forgettable. How had she ended up in bayou-and-alligator country with such a flamboyant best friend? It was one of the mysteries of the universe. Trish immediately set the gift aside and picked up a package wrapped in sparkly blue paper.

"Have you checked your e-mail today?" Sylvia asked.

Louise tried a bite of miniature quiche. "Are you off your meds? I just managed to dress myself and make the house minimally presentable before the babysitter came."

"We got a campus-wide e-mail. There are going to be big cuts at A&M."

"What do you mean?"

"Budget cuts. You know about that, right? Economic crisis? A&M's budget reduced by twenty percent?"

"Yes."

Sales tax revenues were down with the shrinking economy, and the governor had targeted the university for reduction. The previous week, all the faculty and staff had received an e-mail warning them that cuts were coming. No one knew exactly what would happen. There were rumors about killing programs, departments even. German seemed vulnerable, as did Classics and Latin. Everyone agreed that there would be layoffs, at least among the ranks of instructors and adjuncts.

"Well, the library science school is tier three. Which means we might—shoot, probably will—be eliminated," Sylvia said.

"Eliminated? The library school?" Louise nearly spit out a mouthful of quiche.

Sylvia snorted. "Never mind that our graduates run the public libraries, school libraries, and everything else around here. Yes, we are on the chopping block. And guess who still doesn't have tenure."

"Both of us." Louise's stomach sank. She'd just moved to this godforsaken place. For an apparently doomed job.

"Exactly. We are royally and completely screwed, sister."

"But we don't know for sure yet."

"No, but they've already given pink slips to the German and Classics instructors. At the end of the semester, they're out of a job."

Louise set down her plate. She couldn't eat anymore. This was almost worse than when Brendan told her about Julia. She was going to lose the position she'd worked so hard for, the one thing besides the kids that had kept her going after the divorce.

"Time for games!" Trish said, setting the bottles aside.

"Oh God." Sylvia rolled her eyes and popped another mini cheesecake into her mouth.

Connect with U s

Visit us online at
KensingtonBooks.com
to read more from your favorite authors, see books
by series, view reading group guides, and more.

Join us on social media

for sneak peeks, chances to win books and prize packs,
and to share your thoughts with other readers.

facebook.com/kensingtonpublishing
twitter.com/kensingtonbooks

Tell us what you think!

To share your thoughts, submit a review,
or sign up for our eNewsletters, please visit:
KensingtonBooks.com/TellUs.